Forever
Sisters

For Lenore,
my sister of the
heart.

with much love,

27 February 99
San Francisco

Also edited by Claudia O'Keefe

Mother

Forever Sisters

Famous writers celebrate the power of sisterhood with short stories, essays, and memoirs

Edited by

Claudia O'Keefe

POCKET BOOKS
New York London Toronto Sydney Tokyo Singapore

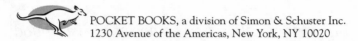
POCKET BOOKS, a division of Simon & Schuster Inc.
1230 Avenue of the Americas, New York, NY 10020

Library of Congress Cataloging-in-Publication Data

    Forever sisters : famous writers celebrate the power of sisterhood
with short stories, essays, and memoirs / edited by Claudia O'Keefe.
      p. cm.
    ISBN 0-671-00792-0
    1. Sisters—United States—Literary collections. 2. American
literature—Women authors. 3. American literature—20th century. 4.
Sisters—United States—Biography. I. O'Keefe, Claudia.
PS509.S43F67   1999
818'.540808352045—dc21   98-43729

First Pocket Books hardcover printing February 1999

10 9 8 7 6 5 4 3 2 1

POCKET and colophon are registered trademarks of Simon & Schuster Inc.

Designed by Irva Mandelbaum

Printed in the U.S.A.

BP/✖

Credits

Credits

For Susan: love ya, sis.

Acknowledgments

My thanks to Kay McCauley for her unswerving commitment; Linda Marrow and Amy Pierpont for their enthusiasm (a very necessary ingredient!); and Greg, Scott, Natalie, Alex, and everyone else at VP, who made editing this book possible. Your understanding was above and beyond the call of duty.

Lastly, my sincerest thanks to the authors who contributed to this book. Writing a short story or essay is not a hugely profitable undertaking, so their belief in this project was and is *greatly* appreciated.

Contents

Contents

Introduction

L ately I have dreamed of my half sister, Lisa. I have had dreams in which we fight over old jealousies, her singles-bar beauty, my supposed ivory-tower intellect, dreams in which I deliver her baby, a Down syndrome child I hug to myself and pronounce perfect, dreams in which we share silly, girlish secrets. I don't remember ever sharing a secret with my sister. Though sometimes girlishly silly on our own, we never indulged in that delightful conspiracy other siblings know.

Why am I dreaming of Lisa? I ask myself. I'm not even certain where she is right now. My sister and I haven't spoken in more than eight years. Nor do I feel the sudden need to find her. To my mind, it's better to leave us whole and happy in our separate lives than to rejoin our old cycle of resentment and mutual petulance.

Perhaps my dreams are similar to those of childless women who suffer from baby hunger. Never having had a close relationship with mine, I suffer from sister hunger. Is it possible that there is such a thing?

When we consider the literary treasures of history that champion relationships between sisters—for instance, Louisa May Alcott's *Little Women*—it is *so* easy to be envious. What a snug, inviting home Meg, Jo, Beth, and Amy inhabit together in the otherwise dreary days following the Civil War. Their fortunes are not fabulous, but sisterhood binds them together in a world of tremendous imagination, and despite fights and the tragic loss of one of their own, an overall sense of contentment and coziness prevails. Whether it's fictional or not, who wouldn't be jealous? What woman wouldn't hunger for the closeness and acceptance found in the story of the March sisters, that feeling of utter safety of the heart when it comes to her foibles and dreams?

Sisters share. That is the myth, and most of the time I believe it is also the truth. They share the joys of a long-hoped-for pregnancy, or the fear that accompanies an unexpected and unwanted one. They entrust each other with their private thoughts about their husbands and lovers. They confess the idiotic things they've done, the brilliant. Like the sisters in Wendy Wasserstein's play *The Sisters Rosensweig*, they bear grudges that can last a lifetime, just as easily as they are equipped to overlook a sibling's faults for the same length of time. They are also stronger for having known each other, because they share the gifts that come from surviving a family's darkest times together.

And yes, unlike Lisa and me, they share secrets. If I were to choose the perfect sister, I'd probably want it to be Eliza Bennett from Jane Austen's *Pride and Prejudice*. What a delightful, caring, and yet sensible woman! What a sense of humor! She is someone who will not compete with, but stick up for, her own—although now that I think about it, as with most of Austen's fiction about that anal retentive time in the pages of British history, it occurs to me that her characters kept just as many secrets to themselves as they shared with each other, often to disastrous ends. Of course, without dangerous harbored secrets, there would be no plot in an Austen novel—nor would there be in modern-day soap operas for that matter, what with their penchant for bringing back identical twin sisters of characters they shouldn't have killed off in the first place but didn't realize were indispens-able until their ratings went into the toilet.

Excuse me, I digress.

This I do know: even if she is not the type to share con-fidences, every woman possesses a *secret self* that only a sister will understand. It doesn't matter if a sister is older or younger or a full, half, or steprelation. She can be near or far, close or estranged, alive and vibrant or someone a woman can speak to only in her prayers. For those women who grew up as an only child or the only female sibling to brothers, she may even be a friend so dear the two might as well be related.

In fact, I do have a sister in whom I will confide when no one else will do. Her name is Susan, and we met in Seattle in our midtwenties. We were both grunts at a fiction writers boot camp, better known as the Clarion West Writers Workshop. For six weeks, we lived across the hall from each other in a dormitory, suffering sheer psychic hell as our fiction was dragged through the mud and barbed wire by our fellow workshop members. It was a pivotal time in both our lives and in some ways like a nativity. It was the birth of what I know will be a lifelong relationship—more than a friendship: a sistership.

I am lucky. I am happy to have found a sister after all.

So saying, what precisely makes a sister a sister? For one thing, she is most often our contemporary. She knows exactly what it was like for us to grow up where we grew up, when we grew up, and with whom we grew up. Also, because she is our contemporary, our relationship with her is often the longest we will have with any other woman. Even in muted form, the tie will last our entire lives, and at its strongest and most beautiful, it is a treasure we hope we will never live without.

We are also curious. Is my sister like your sister? How do our relationships compare? Their bumps and smooth spots?

Introduction

What happens between sisters when one graduates from college and moves away? Or is married? What are the ways in which the bond survives divorce? Breast cancer? Is it strong enough to weather mental illness and retain the fullness of its love? How do sisters fall out with one another and reunite?

We may also wonder what life is like for sisters in other cultures and faiths. Does growing up in Cuba or Russia or growing up in a Jewish family or an Asian household or even a different part of the United States from our own affect the ways sisters relate to one another? What is it like to have a sister who is gay or to be gay and have a sister who's straight? What if you find out that your sister's boyfriend or husband wants you or you want him?

We want answers! Now!

As it happens, these are the themes at the heart of this anthology.

Claudia O'Keefe
Belleair Beach, Florida
April 1998

xvi

Forever Sisters

Seven Sisters

AN ANALYSIS BY NUMBERS

Whitney Otto

1. The Biological Sister

A woman I worked with, named Ellery, was having a baby. Addison, her sister, was giving the shower, and since I volunteered to help, I was asked to arrive an hour earlier than all the other guests.

"You'll really like Addison," said Ellery as we walked to lunch. "She reminds me of Gina—you know, in the art department—unmarried, very personable, pretty, smart but with that sort of restless mind that gives the impression of being in two places at once." She then added, "Actually, Addison is a little like you."

We walked along in silence as I tried to decide if being like "Gina in the art department" was something I wanted. I never even got to the Addison comparison; Ellery said, "I mean it in a good way."

Ellery and I were work friends, that is to say, we seldom saw each other beyond the boundaries of the job. There was the occasional phone call, usually prompted by some unexpected work-related event. And we liked each other. I think, without stating it, we felt that forty hours and lunch once a week was more than enough together time. Besides, there was her husband, Jake, and their child-in-the-making.

* * *

I once asked her how she and her sister got the names Ellery and Addison.

"It's a tradition for the women in my family," she said.

"You mean your names are family names?"

"Not exactly. We have different names. The tradition is we all have boys' names. My mother is Corbett and my two aunts are Dexter and Drew. Well, Dexter *was* Dexter—she died quite young."

"Isn't Drew more of an androgynous name?" I asked.

"These days it is, but not then. Times change."

Addison lived in a great flat. It was one of those places in San Francisco that came available by chance or death. It was full of windows and light, with a working fireplace, two bedrooms, two bathrooms, and a lush little garden behind the sunroom. To list all its features would make it sound like a real estate agent's lie.

"The one thing that could make me leave this flat is moving to Barcelona," Addison told me.

"What about the man of your dreams?" asked Ellery, smiling.

"Only if he lives in Barcelona."

"My sister," said Ellery, "lives what can only be described as 'the conditional life.' "

Addison laughed. "Unlike the suburban life of which my sister is so fond."

"The bland exterior camouflages the hidden wildness," said Ellery.

I should say this exchange had a sense of affectionate ritual about it. As we arranged hors d'oeuvres and flowers, there was further talk about Jake, Ellery's husband, and the fact that Addison had not yet married; about Addison's ambivalence in regard to children, but her undisguised joy at becoming an aunt.

"My little sister, the adult," said Addison, as they continued to lay out their differences for me. "So, what are you
naming my favorite niece?"

"Dexter," said Ellery.

Everything stopped. The goodwill, the fond laughter, the
closeness of the moment. Addison released the flowers,
wiped her hands on her shirt and said, "Will you excuse us?"
Then she looked at Ellery, who dutifully followed her into
another room.

Even if I didn't like to eavesdrop, I was unable to avoid
overhearing their conversation.

"You can't name the baby Dexter," I heard Addison say.

"Why?" asked Ellery.

"Because that's my name. I always said I would name my
baby Dexter."

"No, no. I'm the one who said it."

"You only think it was you," said Addison.

"And you only think because you are the oldest that
everything is yours," said Ellery.

"How can you say that?"

"It's true. You've gone through our entire lives claiming
this and claiming that, and me, knowing whatever you took
for yourself could never, ever, be mine."

"Oh, this is about me?"

"Stop being so egocentric for a minute," said Ellery.
"This is about my baby and our aunt. You don't even know if
you want a child."

"You don't know that I don't," said Addison.

"Oh. So I'm supposed to wait and see what you decide
before I can sift through what is left over? We're not kids.
You're thirty-five."

"Where do you get this?"

"From you, Addison. All my life, everything I have ever
gotten has been from you."

"Fine. But I didn't tell you to run out and live a life opposite of mine."

"Maybe I wanted to set myself apart," said Ellery.

"And did you get what you wanted?"

Ellery hesitated. "I don't know."

"No one's life is free," said Addison with what sounded like a breath of regret. "Are you sorry for your life?"

"No. I love Jake and the baby too much. Still, sometimes I wish—I wonder—"

"—what it would be like to swap places?" asked Addison. "So do I."

The surprise in Ellery's *oh* was unmistakable.

"I was often lonely," said Addison, "and a little envious because you had me in a way I couldn't have you. Maybe you've lived your life as a response to mine, but all I ever had was the unknown and the untried."

"It seemed that you clearly knew where you were going and what you wanted," said Ellery. You appeared that determined to me."

"But you had a lightness I did not feel inside myself. When you made a mistake, it was just a mistake. If I erred, it felt like the world was coming down. There were times when I felt you watching me so intently, with so much admiration, or curiosity, that you failed to see me at all."

"Oh, baby," said Ellery, and I assumed that meant it had moved. The sisters said nothing, then I heard Ellery's voice. She sounded amused. "Look at us," she said, "the old maid and the wife; the one without children and the one with child; madonna and Magdalene; so exactly the same but different."

2. The Fairy-Tale Sister

It is a very bad idea to be the older sister. You are a shrew, you are lazy, selfish, sometimes beautiful with a beauty corrupted by your uncompassionate nature. Your love of jewels and general luxury is so strong it overrides all judgment. You are unloved because it is impossible to love you. As a matter of fact, it is well to leave you behind.

You lack the virtue of your younger, more fair, more honorable sister and it will often be your fate to live off the good graces of one you treated so ill.

The stepsister is a subset of the fairy-tale sister. Before my parents divorced and remarried other people, I was the oldest daughter. After the rearrangement of spouses, I found myself with two stepsisters, older than me, no longer living at home.

This turned out well, since one was plain and bitter and the other was pretty and mean, with toads and snakes that fell from her lips every time she spoke.

3. The Sister-in-Law

I read somewhere that two parents can produce an almost endless variety of offspring. And that our similarities to our siblings is more surprising than our differences.

Take three brothers and, for the sake of argument, say that these three brothers share a number of traits (even as they share as many dissimilarities), and all of them are heterosexual, and all of them are the marrying kind. The question is this: Will their wives be alike in any way (a sort of correlation to the brothers' own similarities) or will the women be a personification of the brothers' diverse traits?

Further, is it possible to know the brothers better through their choice of women?

For example, if one of the brothers is exacting and difficult but marries a woman of wit and warmth, can it be assumed that he has married his other half (his opposite), or is she the image of the deepest part of himself? A self so hidden that no one knows it is there?

Will the wives like each other? Will their discord and

their camaraderie mirror their husbands' discord and camaraderie, as if all the brothers' loves and battles have been
drawn into the open but are now spoken in the softness of a
woman's voice?

4. The Sorority Sister

When I was in college, I did not join a sorority. It was
my disinclination to join almost anything, even as I end-
lessly longed to be a part of everything. I'm one of those
souls who wants an invitation to every party I have no
intention of attending. This has to do with wanting to be
included, not wanting to reject the inclusion. I'm also convinced that some fabulous life party is being held all around
me and it is my obligation to want to participate.

Anyway, during my final year of college, I lived in a large
flat with four roommates: an ex-sorority girl, a gay man, a
heterosexual girl flirting with lesbianism, and a sorority girl.
The sorority girl was rather unpleasant to live with, being
both sloppy and selfish (two worlds not that far apart).

She volunteered our flat for some sort of sorority gathering, or initiation, or ritual, something very covenlike. I was
informed that since I wasn't a sorority girl, I would have to
leave for the duration of the meeting.

I was happy to go, though on principle I thought my
roommate had nerve. My ex-sorority sister roommate was
allowed to stay, but she declined and we went to see *The
Turning Point*; my roommate, who had been a student at the
American Ballet Theatre, told me about a girl she knew who
was not a very good dancer but got into the corps of ABT
because she was having an affair with Baryshnikov.

When we returned, the meeting had long since ended,
but the heavy porcelain toilet tank top in the bathroom had
been broken clean in half.

That is all I know about sororities.

5. Sister Sisters

During my senior year in high school, my friend Karen and I had to do a report that included interviews. Though we lived in Los Angeles, it was clear we would not be speaking to celebrities, power brokers, or anyone of interest. But my parents (non-Catholics) were friends with a young, handsome priest with the improbably perfect name of Father Sweet. My mother would curl up on the couch and coyly ask him things like "What do you say when you are at the beach and girls make passes at you?" (Many years later, my friend Jan, who is a Catholic, explained that a priest like Father Sweet is referred to as Father Whatawaste.) This is how Karen and I ended up taking on the Catholic Church as our subject.

I remember saying to Father Sweet, as Karen and I sat in his office, "Let me understand this: if a pregnant woman knows she will die in childbirth, she still should not have an abortion?" Yes, he said, then went on to give me an example that involved a mother, a child, and a burning building where everyone perishes. I felt there was no future here.

We then went to a local convent. It looked like anyone's ordinary home. Where I had been expecting stone and turrets and window grilles and a chapel that could inspire (or frighten) anyone, I got a two-story contemporary with a picture window. The nun we interviewed, like the rest of the nuns in the convent, taught school and wore street clothes. She talked about the economics of running a convent. After a while, she seemed like almost any mother in my neighborhood, discussing supermarket prices and the cost of kids' clothing.

I had come looking for mystery and sacrifice, and I finally asked, "Is there anything nunlike about you?"

She just smiled and held out her left hand. Her "wedding ring" was a soft, worn gold cross that wrapped around her

7

finger so that the top of the cross touched the foot in an unbroken circle.

6. Sisterhood Is Powerful Sisters

Here are my feminist beliefs in a nutshell: a level playing field and equal pay. Anything more always strikes me as so much window dressing.

Still, in my freshman year of college I found myself in an empty classroom once a week, attending a women's consciousness-raising group. It was in this room that I looked into the vagina at the cervix of a classmate named Carla. Carla didn't shave or wear underwear of any sort. She had hopped up onto the teacher's desk, inserted the plastic speculum given out by the free clinic, and voilà! She asked us to note the near arrival of her period.

One evening we passed around photographs of masturbating women. Another time there was quite a flurry of anger as two women sputtered about men who held open doors for them or, worse, referred to their cars as "she."

On Sundays we met with the men's consciousness-raising group so they could talk about how much they wanted to be free to cry.

I was generally silent, partly because I was in various states of disbelief. And I discovered, early on, that laughing out loud was frowned upon. So there I was, resisting the urge to ask, "Is anyone else listening to this?"—or "Is anyone else looking at this?" as the case may be—thinking, *One day I will write it all down.*

7. Friends as Sisters

These are the only sisters you choose. The Biological Sister has to do with perpetuation of the species; the Fairy-Tale Sister teaches us about the world and the imagination; the Sister-in-law is part of the wedding promise where you take someone else's family as family, which means they belong to you now, and, like the Stepsister, she is inherited. The Sorority Sister is a by-product of the club you joined, and the Nun and the Feminist are just like the Sorority Sister, but in a different club.

You can adore all these sisters. And if you are lucky in life, you do. But the friend who becomes your sister is truly a sister of your heart. She shares your sensibility.

The day she migrates from friend to sister is like this: One day you are feeling at odds with her, maybe vaguely disappointed, irritated, wanting to rearrange her personality ever so slightly, but then you let it all go because the bottom line is this: you will always love her, no matter what. Unconditionally.

You go about the rest of your day. But you should mark this moment somewhere inside yourself because it is the moment she becomes your kin.

Whitney Otto

WHEN WHITNEY OTTO *phoned me to tell me about "Seven Sisters: An Analysis by Numbers," she warned me that she didn't know what it was. "It's this weird combination of fiction and memoir," she said.*

She was concerned.

"When I started on it, I wanted to write a straight-ahead story," she further explained, "something straight-forward and lyrical like Amy Bloom or Lorrie Moore or Laurie Colwin," whose work she admires. Instead, she was so bored with her first attempt, she fell asleep at her keyboard.

"It sucked," she said.

Then she began to think about all the different permutations that a sister can take. She came up with a list of seven basic archetypes. Thinking she could do away with the numbers later, she began to flesh out the ingenious roman à clef you've just read, with quasifictional anecdotes from her own life. The numbers stayed.

An unusual, collagelike story structure has become a trademark with Otto, starting with her first novel, How to Make an American Quilt—*translated to the large screen in 1995, starring Winona Ryder, Anne Bancroft, Ellen*

Burstyn, and Jean Simmons—and continued with subsequent titles Now You See Her and The Passion Dream Book.

A native Californian, Otto now lives in a three-story Victorian in Portland, Oregon, with her husband, John Riley; son, Sam; a dog; and a cat who she says "regularly shuns my love."

—C. O.

The Wrong Sister

Caroline Leavitt

*I*n the summer of 1974, when I was fourteen, I lost my older sister Rose to love.

We were living in a suburb of Waltham back then, a green, leafy new development, full of scrubby trees and mowed lawns and clapboard houses painted pastel, just a half-hour bus ride away from Boston. We were a family of women, my father having died four years before. He had had a heart attack, falling in the very garden that had been a selling point when we had bought the house. He left my mother enough insurance so the house was hers, but not enough so that she didn't have to work long hours as a legal secretary, forcing my sister Rose and me to tend to ourselves, often well after dinner.

I didn't mind. There was no other company I wanted to be in more than my sister's. She was beautiful back then, sixteen and reed slender, with my mother's same river of black hair, only hers wasn't tied up into a corporate bun, but skipped to her waist. She had luminous pale skin and eyes as blue and clear as chips of summer sky. I was almost everything Rose and my mother were not—studious and shy, shaped like a soda straw with frizzy hair the color of rust.

Before Rose fell in love, she adored only me. We had

grown up inseparable, a world unto ourselves simply because we didn't like anyone as much as we liked and needed each other. When I tagged along with Rose, anything was possible. We roamed the woods behind our house looking for the secret landing places of flying saucers. We walked two miles to the Star Market just to steal fashion magazines and candy and cheap gold-tone jewelry we wouldn't be caught dead wearing, for the pure shocking thrill of doing something dangerous. We ate ice cream for dinner with my mother's wine poured over it as a sauce. We dialed stray numbers on the phone and talked enthusiastically to whoever picked up, pretending we were exchange students from France looking for a dangerous liaison or two. "Adventure is the code we live by," Rose declared, hooking her little finger about mine to shake on it. We were always going to be together. We were both going to be famous writers, living in the same mansion in Paris, scandalizing everyone by the hard, fast way we lived. We plotted out our books together. They were always about young girls like us on some quest or another, for stolen diamonds or lost love, and the only difference between my books and Rose's was that Rose's heroines always ended up riding off on the back of a motorcycle with any boy she felt like kissing, and mine were always teaching school in some quaint little town in Vermont, with two Persian cats warming themselves at her feet.

And then Rose met Daniel, and everything changed for all three of us.

Daniel Richmond was a senior in Rose's high school, a science major who loved cells and combustions, who said words like *mitochondria* and *endoplasmic reticulum* as if they were poetry. Rose had met him the first day she started tenth grade, when she had wandered into the wrong room and found him there peering into a microscope. The first time Daniel saw her, he looked stunned. "I'll take you to the right room," he said, and by the time he got her there, going the longest way he could manage, he had her phone number, and a date for the following night.

He was Rose's first boyfriend. She was giddy with the incredulous joy of it. She walked with a new bounce. She brushed her hair a hundred times each night and stared dreamily at herself in the mirror. When Daniel called her, she curled protectively around the phone. She whispered into it, and even after she had said good-bye to him, she held the phone receiver up against her cheek. "Wait until you meet him, Stella," she told me, out of breath. "You're going to die."

The first time he came over, I didn't know what to do. I wanted to dress up, to shine the same way my sister did. Both Rose and I tried on three different outfits. We both braided our hair and took it out again, put on perfume and washed it off, and when the doorbell finally rang, we went to the front door together.

Rose was beaming. She seemed lit from within. "I told you about each other," she said to both of us, and pushed Daniel toward me. He was taller than she was and the handsomest boy I had ever seen, with shiny brown hair so long it fell into his collar, and lashes so lush they seemed to leave shadows across his face.

"Stella, so you like science fiction," he said, and handed me a book, *Brave New World*. I had never read it, had never even heard of it back then, and I took it gratefully.

"I'll be careful with it."

He shook his head. "No, it's yours."

Astonished, I turned the book over and over in my hands. It was brand new. The spine hadn't even been cracked and broken in the way I liked; the pages hadn't been stained with fruit juice or chocolate, torn by my own two careless hands. *A virgin book*, I thought, and blushed.

"See, Stella, I told you you'd like him," Rose said. Her hands reached out to touch Daniel's shirtsleeve, his hand, the bare back of his neck, and could only let go to reach on for another part of him. My mother came in, still in her silvery corporate suit, her makeup, and Daniel handed her a bottle of wine. "Rose said you favor red."

My mother smiled. She undid her top button and gave Rose an approving glance. "You come for dinner tomorrow," she ordered Daniel. "Late dinner. The way they do in Europe. Say around nine."

He came for late dinner the next night, and almost every other night after. It became a sort of ritual. We'd all eat late dinner, huge lavish spreads my mother was delighted to cook for all of us. She loved the way Daniel would engage her in conversation, the way he'd sometimes bring her books he thought she'd like or flowers. "You're over here so often, we ought to charge you rent," she said, but she smiled at him. She told him he'd have to taste the beef Wellington she was planning to make the next night.

One day, though, I came home to find the house quiet. "Where're Rose and Daniel?"

My mother shrugged; she put hamburgers into a pan. "They're out on their own tonight," she said.

"They are?"

We sat down to dinner, to fries and burgers and a salad, and although my mother put on the radio to make the meal more festive, although she chattered brightly about her new boss, who had taken her out to lunch and flirted with her, who she was sure might not be married, something felt wrong. I kept looking at the two empty seats and I was suddenly not hungry anymore. My mother tapped her fork against the table. "It's not a tragedy, Stella," she said sternly.

I put my burger down. "I had a big lunch."

Daniel and Rose began spending more and more time alone. I watched them walking away from our house, and away from me, their hands so tightly clasped, I was sure they must be leaving marks. They couldn't seem to be together without touching, hands or shoulders or heads. They couldn't seem to talk but instead were whispering, as if everything they shared were some great, perfect secret, as if they were in a foreign country where I didn't speak the language or know the customs. That summer they sat out under the peach tree in back, a thermos of lemonade between them, and every time I walked by the kitchen, I peered out the back window until I saw them lying on the ground, entwined as if they were one body, kissing, so still, I thought for a moment they were dead. I watched them when they were sitting across from each other at our table for dinner, how Daniel couldn't pass Rose the salt without touching her shoulder. And even when he brought her home, I peered from the front window and watched them in his car, rolling together, kissing, taking their time before Rose would run back upstairs, back to me.

"Where did you go? What did you do?" I perched on the edge of her bed, but she was suddenly dreamy and distant.

"Stella, it was unbelievable," she said. "No one's ever loved me the way Daniel does." And then she was silent.

They were almost never apart. They even began dressing alike, in the same black turtlenecks and blue jeans, the same white high-top sneakers. She wore his tweedy jackets; he borrowed her oversized Harvard sweatshirt. He sent her love letters that flopped in through the mail slot almost every day, letters she read in astonishment, one hand flying to her face. She kept them hidden so well that even I couldn't find them. He bought her flowers and wind-up toys. By the time Rose was a high-school senior and Daniel was at Boston University, he was at our house by seven every morning, and he sometimes didn't leave until well after midnight. The neighbors got used to seeing him sitting reading on our front porch, not wanting to wake anyone. They got to know his bruised-looking green car parked in front of our house for hours on end. He didn't care that Rose never got up until ten; he'd talk to my mother and make her breakfast; he'd talk to me. He didn't treat me like a younger sister meant to be tolerated. "How could I be mean to Rose's sister?" he asked. Instead, he asked me what I was reading, who I was listening to. We'd be in conversation so deep, he sometimes didn't even see Rose until she was right there in front of us, and then he would jump up, electrified, kissing her, touching her hair, her face, the tips of her fingers. The two of them would move together, joining like a seam.

I frittered away my time waiting for Rose, waiting for my mother to get home, by reading or watching old movies on TV until my eyes hurt. If I were lucky, I could grab bits of Rose's time, parts of Daniel's.

One day, while waiting for Rose, Daniel decided to teach me to drive.

"I don't even have my learner's permit yet."

He laughed. "I thought you and Rose liked to live dangerously."

I sat in the driver's seat. He moved close beside me. "Turn on the ignition," he said. "Power up." He put his hands over mine on the wheel. "Here we go."

I drove around the block, stupefied, once, twice . . . and the third time, Rose was standing out front, in a sheer summer dress, her hair frilling out, her face pinched with an annoyance I had never seen before. She ran to the car and leaned over. "Where were you? I've been *waiting*." She glanced over at me. "What are you doing in the car?"

"Daniel's teaching me to drive."

"We're late." She opened my door pointedly, waiting for me to get out.

"Another time—" Daniel said to me, and then Rose slid into the car, so close to Daniel she could unbuckle his seat belt. She moved closer and slid the belt around herself, buckling them both in together. "There. That's better."

They drove off, leaving me on the hot sidewalk, and when I went back inside, I roamed around Rose's room. I picked up the perfume on her dresser and opened it, daubing it along my neck, behind my knees the way she did. I slid out of my clothes and went to her closet and put on her blue minidress and stared at myself in front of the mirror. I lifted an imaginary wineglass in a toast. "There. That's better," I said.

If Rose was to be lost to me with a boyfriend, it was time I began to think of getting a boyfriend of my own. I was finally in high school. It was the fall, the beginning of a whole new term when anything might happen. Rose and Daniel had been in love a year. I was fifteen and there was nothing to stop me from falling in love, too. There was a dance that September, held in the school gym, and so I went, wearing a blue dress of Rose's and her long dangling Indian earrings.

The gym looked funny without the usual equipment, the ropes, the volleyball nets. Neon-colored balloons floated from the ceiling. Red and gold crepe paper hung along the walls, and the entire floor was sprinkled with silver glitter. There was no food table, no punch bowl, nothing but too many people for one room and the pulse and beat of an out-of-town band called the Paradox. I leaned against the wall in the sweating heat, my hair pasting along my neck, watching the couples gliding by, pretending I was too interested in the terrible band to care that no one was asking me to dance. Sweat prickled along my back, and I was finally about to leave when a boy stood in front of me. I had never seen him before. He was wearing dark glasses and he smelled of cigarettes. "Dance?" he said, and took my hand. "So Happy Together" was playing, and he repositioned his grip, clutching me. I was in heaven, right up until another couple danced beside us. The girl was pretty, with a flash of white-blond hair. "Hey, Bobby," she said, smirking. The boy with her laughed and nodded at me. "New girlfriend, Bobby?" he said pleasantly. Bobby glowered and pressed me closer, his hands scuttling along my back like a crab. "So, uh, having a good time?" the other boy said, and Bobby let go of me. "Thanks for the dance." He bit off his words and turned, leaving with his friends, leaving me standing in the middle of the dance floor.

I kept dancing, by myself, as if it were a deliberate choice, as if I were too cool for a partner, as if I were one of Rose's heroines from the books we used to write. I smiled until my teeth ached, and then I danced myself to the doorway and stumbled down the stairs and out into the night.

I walked home to an empty house. I took off Rose's dress and put it in her closet. By the time I went to my room and closed the door, I was crying. My mother was out and Rose was with Daniel, and I banged my hands on the bed, when suddenly I heard a noise in the house. Footsteps. I bunched the pillow over my head.

The door opened. "Stella?" Rose's voice. I didn't move. "Daniel's here with me. Is it okay if we come in?"

"No. Go away." I heard their footsteps. I felt her sit on the bed beside me, and then for the first time in a long while, she put one hand on my back. I felt the heat of it through my blouse.

"You have to get up," Rose said quietly.

"Why."

"Because you're going out with us now."

Nobody ever really understood the relationship we three had. Every evening, when Daniel showed up, he showed up for me as well as for Rose. We three went to movies and concerts and restaurants. We walked around Harvard Square, Daniel in the middle, one arm looped about my shoulders, the other around Rose. "Man oh man, two of them!" a boy called, passing us on the street. "Lend one to me, would you?" I flushed, pleased, telling myself that I might have been the one he wished to borrow.

I told myself that you really couldn't tell who was with who, not until late at night, when Daniel dropped us off. I always got out first, running up the front walk, letting myself in to my mother's confused questions. Rose stayed behind with Daniel, sometimes for as long as an hour, the two of them talking. Sometimes he drove off again with her, not coming back until three in the morning. Then Rose would creep into my room and wake me up and I would relive her life through her. "We went skinny-dipping," she breathed. She smelled of chlorine. "We broke into the pool at BU and swam. No one else was there." She laughed. "Guess what?" Rose moved closer. "We're going to get married. When we're through college. We went to Sudbury. It's exactly like living out in the country, only it's close to Boston. We're going to have two dogs and three kids, and he'll do research and I'll write books."

I plucked at the sheets, pushing her away. "You're getting my bed all wet."

Rose looked startled. "I am?" She turned to leave, but even after she was gone, my sheets smelled of chlorine. I held them up against my face.

And then, when I turned sixteen, Rose went off to college herself. She didn't get into BU, where Daniel was, but she got into a school thirty miles away. She lived at school because she said she wanted the experience of living in a dorm, but I thought it was just because she wanted to spend her nights with Daniel. The day she left, I didn't know what to do with myself. I walked to the Star Market and stole a magazine that I threw out as soon as I left the store. I walked to the Dairy Dip and got a cone, and then I walked back home, where the house seemed so empty I was drowning in it. "She'll be home weekends," my mother told me. She sighed. "Do you want to go shopping?"

"I don't know."

"You should get some new clothes. You look like a raga-muffin."

I turned away from her. "I have to study."

Rose didn't come home that first weekend or the next. "I have a paper," she claimed. "I have to study."

"So do it at home," my mother said, but Rose was immovable.

With Rose gone, you would have thought Daniel would be gone, too, but that wasn't really the case. He was up at Rose's school almost all the time, but he still came by for dinner once a week, he still called, and as soon as he walked in our door, we asked him for news about Rose, news we were sure that he, of all people, would surely have.

"Something's wrong," Daniel insisted. "That school is bad for her."

"How is it bad?"

Daniel hesitated. "She's not herself anymore. She's con-fused."

"How is she not herself?" I wondered.

Daniel looked uncomfortable. "I don't know. I haven't figured it out yet." He sighed and looked at my mother. "You should bring her home."

But there was nothing my mother could do to convince Rose to come home. "I love school," was all she would say. She wouldn't talk about Daniel or what might be going on at school. "Everything's fine," she insisted. She took her own time, and when Rose finally arrived back to us, it was winter and everything seemed changed. She came home looking different, more beautiful, but more distant. "Jesus, do you have to wear those slippers?" she said to me in disdain. Daniel was coming over to see her. It was the first time he had seen her in a while, and I wasn't going to go with them.

The phone began ringing, and every time I picked it up, it was another male voice, asking for her.

"I don't know," she said into the phone, coiling her hand around the cord. "I have another date. Can't we do it another night?" She looked flustered. "Really? You really mean that?" She smiled, considering. "All right. Pick me up at seven."

As soon as Rose hung up the phone, she looked suddenly nervous. "Stella," she begged. "Can you do me this big favor?"

I waited.

"When Daniel comes, can you just tell him I'm sick, that I can't get out of bed?" She motioned to her room. "I'm just going to lie down there."

"You have another date?"

"I'm allowed." She bit her lip. "I'm allowed," she repeated. "Please, I don't want to hurt him. I just— There'll be other dates with him. It's not like this is the one and only time. But this other guy is going home to California tomorrow."

"I thought you were going to get married. I thought it was forever."

"I just—Stella, Daniel was the first boy I ever dated. I was a baby when I met him. Now there's all these things opening up for me." She blew out a breath. "Please. Do it for me. Go get pizza with him or something. I'll make it up to you." She touched my shoulder. "I promise."

And so I did it. When Daniel came, dressed in a new tweed jacket, his hair longer, I lied. I told him Rose was sick, that she was sleeping and couldn't be disturbed. He nodded. "Should I get her tea or ice cream?"

"She can't be disturbed," I lied. I hesitated. "Want to go get pizza?"

He studied me for a moment, and then sighed. "Sure. Why not. Maybe by the time we get back, she'll be up and feeling better." He brightened. "Come on, let's go eat."

We ate pizza at Pie in the Sky in Cambridge, seated in a red leatherette booth in the back. There was a noisy, boisterous crowd of students, and when Daniel talked, he talked about Rose. "I don't think she's happy away at school, do you?"

"She seems to like it."

He put his pizza down. "But she seems different. That's all I'm saying. Or maybe it's just because I haven't seen that much of her. She's always studying. I said I'd study with her, but she says she has to do it alone now. I know what she means. It's hard to concentrate on anything but the person you love."

We didn't order dessert. He drove me home silently. "I'll walk you in," he said, "check on Rose." But when we got in the house, my mother was home, and when she came to the door, her face was apologetic. "She went out," she said quietly. Daniel didn't even ask where Rose was. He said goodbye and walked back to the car. I peeked at him through the front window. For a long while, he just sat in the front seat, staring out ahead of him.

Rose began coming home less and less. But Daniel showed up at our house more and more. "We should bring Rose home," he kept insisting. He moped about our house. He helped me with my science papers; he stayed for dinner. My mother was happy to have someone to cook late dinners for, someone who appreciated the chicken Français, her duck à la Waltham. "It's a phase with Rose," she told Daniel. "You mark my words. She's just feeling her oats."

After dinner, we would all play Scrabble or sometimes go to the movies, and finally, when it hit midnight, Daniel would go home. I got used to his being at the house and I told myself that I was angry at Rose for denying him. I called her at her dorm. "She's out," a voice said. I left my name, I said it was important, and although I waited, she never called back.

* * *

Rose came home for spring break with her hair three inches longer and a whole pool of new boys who were in love with her. "Should we have Daniel for dinner?" my mother asked.

Rose sighed, exasperated. "I broke up with him last month."

"You didn't!" My mother shook her head.

"He was just here last night. He didn't say that—" I said, and Rose shot me a look.

"He shouldn't be coming here anymore." She flung her hair back, annoyed. She got up from her chair and stared out the window. "You don't know what it's like," she said. "Everywhere I look, there he is. He won't leave me alone. He's obsessed. He's making me hate him." She turned to me, accusing. "Did you know that he follows me around at school? I'll be coming out of class and he'll be there, skulking in the halls, waiting. I'll come home from a date to find his car parked in front of the dorm, watching, waiting. Every morning, no matter how early I wake up, he's somehow there. He calls me up a million times a day and night just to check up on me, make sure I'm there, and even then he doesn't trust me. He saw me hugging a friend of mine, congratulating him on getting engaged, for God's sake, but do you think he could understand that? Not Daniel. He called me five times that night, asking me over and over why did I hug someone else, what did it mean, why was I walking with another man, why was I lying, didn't I trust him enough to tell him the truth? God! Every day there are five notes from him taped to my door. There are love letters six pages long slid under my door. Doesn't he go to school? Doesn't he have a life? I'm allowed to see whoever I want." She flung off her scarf.

"He loves you," I said.

"I'm having dinner tonight with this boy who wants to take me to Spain. Next week I'm going to a play with this other boy who's writing a novel about me. And my English professor is going to let me walk Meredith, his sheepdog, in the Boston Commons with him on Sunday." Her eyes sparkled like constellations. "And tonight, in less than an hour, I'm going out to dinner with a boy from England."

She breezed out of the house that night. My mother shook her head. "Poor Daniel," she said sadly.

I felt sorry for Daniel, too, but I also felt something else. Wonder. That a boy would love you so much that he might ruin himself over you, that a boy would risk his own education and maybe his life to be with you and that it all might last forever, love never dying.

Rose might have been orbiting away from me, but now that she knew I was friendly with Daniel, she was openly hostile. "Don't give him any false hope about me," she said. "He'll just hang around me even more." She was suddenly too popular to go into Harvard Square with me. She scrutinized me. "You could do something about your hair, you know," she said. She sniffed with disdain at the music I listened to. "Rock and roll—barf!" she said. When I ran into her in Boston, she ignored me. She couldn't wait to get back to school. Her conversation with my mother was peppered with new names. David. Roger. Ben. Any name but Daniel's. Any name but mine.

Gradually, Daniel stopped coming to the house. He stopped calling. My mother stopped making exotic late-dinner menus and went back to her workaday pastas, her ready-in-ten-minutes burgers. "What a shame," she said, but Rose was immovable. Rose even said Daniel had stopped showing up on her campus, trailing after her. Her mailbox wasn't full of his love notes anymore. There weren't two dozen phone messages from him, or personal notes he had scribbled himself, taped up across her dorm room door. "Thank God," she said, pulling her hair into a ponytail.

"I don't know," my mother said. "He was a nice boy. I miss him." Then I thought, *I really miss him, too.* I really had lost Rose, and I had lost Daniel, too.

It was May and school was nearly over for the summer. I was coming out of school, walking down the grassy backyard to the buses. Just that day, a girl in my gym class had threatened to beat me up because she didn't like the peace-sign necklace I was wearing. I was saved when she had been caught phoning in a bomb threat. I kept to myself. I told myself that soon, soon things would be different, I was going to go away to New York City to college. I would be a famous writer, by myself, without Rose. I would have many boyfriends because at college, boys might appreciate a quick wit and a smart mind; curly hair might be beautiful there. I was deep in reverie, and then I heard two blond girls whispering, pointing, and flirting. I looked over, and there was Daniel, walking across the grass toward me ignoring them altogether. He gave me a big hug, and over his shoulders, I saw the blondes staring at me. I put my arm about Daniel and we walked along, the blondes still watching.

"You know," he said. "I missed you."

"God, me, too."

I waited for him to ask me about Rose, what was she doing, who was she seeing, did she miss him at all? Or maybe he might suggest we go visit her, united we stand, both of us pulling her back to us, but he never did any of that. Instead, he took me to his car. "Let's go get some muffins," he said.

We went to the Pewter Pot in Cambridge, where there were not waitresses but "wenches," dressed in tight black corsets and red skirts, bonnets bobbing on their heads. We ordered fudge muffins and cranberry butter and hot chocolate with whipped cream. I felt flushed with happiness seeing him.

Daniel drew a double helix in a spill of salt on the table. He smiled. "What's the gene for stupidity? For false hope?" He smiled again and then reached over and touched my hand. "I'm having a good time."

"Me, too."

"Maybe I fell in love with the wrong sister."

He smiled, the same Daniel, easy, smart, funny. The wench appeared, refilling our water glasses. Tendrils of blond hair were falling from her bonnet. Her pink lipstick was smeared.

"So," he said slowly. "Joni Mitchell's playing at BU. Want to go?"

"Yes, of course I do! It'll be like old times."

He shook his head. "No. Not like old times. Like new times."

He reached over and took my hand again and this time, I let him. The wench walked by and winked at me.

I went home in a confusion. Rose was there on a surprise visit, with a new boyfriend in tow, a blond named Merle who was singing a song he had written about her. "Raven hair and eyes like a stormy sky," he sang. They both ignored me.

"I had cocoa with Daniel," I said, and Rose looked up, seeing me for the first time. She raised one brow.

"He thinks he might have been with the wrong sister," I said. My heart skated against my ribs. Merle looked at me quizzically. "We're going to a movie Friday."

Rose seemed to go rigid. "So?"

"It's a date."

She grew silent and then she looped one arm around Merle's shoulder. "Date whomever you please. It has nothing to do with me."

The next day, the news that an older handsome man had come to the school to pick me up, throwing an arm about me, was all over school. Ned Thompson, the boy who sat behind me in home room, who used to amuse himself mornings by whispering "ugly, ugly" at me like a mantra, looked at me with new respect and interest. "What a nice day, huh?" he said pleasantly. Later, in the girls' room, while I was staring at my reflection in the mirror, Debby Ryan, a cheerleader, strode in. "I like that shade of lipstick," she said, nodding at my open mouth.

I felt as if I had tumbled into the wrong school, but all day, things felt different, and I knew it was because of Daniel.

"So who was that guy?" Marisa Filbert asked me in history class.

I grinned, blushing. "Daniel." A thrill shot through me.

"Is your boyfriend a college guy?" She leaned closer.

I nodded. *Boyfriend.* "We're going to see Joni Mitchell Friday."

"What a hunk." Her admiration washed over me like a cool pour of water.

The night of the date, my mother was out of town on business, but Rose was home again, getting ready for a date of her own. She was in a bare black dress, her hair braided down her back, a single red glass earring dangling from her left ear. She watched me struggling with my outfit, pulling on a new blue minidress printed with yellow peace signs, a dress I now had serious doubts about, especially next to Rose. She frowned as I smeared on lipstick, as I tried to flatten my unruly hair with my sweaty palms. Rose leaned along the doorjamb. "I just want to tell you," Rose said slowly, "that I think you are insane."

I ignored her.

"He doesn't want to date you. He's doing this to get at me. You're making a mistake." She frowned. "He was *my* boyfriend."

"Not anymore."

She threw up her hands. "Fine. Do what you want."

When Daniel arrived, Rose made sure to be in her room, with the door firmly closed. I told myself it didn't matter where she was, because Daniel stepped inside, dressed in a tweed jacket I had seen a million times before, but suddenly it took on new importance. Suddenly even the way he had brushed his hair seemed new and different and wonderful to me. "You look great," he said. He opened the door for me, and then I stepped out of my house with Daniel and into a whole new life, not once looking back to see if Rose had somehow snuck out of her room to watch us, to feel the same jab of envy I used to feel toward her.

The concert was in an auditorium at the college, so crowded that we ended up sitting on the floor. Joni Mitchell was a pinprick on the landscape. I could barely hear her. I could barely see. The whole time, all I could think about was how much older everyone was around me, how the girls seemed to know something I didn't, just in the way they flipped their hair back or gazed at their boyfriends or whispered to one another. These were girls in blue jeans or long skirts, girls with no makeup and straight hair, and there I was in lipstick and my fizz of curls, in a dress so short I had to keep tugging it down over my thighs. In front of us, a red-head and a boy with a heavy beard began kissing. He touched her neck; he pulled down the neckline of her dress and kissed her shoulder. His mouth was open and wet. She licked at his ear. I stared down at my hands, at the nails I had bitten to the quick. Daniel's foot touched mine, and I drew my legs under me as tightly as I could.

I was glad when the concert was over, when Daniel pulled me to my feet. I wanted to go home to process this, to think how I felt, what I wanted to do. "Come on," he said.

He took my hand and we went to someone's dorm room. The door was wide open and there was a couple lying on a narrow bed together. They were rumpled and laughing, half dressed, and the sight of them was as intimate and shocking to me as a slap. I started, stepping back, unsure of what to do.

"This is Rita and Mike," Daniel nodded at them. They rolled closer together on the bed, smiling lazily up at me. Mike swept one hand over Rita's face. Rita yawned and stretched and snuggled against him. Her white T-shirt rode up, showing a band of pale stomach. "Don't think us rude, but we absolutely cannot get up," she said. Mike took a rope of her long pale hair and tickled her nose with it.

"That's all right. We're going for a drive anyway."

A drive. I followed Daniel out of the dormitory and back into his car. He was talking nonstop, but I couldn't snag my attention on any of his words. I put my hands deep into my cotton pockets. The night was thick with clouds. The air was so warm and heavy and yet I was shivering. I suddenly wanted things back the way they had been before, back when he was my big brother, bringing me books and chocolates, teaching me the best way to cook shrimp creole, how to appreciate a foreign film. I hadn't minded when he had looped his arm about me when we were walking down the streets with Rose, when he had come to get me at school, with an intrigued audience making us indelible in their minds, but now, with the two of us alone, his arm felt like a weight on me. His interest made me want to flee.

We drove. I sat as close to the window as I could. He put on some music, guitars and flutes. "Let's drive to Sudbury," he said enthusiastically. I moved closer to the window. He glanced at me. "You all right?" he said pleasantly.

It started to rain, droplets smearing across the window. When I was little, I used to try to match up all the raindrops. I wanted them to all have partners, to never be alone.

"Come sit closer."

"I think something feels wrong about this."

He drove deeper into Sudbury. The houses were spread out. The land looked rich. He turned and gave me a half smile. "I think maybe you're afraid of things you shouldn't be afraid of."

"What does that mean?"

He smiled again. "Stella." He lifted one hand and brushed back my bangs, so my forehead was clear, like Rose's.

"I'm not my sister."

"I have always loved you," he said simply. "You. Your sister. Your mother. Your whole family. I even loved your house."

I opened the window. The hot, moist air struck my face. The rain beat in. My hair would frizz even more in minutes, but I didn't care.

"I loved your backyard."

"Can you just drive me home now?"

"No, not until you talk to me about this."

"I don't think this is going to work out."

"People say that when they're afraid to even try. But there's nothing to be afraid of. I love you. I do."

He drove faster. "Where are we going?" I said.

"I want to show you the houses out here, how pretty it is." And then suddenly, I felt like what it must have been to be Rose, but in a different, more dangerous way. A Chevy slammed on its horn beside us.

"Can you slow down?" I asked.

Daniel slowed but he kept going. "You don't love me, but that's all right. There's an art to loving. Have you read that book? *The Art of Loving*? Erich Fromm? I'll bring you a copy." He looked over at me. His voice was smooth, modulated. It sounded liquid. "Don't you think I have enough love for both of us?"

I looked out at the road, bordered by tall grassy fields. Cars hummed behind and ahead of us. "You're not going to take me home?"

"Of course I am. But not while you're this upset. We have to talk about this. Talking solves things. The problem with Rose and me was we never talked it out toward the end." He turned the wheel. "I'll park the car and we'll talk. How about that?"

"I want to go home. Now."

"No one will love you like I do." His voice was matter-of-fact. He turned to look at me. "You have very pretty hair, all misted in the rain like that. Hair to write a poem about."

"Please. I don't feel good. I have to go home."

"Listen to me, Stella—"

"Let me out. I have to get out." I gripped the door handle.

He leaned across and grabbed at my hand. "Stella, listen—" he said. "Listen to me—you don't understand—"

But I couldn't listen. I couldn't understand. Not anymore. I opened the car door. The road spun out before me. Less than a foot away was the grass, and then, without thinking, I tumbled from the car.

I curled up and hit the pavement and a bolt of pain zigzagged through me. I rolled toward the grass. I was soaking wet; my tights were torn. I could hear Daniel shouting at me, trying to stop the car, to pull over. The other cars were honking, but I got up, and I saw his car, and then I saw him getting out, coming after me, and then I was all legs and arms and jagged breath, running.

This was suburbia after all, not the country Daniel had proclaimed it. There were lit houses and convenience stores and an open-all-night Store 24 where as soon as I ran inside, the cashier, a clean-scrubbed girl with a brunette ponytail, reached for the phone and held it out to me. My tights were ripped. I had a gash across one arm and my mascara rac-cooned along my eyes. My dress and stockings were torn, and my shoes, ballerina flats from Pappagallo with ribbon ankle ties, the same shoes that had cost me two months' allowance, were ruined. The thin soles had come right off and one of my feet was bleeding. I told her I was all right, that all I wanted to do was call a cab and go home. "Honey, you sure?" she said.

It didn't take me long to get home. The cabdriver was an older man who didn't seem the least bit surprised by my appearance. He didn't say a single word to me except "that will be ten-fifty" when we got to my house. As soon as I got out of the cab, he sped away.

The lights were out except for the one my mother kept on at night, to let prowlers know this was not an empty house, even when it sometimes was. It was eleven. My mother wouldn't be home until morning. Rose would still be out, if she came home at all. I let myself in as quietly as I could and walked toward my room, wanting only to burrow under the quilt, to sleep, to forget everything about my life, when there, suddenly, was Rose, in the corridor.

I waited for her to tell me that she had told me so, that I got what I deserved, that the real question was just who did I think I was? Or maybe she might leave me to my own devices and instead go to the phone and call Daniel and demand an explanation. I wavered in the hall. I felt myself listing. Behind me, the phone rang, a sound stinging the air, and for the first time that I could remember in a long time, Rose didn't rush to answer it. And then Rose moved forward and for a moment, because her face was so unreadable, I thought she was going to strike me, and I put my hands up, to shield my face.

Her arms hooped about me. I felt her warmth, the slow slide of her hair as it spilled against me. She led me toward the bathroom, not letting go. She kept whispering, ignoring the doorbell that made me jump. She whispered, but it might as well have been Morse code, because all I could hear was the soothing hiss of sound, mesmerizing me. She took off my clothes and wadded them into the trash. Then she drew me a bath, all the while still whispering to me. The doorbell stopped. The phone was silent. She held up one finger for me to wait, and disappeared, and when she came back, she held up a blue packet with some French writing scribbled across it. She tore the top and then poured cobalt-colored crystals into the bath, stroking one hand through the water until it bubbled up blue. There was the smell and tang of citrus. She helped me step in, lowering me into the tub as gently as a fine piece of silk. The phone rang again and I stiffened. I tried to talk, but she simply put her hand to her mouth. "Shhhh," she said.

And when I started to cry, she sluiced back my hair with her fingers. "We're always sisters," she said quietly, and then I shut my eyes, and then I didn't hear the phone anymore. Instead, I gripped the hand she offered me, holding fast to her even as the slow, steady waves of the bathwater washed over me like a tide.

Caroline Leavitt

CAROLINE LEAVITT is one of those hidden treasures you're happy to have come across. Though not a household name, her most recent novel, Living Other Lives, received a starred review from Publishers Weekly. The New York Times Sunday Book Review, as well, has praised her for "her ability to create believable characters who can behave badly without forfeiting the reader's sympathy," a talent echoed in "The Wrong Sister."

This novelette is based loosely on real events, Leavitt says. "My sister is a story I always feel compelled to tell. This one, written in a fever in two days, sums up the nature of our relationship—i.e., that no matter what, our bond is unbreakable."

Currently working on her seventh novel, some of Leavitt's award-winning other novels include: Family, Jealousies, Into Thin Air and Lifelines. Her short prose, for which she is a National Magazine Award nominee, has appeared in Parenting, New Woman, and Salon magazine. She is also one of the authors of the Wishbone mystery series for children, companion books to the award-winning PBS program, a legacy her baby son, Max, will no doubt enjoy. She, Max, and her husband, Jeff Tamarkin, live in Hoboken, New Jersey.

—C. O.

Two Sisters

A PERSONAL ESSAY

Olivia Goldsmith

. . . treachery is the other side of dailiness.
—Alice Munro

*E*veryone called my maternal grandmother and great-aunt "the sisters." My Nana Rose, the eldest daughter of eight children, lived with her sister Anna throughout her childhood and almost all of their adult lives. Neither one was, as you might first guess, a spinster who existed as the unmarried auntie appended to a sibling's family. Both women married, then set up housekeeping, raised their children, and lived in the same home until my grandmother's horrific death.

Rose had married first. Her husband Abraham was a very tall, very silent man who seemed satisfied to let Rose—just five feet, talkative, and dynamic—run everything. Early in their marriage, Abe had worked as a teamster but was lucky enough in those Depression days to get a job with the post office. He spoke rarely, and when he did, it was most often in unusual clichés from his family's Liverpool beginnings. If he hadn't seen us in a while—any amount of time that varied from fifteen minutes to a week—he'd greet us with "Where ya been? China?" Or if the weather had turned wet or freezing, he'd ask, "Are you cold as Kelsey's Jibbers?" The rest of the time, he sat in the living room in his easy chair—the one without an ottoman—and smoked an unending series of El Producto cigars.

Two Sisters

The other easy chair, the one with an ottoman, went to Anna's husband Jack. It seemed to me that that was the main chair, and Jack reigned from it, at least when we knew him. In those days before remote control, he still decided what was watched on the big console television (every Western movie that was ever shown, along with *Have Gun, Will Travel; Bonanza; Gunsmoke; Wanted: Dead or Alive;* and *Rawhide*). If Abe or the sisters ever objected to the steady visual Tex-Mex diet, I never heard any of them say so.

The sisters had done everything together, or so the legend went. They lived in a two-family house on Pelham Parkway in the Bronx, but they didn't live in it as if it were a two-family house. The top floor had Anna and Jack's bedroom in the front and, separated by a guest room, Rose and Abe's bedroom in the back. The steep staircase brought one down to the main floor where there was, to me, an elegant arched entrance to the living room and dining room along with a large, long kitchen. Downstairs, in what had been built as a separate apartment, were the bedrooms for the children. My grandmother had two daughters. Anna had two, as well as a middle son. They were all raised together, certainly more like siblings than cousins.

And it moved into the next generation. My siblings and my cousins called my grandmother "Nana" and her sister "Auntie Nana." Whether at one time that had been only "Auntie Anna," I don't remember, but the invented sobriquet described well the relationship so much closer than a great-aunt. Anna's grandchildren, though, merely called my grandmother "Aunt Rose."

Rose and Anna seemed to work in utmost harmony and divided the housework very clearly: Rose did all the cooking—a prodigious amount. One of my most frequent memories is of her over the double sink with her hand buried to the wrist in a raw chicken. Anna did all the cleaning, and the house was always spotless, the figurines dusted, the huge mirror over the fireplace and the glass shelves beside it always glistening. I don't remember that they had any outside help.

Rose was a good cook in the heavy European Jewish way, which was odd because she had no sense of smell. As kids, we were all fascinated by this fact. When we drove with her on long-distance trips through industrial sections and the stink of chemicals filled the air, she'd tease us by taking deep breaths and saying, "Um-m-m-m. Delicious!" while we choked and gagged. She explained how she had smallpox when she was a little girl and how, after she recovered, her ability to smell was gone. Her taste must have been affected, too, so as she cooked, she would always call for Anna and spoon a taste of the potatoes or carrot *tsimmis* or pot roast at her. I remember Anna feeding from the spoon like a plump bird, then telling Rose to add more salt or approving the dish as it was.

Rose had always been social and enjoyed a party and a good time. She was also, as the eldest sister, the one that the brothers called. It was Rose who listened to problems, organized dinners for the cousins' club, spoke on the phone for hours to friends and distant relations. Anna was far from shy—her opinions were strongly, sometimes harshly, given—but she was not the center of the extended family life.

There was the center she had, though, that Rose seemed without. Rose treated her children the same as Anna's. She allowed no favoritism, and when grandchildren came along, she continued that tradition. I know it caused some resentment (as it should have) with her daughters. Rose always divided the candy evenly, while Anna held some back, some extras for her own. It was clear to me—even as a young child—that Anna put her children and her grandchildren first, but we were told it was her weakness, that it was inappropriate but should be overlooked. Anna also deferred to her husband, while Rose seemed to dominate quiet Abe.

Jack called his wife "Babe" and certainly seemed to give her more gifts and attention than Rose received from my grandfather. There was something in the bonding of Anna and Jack's marriage that, for Anna, took precedence over the sisterhood. But I don't think that was true for Rose. She would hear no criticism of her younger sister Anna and always denied any injustice on Anna's part.

And so the family myth developed of generous, evenhanded, good-hearted Rose, and Anna who was just a little less of all those desirable things. Only now, twenty years after Rose's shocking death, does it occur to me that it was Rose's behavior that was inappropriate: that a mother should naturally favor her children over her nieces and nephews and her husband over her sister. It wasn't a moral failing in Anna. If Rose turned to Anna out of a lack in her marriage, the gap might have been filled for her, but at a tremendous longer-term cost.

Every decision was, at one point, mutual. I remember shopping with the women on White Plains Road. They had a bakery they would buy their bread orders from, but both agreed never to stoop to buying cakes there. It was the Snowflake for cakes. As well, they agreed on vendors of vegetables, smoked fish, poultry, and meat. "His lamb is good, but never trust his chopped meat," they would counsel each other and us, nodding. They decorated the house together, with big down-filled upholstered pieces and multitiered pie-crust occasional tables; and a dining room furnished with chairs so heavy a grandchild could barely pull them out. Nana alone, it was true, tended what she called her "geranibums," lush plants she kept flowering through the winter that Anna seemed to dislike because of their pungent scent, but I never heard them argue or disagree about anything else except who had last used the favorite knife. It was a worn but sharp piece of cutlery that had been bought in New Jersey and was always referred to by its origins. "Anna, what did you do with the Jersey knife?" Rose would call.

"I didn't touch it. *You* had it last for the children."

"No. *You* used it when you cut the sandwiches."

"Rose, I didn't touch the Jersey knife."

I remember that we once, in the interest of perfect peace, bought them another knife in New Jersey, hoping to make that one issue dissolve, but the new knife, as the saying goes, didn't cut the mustard—or anything else. It lay in a kitchen drawer while the two sisters still argued over the whereabouts of the real Jersey knife.

There must have been some more visible disagreements, but I and my sisters don't remember them. What did become clear was that under the seemingly still surface of familial peace, a lifetime of stored resentments had begun to appear. For a while, as with an unsound piece of furniture, the structural problems of rotting underpinnings were covered by the smooth veneer, but eventually, it buckled.

Perhaps it was a class issue that divided the sisters in the end. Abe had gotten Jack his job from the owners of the trucking firm Abe had once worked for. While Abe continued with his secure but unremunerative work at the P.O., imprisoning my grandmother in the middle and then lower-middle class, Jack's genius at mechanics moved him up and made him invaluable to the firm he was employed by. When they bought a fleet of taxis, Jack kept them running, even through World War II when parts and labor were both virtually impossible to find. He was brilliant at improvisation and was soon running the operations of the company, his affluence increasing, though his hands were always blackened under the nails from engine grease. He was, I believe, eventually rewarded with not just generous bonuses (which he invested well) but also a small ownership position in the company. In time, he must have been outearning my grandfather by four, or maybe ten, to one.

Anna's good fortune didn't immediately change the sisters' living situation. As their kids grew up and married, the sisters and their husbands continued to live in the big house together; but we knew there was a difference in the families. Anna's children married better, with more elegant weddings. Jack and Anna owned a Cadillac, and when the two couples traveled, Jack always drove it. But at Chanukah, Auntie Nana continued to give each of us a gift envelope with only two dollars. "I wish it could be more," she would say, year after year, until we, as young teenagers, started muttering, "We wish it could be more, too."

But Jack and Anna showed their affluence in other ways. They abandoned the synagogue their parents and Rose and Abe still attended and became board members of a new smaller one.

Yet their changed financial status never seemed a problem between the sisters until the day Anna decided that new carpeting should be laid in the living and dining rooms. Rose agreed but couldn't pay for her share at the time. So as the story I heard went, Anna went alone and paid for and picked out the persimmon wall-to-wall nylon that went down on the floor. We all hated it, but I believe Rose was decimated, not by Anna's decision but by what she saw as more than insensitivity. It was a betrayal. Rose had to live with the persimmon carpet for the rest of her life—along with marble tile Anna installed in the hall.

Next there was a change in travel. The couples had always summered and vacationed together. But they had never traveled abroad. Anna and Jack decided they wanted to visit Israel. It was also a dream of my grandmother's, but not something she and Abe could afford. And so Jack and Anna made reservations for themselves. Anna didn't invite her sister. Rose was stunned when Anna and Jack left for two weeks. Usually so upbeat, so energetic, my Nana was reduced to silence and lethargy. Alone with Abe, who had grown only more quiet over the years, terrible thoughts must have run through her head. Abe had become forgetful. His mind wandered. (None of us knew it was the onset of Alzheimer's.) Rose sat with him. What she did know was that her sister was realizing her life's dream and had preferred to do it without her. Rose had believed they shared everything. She'd been wrong. This act was a statement by Anna that made it clear that Anna's independent life took precedence, or would from then on.

Of course, we, Rose's children and grandchildren, saw Anna's trip as scandalously selfish, but why should Anna take on Rose and Abe's expenses? And perhaps she and her husband were tired of Abe's increasing passivity and non sequiturs. Or perhaps it was Anna's way of finally becoming the dominant sister. She returned from abroad and changes continued. She dressed like the wealthy matron she was. She had her hair dyed the same persimmon color as the new carpet. She got a mink stole, something my grandmother had craved for years but had never managed to obtain. And Rose seemed to diminish as her sister preened. Her energy lagged. She still smiled at jokes, but her laugh, an irresistible deep chuckle, became rare.

Anna and Jack were away on another trip when the accident happened. Apparently my grandfather, still tall and broad but less steady on his feet than little Rose, was making his way up the long stairway to the bedroom when he lost his grip or his balance. He must have flailed out, but he didn't fall. Rose was right behind him, carrying a basket of laundry. She fell, all the way down the stairs, to bash her head on the new marble floor. My grandfather managed to dial 911 and attendants came and took her to the hospital by ambulance. My grandfather was left in the living room, in his chair, in the dark. He didn't telephone the hospital or his children. After not hearing from their mother for two days, Rose's daughters finally reached a neighbor, who went into the house and found my grandfather, disoriented, sitting in his chair. My grandmother's clean abandoned laundry, along with her blood, was on the floor. Abe's account was garbled, but my mother called the local hospitals. My grandmother had been pronounced dead on arrival and had been in the morgue for almost two days.

I can't imagine what Anna felt when she returned from her trip, but her guilt and pain were so great that she physically attacked my grandfather, who was still completely dazed, and yelled, "You killed my sister! You killed my sister!" I remember nothing at all of the funeral. Neither do my two sisters.

The dissolution afterward was very quick. My grandfather's mind either deteriorated more rapidly because of the trauma or Rose had covered for him more than we ever understood. At any rate, he went to live with my aunt for the winters and my mother for the summers. He spoke to Rose often or asked where she was. My cousins and sisters and I stood silent when he did.

Meanwhile, the sisters' house and its contents remained as the only tangible property he and my grandmother had owned. But Jack and Anna continued to live in it and it seemed they were reluctant to appraise it or pay for the other half. After some time went by, a settlement was made, and I remember that my mother and at least one of my sisters went to see Anna and Jack and go through the house to pick up Rose's property. But when my sister wanted to take a china cup and saucer emblazoned with "Remember Me" that she had bought my grandmother at a bazaar, Great-Aunt Anna refused, saying it was hers. So apparently were the Meissen statuettes of a shepherd and shepherdess that stood on the mantle. So, in fact, was the French porcelain lamp beside my grandfather's chair. So she claimed, was every knickknack, picture, bowl, and cup that Rose's daughters selected as keepsakes. Anna owned it all. My sister watched our mother and aunt as they were denied each selection. In retaliation, she stole the Jersey knife when Anna wasn't looking.

I have nothing at all of my grandmother's, except the old rugs they threw away when Anna carpeted the living room. Rose's daughters have only her jewelry and their pride. They didn't argue. They went mute. I never spoke to my great-aunt Anna or Jack or their children and grandchildren again, though I had spent every holiday, every vacation of my early life with them. It wasn't a feud. There were no sallies back and forth, no sides taken. It was ended. And my mother and her sister lost not only their birth mother but the other woman who had raised them, nursed them, and knew them from birth.

Women without sisters have often told me how they long for them. "I know I wouldn't be lonely if I had a sister like yours," my friend Sue recently told me. And my sisters, at different times in my life, have been my closest friends.

But then I think of Rose. Rose had lived her whole life with not only a husband and two children but a brother-in-law, two nieces, and a nephew always around her, as well as constant visitations of brothers, their wives and kids, and eventually grandchildren and grandnieces and nephews. Most importantly, she spent her days with her sister, talking, working, shopping, housekeeping. Yet somehow the bond of sisterhood she seemed to count on most had not held. Worse, she died alone, either on the marble floor, in the ambulance on the way to the hospital, or perhaps in the hallway of the emergency room. I hope it was the first choice, the instantaneous death without time for reflection.

Olivia Goldsmith

AT AGE 33, *divorced and childless, Olivia Goldsmith had become so dissatisfied with her career as a New York City management consultant, and her life in general, that she left for Vermont and hunkered down to try to make it as a novelist. Though she had already had some success writing magazine articles, it was a huge risk. She gave herself three years to get published and lived off stock options.*

At the end of those three years, she had amassed $40,000 in debt and 27 rejection letters. Things, to put it succinctly, looked bleak.

Then came the unexpected call that the novel New York publishers had had been embraced by Hollywood and three of its most popular leading ladies. The First Wives Club, starring Goldie Hawn, Diane Keaton, and Bette Midler, premiered and became a hit in 1996, as did the book.

Now in her midforties, Goldsmith's best-selling status includes six other novels, Switcheroo, The Bestseller, Marrying Mom, Fashionably Late, Flavor of the Month, and Simple Isn't Easy. A sequel to First Wives is due out in 2000.

What, after all her travails, would Goldsmith advise women to do to encourage their own successes? "Listen to your inner voice," she said in an interview with the Jewish Exponent's Melissa Solomon. "I look at the very serious problems women face and try to write with humor. Otherwise, it's too painful. Women deal with thorny, depressing issues. We all deserve an award for grappling with them."

—C. O.

Venus Flygirls

A NOVEL EXCERPT

Lolita Files

"So how you feelin'?"

I sat up in bed, my head slightly throbbing. Reesy handed me a glass of pineapple juice with ice in it. She knew I always liked my juice with ice. I took a sip. The cool sensation of the liquid coursing over my tongue with its acidy sweetness was invigorating.

"Better," I said.

"That's good. You look a lot better today than you have in the past few weeks. Your skin's got a little color to it."

I rolled my eyes up at her and snickered at this remark.

"What the hell is that supposed to mean?" I asked in exasperation. "Of course my skin has some color to it. I'm brown."

I continued to sip my pineapple juice.

Reesy looked surprised.

"You know what I meant, you mean heffah. You look like you've got a little bit of life to you today."

"You need to say what you mean," I mumbled.

"I thought I did," she replied.

"Well, it's not like I'm white or something. I'm always gonna have a little color to me. That was such a stupid thing to say."

I took another sip of juice.

Reesy just stared at me.

"So is *this* it?" Reesy asked.

"Is *what* it?" I didn't even look up. I just kept sipping my juice.

"*This!*" she snapped, waving her hand over me in a sweeping motion.

"I don't know exactly what you mean," I said dully.

"I mean, is *this* what you've become now? You crawled into your little cocoon three weeks ago, all beat-down and pitiful, and *this* is what emerged? A bitter bitch who doesn't have the sense of humor God gave a goat?"

I pretended to drink the juice. My lips lingered on the rim of the glass. I felt a little sheepish.

Reesy kept on.

"I've been your friend through all this. I sat here and listened to you cry day in and day out. You call me from work whining. You crawl into bed as soon as you get home. You won't have lunch with Cleotis. Do you know he called me? I don't even know how he got my phone number."

I looked up at her.

"What'd he want?"

"He wanted to know what the fuck was wrong with you!"

"What'd you tell him?" I asked with concern.

The last thing I wanted was everyone at work knowing about what happened.

"I told him not to worry. You'd be all right."

I looked back down into my glass of juice.

"People have been noticing what's going on with you at work. You're crazy if you think they haven't. You've lost weight. You half-fix your hair when you go to the office."

I played with my juice glass.

"Why do you think I've been staying over here with you like this?" she asked. "I didn't say shit about Roman or do anything to make you hurt any more than you had to, because, hell, Misty, I've been feeling your hurt for you. You don't know what it's like to sit around and watch your friend fall into a hole right in front of your eyes."

"You could have gone," I muttered meanly. "You didn't have to watch."

She sighed deeply.

"Do you think I like seeing you laying around suffering like this? You're my girl. You're my role model. You've got more ambition in your thumbnail than I'll probably ever have in my whole lifetime."

I looked up at her sidelong, surprised to hear such a confession from her.

"You're the role model, Miss Shake Your Groove Thang," I said with bitter sarcasm.

It was a rotten thing to say. I didn't really mean it. I was actually somewhat jealous. Learning that your best friend was an exotic dancer was a giant pill to swallow.

When I saw her in action, I was surprised at what I saw. Reesy was good. *Damn good.* And men *loved* her. Something I seemed to have a problem getting them to do.

Yeah. I was jealous of her in a big way.

"Go ahead," she said. "Be nasty to me, if it'll make you feel any better. But you need to change your program, girl."

I listened, my demeanor morose.

"I see you meet these guys, and they're losers. You have so many things going for you in your life, but you keep meeting these lyin', schemin', punchin', cheatin', layin'-up-in-the-cut-ass niggas who make you think there's something wrong with you. It's not your fault. You've just got a big heart. But you need to find a way to tie your head into the whole equation."

"*Anyway* . . . ," I interrupted.

"*Anyway*," she continued, "it doesn't matter how many losers you meet, or whatever happens in your life. I'm always here for you. I always listen. Sometimes I say stupid stuff that I'm really sorry for, but I've got a big mouth. I speak my mind. I'm frank and I'm harsh. But you've known me for twenty-three years. It comes with the package."

"So what's your point?" I said quietly, my lips nibbling around the edge of the glass.

Reesy had her hand on her hip, her finger pointed skyward.

"My point to you, my sistah, is this: I'm gon' be here for you. It's not fair for you to turn on me, 'cause I'm gon' be here to wipe your ass, fix your tea, change your sheets, comb your nappy ass head, and hold your hand when all them niggas don't call, show up, or run off to San Diego and get married."

That smarted. It smarted real bad.

Reesy knew it did. And I deserved it.

"I'm not saying this to hurt your feelings, Miss Divine. I'm not. I'm just hurt 'cause you're laying up here snappin' at me, and I'm not the one who did you wrong. We sistahs need to know how to properly direct our anger. If a man hurts you, get mad at the man. Not me."

"I'm sorry, Reesy. I didn't mean to snap at you like that," I said softly. "I appreciate you being here for me like this."

She plopped down on the bed.

"Well, I didn't mean to hurt your feelings, either, Misty. I'm mad about what that asshole did. I'm really mad. And to have you sit here and be mean to me instead of him ain't right. I shouldn't be taking the stabs. He should be taking 'em. Right in the fucking nuts."

"I know," I said. "I'm coping, Reesy, all right? It's hard. I took a sharp blow to my ego. And my heart. That's a year out of my life I'll never get back."

She rubbed my back.

"Yeah, girl. I hear ya. But it's gon' be all right. You'll bounce back like it was nothin'. I know you."

She smiled into my face brightly, her perky yellow face all teeth and dimples.

"After months of therapy," I added. "Some Prozac maybe. A lobotomy."

We both laughed.

"Silly. Girl, you don't need no lobotomy, and you damn shole don't need no Prozac. All you need is a trip to the beauty parlor and the mall. Get your hair done, have them do your nails. Maybe get a pedicure. Then we'll do some major shopping. That's always good for a purge. Go to Lenox and hit the stores."

"I don't think I want to go to the mall for a while, Reesy. Especially not Lenox."

She put her hand on my tangled head.

"See there? Look at how you're misdirecting your anger. The Lenox Mall ain't got nothin' to do with what Roman did."

"Association," I said. "Right now I don't need the association."

"Just because we were in the mall when you found out what an ass he is, don't let that keep you from going back. That's crazy."

I put the empty glass on the nightstand.

"I know it's crazy, Reesy. The mind's a crazy thing. Right now, I think I need to stay as far away from the Lenox Mall as I possibly can."

She sighed helplessly.

"Whatever," she said.

She ran her fingers through the matted mass of hair on my head.

"So are you gonna stay in bed all day?" she asked.

I shrugged my shoulders.

She turned sideways, facing me, all smiles.

"Whatsay we get up, wash your hair, and I'll fix it up real cute. We can go for a drive, or ride out to Piedmont Park.

Maybe even go down to Little Five Points, to that record store you love so much. The one where they have all that music from the seventies and eighties on CD for so cheap. What's the name of it?"

"Wax 'n' Facts," I droned dully.

"Yeah. That's the place. Maybe I can find those old Rufus and Chaka Khan albums I been looking for. I can't find *Ask Rufus* on CD to save my life."

I listened to her, but my mind was going a mile a minute. I'd already come to a decision about what I wanted to do. And it didn't include riding out to Piedmont Park or trolling record stores in Little Five Points.

"So what do you say?" Reesy asked, all animated.

"I want to leave Atlanta," I announced.

"*What?*" she asked, totally taken aback. "Where did *that* come from?"

"It's been there for a while. I've been thinking about it a lot lately, and it's what I decided I want to do."

Reesy was quiet for a moment. Her lips were pressed tightly together.

I slumped back deep into my pillows, waiting for the barrage of comments I knew was about to come flying out of her mouth. I could practically hear the wheels a-turning in that tightly braided-up head of hers. I knew it was a matter of seconds before it all came pouring out.

"You know, you shouldn't let some nigga run you out of town like that," she said softly.

I was stunned. I wasn't expecting her to come at me so strong.

"I'm *not* letting Roman run me out of town!" I snapped. "He doesn't even live here anymore, so what does *he* have to do with it?"

"*Exactly!*" Reesy said. "He doesn't even *live* here anymore. So why do you have to leave? Let me guess. Association, right?"

I didn't say anything. I found myself getting angry at Reesy again, but I checked it because I wanted to make sure I was directing my anger at the right source. She took my silence as defiance and kept prattling on.

"That nigga wasn't *shit*, Misty. He damn shole ain't worth leaving Atlanta for. This city has so much to offer people of color. I mean, we actually have the opportunity to own things here. We run government here. We're *the shit* here. These are the kinds of positive images we need as sistahs and as a people. That's what you said when you moved here, and that's what you said when you talked me into moving here, too, I might remind you."

I rolled my eyes at her. She knew damn well I didn't talk her into moving here. She came of her own, ain't-got-no-damn-direction accord.

She huffed indignantly.

"I can't believe you're letting that asshole make you move away from a city big enough to swallow a million assholes like him whole without anybody noticing it."

I watched her, sitting next to me pitching a fit. She acted like I said I was going to kill myself or something. All I wanted to do was make a fresh start. Atlanta was cool and all, but I needed to get away from it for a while. It was association like a mug, though I couldn't tell Reesy that right now.

"Roman isn't the reason I'm leaving Atlanta," I stated calmly.

It wasn't actually a lie. Just partially one.

"I thought you liked it here," Reesy argued.

"I do. But I think it's time for me to make a change."

She shook her head in disbelief.

"You've only lived here two years. You have a good job, a nice future, everybody likes you. Why the hell would you want to leave all that?"

"I did it when I moved before."

"Oh," Reesy mused. "So you're gonna spend your life just hoppin' around from place to place every time things don't go the way you want them to romantically?"

"I'm not gonna sit here and defend to you all the reasons I have for wanting a change in my life. You know I moved here because of my job."

"And to get away from crazy Stefan."

I sighed in frustration.

"I'm not gonna even have this verbal joust with you. You know why I moved here. I think Atlanta is great. I like it a lot. It has a lot of things going on for us as a people. And I've had a chance to learn a lot and move up the corporate ladder. I learned stuff that I can take with me anywhere."

I brought my knees up to my chest.

"So what's your beef?" she asked.

"I'm just ready to go."

Reesy was quiet.

"So what are you gonna do about your job?"

"Leave."

She looked at me like I was crazy.

"*Just like that,* you're gonna walk away from your job? After Rich Landey flew down to Fort Lauderdale, practically begged your ass to take it, then moved you up here for free? You don't get opportunities like that, or people flying *to you* to extend them, every day. And you're gonna just walk away?"

I nodded.

"I've never had a problem getting a job. I can get another one."

She shook her head in disbelief.

"Misty, you done lost your mind."

"I'm gonna give notice," I said. "Plus, I have some leave time."

Reesy got up from the bed. She wandered around the room. She went over to the window and peered out.

"Why is this miniblind bent back like this?" she asked.

"I'on know," I lied, remembering the many nights I had peeked out, waiting for Roman to drive up.

We were both silent for a long time. I sat in my bed playing with my fingernails. They were long and hard, probably the only thing about me that was still in admirable condition.

"It's a beautiful day outside," she said finally. "If you got out of this depressing apartment and let the sun hit you for a minute, you might come to your senses, you know."

I sighed loudly.

"Reesy, I *have* come to my senses. I'm leaving Atlanta. That's all there is to it."

I didn't even bother to look up from my nails as I said this.

She turned around and studied my face. The zillions of braids that had defined her hair for the last two decades were twisted into a bun piled high on her head. She stood there, giving me a quizzical look that was part concern, part resignation. Reesy knew me. She's seen me move before. She knew that once I made a declaration like this, it was useless.

Mentally, she knew, I was already out of Atlanta.

"Damn, Misty! Here we go with *this* shit again!"

I looked up from picking my nails, taken aback by her comment.

"What do you mean, *this* shit?"

"I mean, here I go, gotta find me a new job in a new city. Just because my girl's got wanderlust and can't keep her hot little ass settled down in one place."

I scanned her face. This girl was dead serious. Inside of me, I smiled. I was elated. If I had really thought about it, I should have known Reesy was coming with me wherever I was going. She was my sistah.

Anybody else might have thought we had some kind of

55

weird, kinky thing going on, with her picking up and going every time I did. But our relationship was so special to me.

No matter what, I knew Reesy wasn't going to let me be out there alone.

"So where we moving to *this* time?" she asked, matter-of-factly.

I smiled at her, my long-nailed hands now folded in my lap.

"New York?" I said. Part question, part statement.

"*Godddddamm!*" She laughed, shaking her head. "Heaven help us, heffah! Heaven help us!"

"Why do you want to resign, Misty?" Rich asked. "You've been with the company two years now. You're one of the best managers I've got. Look at how you've built up your portfolio. The guys are even jealous because I give most of the important accounts to you. There's definitely room for growth for you with us."

I listened to him talk to me with sincerity and warmth. He was the quintessential corporate American vice president: a neatly trimmed, military haircut that was frosty only around the temples; politically correct in his tailored blue suit, yellow power tie, and crisp white cotton shirt. Rich jogged ten miles every day and was a strict vegetarian. He had two Miss America–looking daughters in college whom the sun rose and set upon, and an anorexic, way-too-tanned wife who spent her days doing the country club thing.

His small eyes peered at me out of a ruddy, post-fiftyish face. Rich Landey was a good-looking man, if older white men was your thing. It wasn't mine. Even though he did flirt with me quite often, in an inoffensive kind of way.

"There's no way I can talk you into staying on here? There are going to be some fantastic opportunities coming up in the near future. We're buying properties and investing in real estate like crazy."

I looked at him, so earnest and tenacious in his efforts to get me to stay.

No dice. Atlanta had been officially stricken off my list.

I shook my head slowly.

"No, Rich. I don't think so. I've made up my mind. Atlanta's had an impact on me lately in a way that makes me believe it's not meant for me to be here. I need a life change. I think it's time for me to make my home in a place where I feel there's a better fit."

Rich nodded as if he understood. He rubbed his chin pensively.

"You know, Misty, I went through the same thing ten years ago. Everyone thought I was crazy, wanting a change like that at forty-five, especially my family. But I did it. Uprooted my wife and daughters, and it was the best thing I ever did for my career and my life."

This made me feel somewhat encouraged, although realistically I knew that uprootings were probably far easier for a successful, well-educated white man than for me.

"Do you know where you're going, Misty?" he asked. "Perhaps I can put out some feelers for you, give you a reference. Maybe call up some friends in the business. That is, if you're not considering changing careers as well as locales."

I should have known he would say something like this. I'd gotten to know him well, and he had turned out to be my second-best ally. After Reesy.

"I'm really flattered you would do that for me," I said and smiled shyly.

He casually waved his hand.

"Don't you know what kind of contribution you've made to this company?"

"Well . . . yeah," I grinned.

"I'm sorry I haven't been able to spend the kind of time with you I did during your first year," he said pensively. "I've been so busy chasing down deals and concentrating on corporate expansion. I think we lost touch with each other a little."

"It's okay, Rich. I always knew you were in my corner. You didn't have to always be in my face for me to know that."

"Good," he said. "I'm glad you know how I feel."

I casually looked away, out of the window behind him. It was a breathtaking view of the Atlanta skyline. In the distance, I swear I thought I could see Stone Mountain.

"Rich, can I ask you a frank question?"

"Sure," he said, his expression earnest and intense.

"I guess I need to tell you up front, it's a racial question."

"Shoot," he replied.

"I know I've done a great job for you; I mean, heck, that's why you moved me up here in the first place. I can only guess that's why you've given me such a big portfolio now."

"Right," he agreed.

I looked down at my nails, then up at him again.

"You'll probably think this is a crazy question."

"No, I won't, Misty. Go ahead."

I smiled.

"I'm only asking you this because I feel like I can talk to you. About almost anything."

"Almost anything?" he smiled.

"Yeah. Almost anything."

"So? What's your crazy question?"

"Why aren't there any black males in the company that are being given the opportunities I am?"

His brow shot up quizzically.

I quickly tried to clarify.

"I mean, I know there are some out there who are capable. I keep moving up, up, up, and believe me, I've got no complaints about that. But I've been here for two years and haven't seen any black men in this whole big company getting the breaks that I am. I just see people who look like Jeremy."

He nodded.

"You're right, Misty. But that's not by design. There aren't a lot of black men out there that we've found qualified to do the level of work you're doing."

"C'mon, Rich, really. I know I'm good, but I don't think I'm that unique. Are we doing the kind of recruiting that would even reach the black men that are qualified? Or is it all done in an inside way, like how you got me? From a management company."

He pressed his lips together.

"You know, I've never really thought about it."

"I guess there's no reason you would have," I said absently. "I just think it would be nice to see more African-Americans in companies like this, representing both genders. This has been such a wonderful place to work. It's a place where a person can really feel like they're making a contribution."

"Maybe I should pay more attention to it," he said.

I studied his face.

"I didn't say that to take a stab at you," I explained. "It's just something I've thought about. I mean, I see people in positions like Cleotis's all the time. But I know there are plenty of black males out there who are very capable managers as well."

"Thanks for saying that, Misty. I'll remember it. But even now, I could show you some places in this company where you'll find some of the examples you're talking about."

"Yeah," I said. "Oh well . . ."

We were both quiet for a moment.

"You never did answer me. Are you making a break from

59

this business, or can I help you out in any way wherever you plan on going?"

I answered quickly.

"No, I don't plan on changing careers. Not at all. In fact, I'm hoping I have a pretty good chance of finding work in New York, especially since corporate asset management is such a big deal there."

Rich burst out laughing, abruptly changing the mood of the room. A deep, hearty, gut-busting laugh.

"You're moving to *New York*, Misty?" he laughed.

"Yes," I said, surprised at his laughter. "Why?"

"*New York City?*" he questioned again.

"Yes. New York City," I repeated, puzzled.

"So you think you'll have a better fit in New York than in Atlanta?" he asked, his face contorted in disbelief. "The people there are cretins, Misty! Absolute asses!"

"Then, for the most part, Rich, it should be a smooth transition," I stated.

He quieted his laughter and began to rub his chin, a smile still haunting his face.

"That's an interesting comment, Misty. I won't pry and ask its etymology."

"Don't. It's too time-consuming and pathetic for me to go into."

He rose from his chair and started walking around the huge office.

"You know what, Misty?" his eyes were twinkling, like he'd just had a vision.

"What, Rich?"

"How about a transfer?"

"We don't have an office in New York, do we?" I asked.

"Well, yes, and no," Rich said. "Remember six months ago we bought out the Burch Financial Group?"

"Y-y-yesss," I said slowly, picking my brain for details of that particular deal. "I remember you spent a lot of time going back and forth out of town negotiating it, but you spent most of your time in Canada, I thought."

"That's because their former parent company, Gulfstream World Enterprises, is based there."

"Oh," I said.

"Well, the Burch Group is ours. It's headquartered in downtown Manhattan. We're the parent company now, and it's given us a stronghold in cities like New York without having to go in and try to build a reputation from scratch."

"I understand," I nodded.

"In the past few months we've been turning over personnel and transitioning Burch's standards to fall in line with ours."

I kept nodding, seeing a potential positive development out of all this.

"Remember Bob Blanculowitz?" he asked.

"I think so. Didn't he come here once? You took him on a tour of the department?"

"*Yes!* Not long after we closed the deal."

"I remember that," I said. "He was a tall, stiff-looking kinda guy. Like he never laughed a day in his life."

Rich chuckled.

"That's Bob," he laughed. "I don't believe he's really as anal as he seems, though. He was just trying to impress the boss. That's me."

"I see," I said.

I wasn't sure I did.

"Let me cut to the chase, Misty. Bob used to be the VP of diversification for Burch Financial. His job was pretty much the equivalent of mine here, so when we took over, he began to report to me. His title is now comptroller for Burch, even though he's still handling diversification. With my guidance and supervision, of course."

"Uh-huh," I said, trying to follow where he was heading.

"We're going to be adding more asset managers at Burch.

Right now the load on the existing managers is way too heavy for the type of concentration they need to be doing on their portfolios. I'm also having Bob turn over some of the less productive managers. We need aggressive people in our company, not slough-offs."

I nodded, a slight smile forming on my lips.

"Obviously you see where I'm going with this," he said.

"Possibly," I said.

"Well, Misty, I'm offering you one of those positions, if you'll take it. But there's a catch: I'd like to make you a senior asset manager. With a possible chance to take over Bob's job in the near future."

"Are you serious, Rich?" I exclaimed. *"You're going to give me his job?"*

"It's yours if you want it," he replied. "I think you're more than ready to move on to the next level."

Shit!

My heart was pumping wildly. I was finally going to get a chance at what I'd been working so hard for.

The skin on my arms had raised up in a million little goose pimples.

"What about Bob?" I asked.

His expression was intense.

"Bob's too set in his ways. He's not very open to new ideas and that makes it hard for us to make any progress. I need someone with a fresh approach. You've got just what it takes to get in there and do the job."

"I'll do my best, that's for sure."

"I know you will," he said. "That's why I'm offering you the job."

I nodded, in a daze, already picturing myself in New York running things.

"So what do you think?" Rich asked. "Are you ready to take on the Big Apple?"

"Are you kidding?" I exclaimed. "When can I start?"

* * *

"*Unbelievable!*" Reesy cried. "*Un-fucking-*believable!"

"What?" I asked innocently, knowing full well what she was talking about.

Reesy paced around erratically in my living room that evening, shaking her head.

"I can't fucking believe how your life *sucks* to high heaven, yet shit just *drops* into your lap when it comes to your career!"

I didn't know whether to be flattered or insulted by her comment.

"My love life doesn't suck, Reesy," I said shortly. "And I don't exactly see you in a Cinderella relationship right now either."

"*Black*arella, honey. Ain't nothin' *Cinder*ella 'bout me," she quipped.

Amazing how yellow negroes were also so militant.

"Well, you ain't no *Black*arella right now either, Miss Thang, so far as I can see."

"Yeah, but I'm running the shit I do have going on. Niggas know they can't play me for no dummy. They got to come hard when they're steppin' to the Reesy!"

She patted herself on the chest as she strutted around the room like a cocky little peahen. Talking that ghetto talk again.

"You'd stop doing that if you knew how foolish you looked," I laughed.

"You're just jealous, bitch. 'Cause you know I'm *all* that." She grinned.

"Of course you are, Reesy. Of course you are." I rolled my eyes as I said this. "But this ain't the Magic City. Ain't no stripping going to be going on in here."

"*Exotic dancing,*" she corrected.

"Whatever," I said.

She came over to the arm of the chair where I was sitting. She looked at me, shaking her zillions of braids vigorously.

"Now, don't try to change the subject, heffah," she said. "I want to know how you always manage to get great jobs to just fall in your lap, while the rest of us sistahs are out here scrugglin' like a muhfucka."

I looked up at her, amazed.

"I didn't try to change the subject, Reesy." I laughed.

"Yes you did, bitch. You're doing it now."

"You know, you curse way too much. No wonder men are scared of you."

She chuckled.

"They're not scared of me, honey. They *respect* me." She worked her head sharply. "There's a difference, you know."

"Who's changing the subject now?" I asked.

"Quit playing, Misty," she snapped anxiously. "Now, you tell me how it is your boss offers you a job taking over an office in Manhattan, *just like that?* You go in there and tell his ass good-bye, and come out a fucking CFO. That shit ain't normal."

"It's not a CFO," I protested. "It's a senior asset manager."

"What difference does it make?" she returned. "You're gonna be running the office eventually. You must have given him some pussy once or something, for him to be carving out your career the way he is."

I glared at her, then shoved her off the arm of the chair.

"Get away from me with your little nasty mouth!" I huffed. "What would even make you say some stupid shit like that?"

"I'on know, girl," she said apologetically, realizing I was serious. "I was just playin'. But why else would a white man give you such a prize job? They're not ones to give us shit. There's usually a catch. And most times with black women, it's pussy."

"Did it ever dawn on you that maybe I'm good at what I

do? That maybe he saw a fit for me with the position in New York?"

She shrugged.

"Whatever," she said.

She hesitated a moment, then said, "How come everything with you is all about a *fit*, Misty?"

"Because, if it doesn't feel right, I have to move on."

"Then how come you never got hip to Roman and his shit?" she asked.

I didn't say anything. I actually had to think about that for a moment.

"Don't tell me you thought that nigga was a fit for you?"

I stared off into the nothingness ahead of me.

"Huh?" she persisted.

"No, Reesy," I conceded. "Roman wasn't a fit. You know that. I don't know why you're asking me that stupid question."

She plopped down on the couch across from me.

"I just don't understand why you put up with that mess for a year."

She shook her head in amazement, as if I wasn't even there.

"As sharp and driven as you are, for the life of me, I just can't understand it, girl."

"Yeah," I said softly. "I can't either."

Suddenly her tone was upbeat.

"Oh well, it don't matter now. Looks like it worked out to your advantage. You're about to go off to a big-ass, hot-shot job in Noo Yawk Siddy. *Gon', girl! Do your thang!*"

"You're so silly, Reesy!" I giggled.

"I'm for real. I'm proud of you, even though you ain't got no sense when it comes to men."

I threw a pillow from my armchair at her.

"*Quit!*" She laughed, ducking from the pillow. "You gon' need me in Noo Yawk, so you better not hurt me."

"Is that right?" I asked rhetorically.

She nodded, her head moving so swiftly, it made her look goofy.

"Well, if you know what's good for you," I said, "you better stop saying the first thing that comes out of your mouth to people. You'll get shot up for that mess in New York with a quickness."

Reesy clucked her tongue.

"*Honey, please!* she exclaimed. "I'll be fine. I'll fit in perfectly with all those assholes in Noo Yawk!"

"You're right about that," I laughed.

"You're the one I'm worried about," she added. "What's gonna happen when Pollyanna Purebred hits the streets of Manhattan? The niggas are gonna be knee deep with numbers standing in line to take a crack at your naive ass."

I laughed at that. I was feeling so much better now that I knew I, thanks to Rich Landey, once again had the opportunity of a lifetime to look forward to.

One that would include a relocation package.

This was a good thing, I realized. It was helping considerably in diminishing my concentration on the legacy of pain and hurt Roman had left me with.

"But it's all right, girl," Reesy continued, still wrapped up in our conversation. "I got your back."

"Do you now?" I asked sarcastically.

"Yep," she said, jumping up from the sofa. She walked over to her big heavy shoulderbag, which she had parked by the front door.

"Which reminds me," she said brightly. "I bought you something today. I almost forgot about it."

I was suddenly filled with affection for her. Even though she cursed like a sailor, and was way too frank and harsh with me most times, Reesy was always thinking about me. She always had my best interests at heart.

She pulled a plastic bag from the purse. She walked over and stood just above me.

I looked up at her, warmth and the spirit of camaraderie rushing over me, oozing through my very pores.

"I love you, Reesy," I said matter-of-factly.

"I love you, too, girl," she returned.

She pulled a book from the plastic bag. I smiled. Reesy knew I loved to read. She knew books often replaced boyfriends in the empty space that I loosely called my love life. She handed it to me.

I reached for it, staring at the cover for a few seconds before I actually focused on the title. When I finally did, my eyes were like saucers.

Smart Women, Foolish Choices.

That damn Reesy. She just never, ever quit.

I was packing up my things, excited at the prospect of something new, someplace different. This would be the *third* time I had moved to a major city in less than ten years. When I told my parents about it, they were very supportive and congratulatory. Mama was worried about me living in New York, but she was glad to hear that Reesy was coming with me.

As I thought about things now, I realized that Cleotis was right. About me being naive enough to think that I could spot a cheating man a mile away.

Roman taught me a lesson. Lesson enough to make me want to move on, away from Atlanta with its well-packaged men and their well-packaged, build-to-suit romantic plans that included the girlfriend du jour. I was not willing to be a part of that scene.

The move to New York would be the best thing for me. I knew it. In a city with nine million people, I could lose myself, take my time and find a man who was right for me.

More than anything else, I could concentrate on my career and build a solid future for myself.

I smiled to myself as I wrapped up my dishes in newspaper. I couldn't wait to get to New York. Starting over again would be a wonderful feeling. Just the feeling I needed to make me forget the shame of what happened with Roman.

It still hurt real bad to think about it. But the hurt was more ego than anything. I couldn't accept that I could be stupid enough to love a man so desperately that I chose to ignore all the signs that he was never really mine.

I had to admit, I always knew something wasn't on the up-and-up. But I figured if I hung in there long enough, all the problems would go away and Roman would be all mine.

I guess God has a way of making us look stupidity in the face, no matter how much we try to run away from the truth. Too bad we can't pick the moment to be confronted with that stupidity.

It hadn't helped that I was squatting over the toilet with my panties in a bunch when the bomb was dropped on me.

I had begun to act as if the whole thing with Roman never happened at all. I knew this was not a good approach, and that one day the dam would break. Then I'd have to face the issue for what it was.

For right now, I chose to tuck it all away inside.

I had a new life to start in a big city far, far away.

"Girl, I at least need to find me a job before I go. I ain't like you with shit just dropping into my lap."

Reesy sat on my couch crosslegged, the *New York Times* classified section open across her lap. There were several ads boldly circled in black.

I was still packing, stowing books, pictures, and towels into boxes. I had already packed up my most important stuff: the African masks, the Senegalese collection of villagers, and my black art.

I alternated between sitting and kneeling on the floor as I stuffed everything away.

"What are you looking for?" I asked. "The same kinda job you have now?"

"Hell no," she snapped. "The last thing I want is to be talking to folks on the phone all day long about stocking their vending machines with more Ding-Dongs and Ho-Hos. That shit's for the fucking birds."

I laughed as I pressed towels down into a box.

"That's not exactly what you do all day, Reesy."

"It's pretty damn close to it," she said.

I closed the box and wrote TOWELS on the outside of it.

"I've earmarked some stuff here in the *Times*. I think I want me a change of venue," she said.

"What about your night job?" I asked. "You're just gonna give that up? There's good money in that business."

She waved her hand, dismissing it all.

"No more exotic dancing for me. That was just a fantasy gig. Something I always wanted to do. Now I can walk away and say *Been there, done that*."

I struggled to get up from the floor, a little sore from all the bending. When I finally stood, I pressed my hands against my lower back and arched into a deep stretch.

"What do you *think* you want to do *now*, Reesy?" I grunted. "You've done it all, from hamburgers to hair. You've done everything but be a hoe. A real one anyway."

She laughed.

"At least, I don't *think* you have," I amended.

"Shut up, wench," she laughed. "And you know damn well I ain't done no hamburgers, so I don't even know why you gon' go there."

I abruptly stopped stretching and looked at her.

"*Reesy, pleez!*" I said. "I can't believe you! You were the burger queen. Miss McDonald's herself. You even got me a job there. You used to make everybody sick bringing all them free, dried-out, day-old hamburgers to school every day. And I'm surprised you ain't got fired for giving away

69

all that free food to your friends when they came through the drive-thru."

"I forgot about that," she said, and smiled.

"Of course you did."

She clucked her tongue and waved her hand at me, stretching her legs out over the arm of the sofa.

"I must have blocked it out," she retorted. "Plus, it don't count anyway. That was when we was in high school. Work before or during college doesn't count in the scheme of what I've done in my life."

I grabbed an armful of knickknacks and some newspaper, and sat back on the floor again.

"Come again?" I said.

"Just what I said," Reesy replied. "What I did before and during college doesn't count."

I began wrapping the knickknacks in newspaper and placing them into a box. I looked up at her, sitting there on my couch with her legs cocked up.

"How is that?" I asked.

"Those weren't real jobs," she said.

I laughed, shaking my head.

"I'll bet the people who hired you to do them thought they were. And if I recall correctly, you got paid for them, which usually qualifies for what is defined as a job."

"But I didn't need the money to survive," Reesy said. "That's what makes the difference. When I worked in high school, I was living with my parents. When I worked in college, that was for extra money to go partying and shopping with."

"And you need the money now to survive?" I cynically asked.

"Yes, Miss Smarty, I do," Reesy said. "My parents haven't given me money since I got out of school."

I rolled my eyes at her. I knew it wasn't a lie. It was just a gross distortion of the truth.

70

"What about that quarterly stipend?" I asked.

She was holding the paper up to her face now, blocking my view of her expression.

"You know that doesn't count," she said dryly. "I barely even get to see that money. I've never even used it."

"Umph," I grunted.

She pulled the paper down from her face.

"What does *that* mean?" she demanded. "You know I don't take money from them."

"Nothing," I said, the pitch of my voice unnaturally high.

She clucked her tongue at me.

"Heffah, I know what you're getting at," she said. "Just because I take stuff from them, that don't mean nothing. I make my own way, and they ain't giving me nothing that contributes to my day-to-day existence."

"Yeah, whatever," I replied.

That was a crock of shit. Those years of stipends out there accruing interest and generating dividends smelled like day-to-day eventual contributions to me.

I stuffed the last knickknack into the box and wrote FRAGILE GLASS on the outside when I sealed it closed.

I stood up and walked into the kitchen.

"You want something to drink?" I asked her.

"Case in point," she kept on, ignoring my question, "this morning I told them I was moving to New York. They asked me if I had a job lined up, and I told them no. They had a fit. Mama tried to talk me out of moving, and when she saw it was futile, she offered me five thousand dollars to help with the move."

I was pouring myself a tumbler of water. When I heard her mention $5,000 for the move, my hand froze, the cup just inches from my mouth.

"And you said . . . ?"

"*No!*" she shrieked, incredulous that I would even ask.

I put the tumbler down and leaned against the counter. I tried to fathom the thought of anyone, especially my parents, *ever* offering me $5,000 *gratis*, and me turning it down. Stuff like this never happened to me.

I peered at her from the kitchen. I studied her closely, like she was an amoeba or some other weird microscopic thing worthy of scrutiny. She stared back at me, her indignation at the offer of money quite comic and ridiculous.

"Just because I've taken trips and furniture doesn't mean they can just throw money at me to make things easy. This move is my thing, not theirs," she said.

"Actually, it's *my* thing," I corrected.

"I know that, heffah, but I'm talking about from their perspective. This has nothing to do with them, so I don't need their money to jump-start me on getting settled in New York."

I picked up the tumbler and drank some water. I needed it.

"Why don't you just take the money as a loan?" I asked. "At least until you find a job. You don't have to use it all."

Reesy shook her head vehemently.

"No way, Miss Divine. I don't want to even get myself in the habit of taking money from my folks, 'cause then it'll be too easy for me to do it again. A lot of the bad habits I have now are because my parents made things too easy for me. I spent my twenties trying to break those habits. Now that I'm thirty, I don't want to spend another decade doing the same thing all over again."

"All right," I said.

I brought the tumbler into the living room and sat down on the chair across from her.

"Do you understand where I'm coming from, Misty?" she asked.

She looked really pained about all this. For the life of me, no, I couldn't understand. But I lied to her. Unlike Reesy, I didn't get my jollies out of being brutal and frank.

72

"Sort of. I didn't grow up with money and there are never any instances in my life where it's being offered to me in chunks of five thousand, so it's hard for me to feel sympathy for you."

"What about this job you're getting in New York? Your boss just handed it to you like it was nothing. People would kill for something like that."

"That's different, Reesy. I work hard for Rich. I've put in sixteen-hour days on many, many, many occasions. I've spent lonely nights in hotel rooms, I've done the O.J. thing, the *old* O.J. thing, not the new one, running through the airport and nearly breaking my neck hundreds of times trying to make connecting flights. Rich didn't just hand this job to me. I've earned it."

She sat there listening to me, but I don't think she could really relate.

"Well, Misty, in your own way, you have people in your life like my parents, making it easy for you whether you want them to or not. Rich Landey is one of those people."

"Rich Landey and your parents are two totally different issues!"

"I beg to differ, sweetie. Believe it or not, they're both the same."

I knew we weren't going to agree, so I steered the conversation back to its original subject.

"So what kind of jobs have you circled?"

She picked up the paper from her lap.

"Well, I figured I'd try something easy at first, like an office manager position. That way I can see what the best jobs in the company are, and target the one I really want to go for."

Why was I not surprised to hear she'd pick something easy?

"Are all those circles office manager positions?"

"Yep."

I stretched out my legs in front of me. They were sore from all the kneeling and sitting I had been doing on the floor.

"Have you done a résumé?"

"Yep."

"When are you going to send them out?"

"I already have." Reesy smiled. "I just brought the paper over here to show you I'm already on it tryna get a job."

"Good for you," I said. I was proud of her initiative. "So have you heard anything from any of them yet?"

"No," she said. "But in the cover letters I told them I would be in New York for one full day on the tenth. I figured I could do all the interviews that day, and we could still go apartment hunting the next day."

That Reesy, I tell you. Leave it to her to set the criteria for an interview. She didn't even know how quickly the people were looking to hire. I wondered how many of them would call her. I also wondered how it would be having her as my roommate.

"So you think you're ready for this, huh?" I asked.

"What, the move?"

"No, living together."

She smiled, waving her hand dismissively.

"Yeah, girl. The question is, are *you* ready?"

I had to stop and think about it. I hadn't lived with anyone since Stefan, with the exception of the bizarre little arrangement Roman and I had going on. I wondered if I was ready for the clashing of personalities, the sharing of space, the synchronizing of menstrual cycles, and the general envy of anything and everything that came when you lived with another woman.

"I guess so," I said contemplatively. "I mean, we've been best friends most of our lives. It shouldn't be that bad."

"But we've never lived together," she warned. "And you know how vocal I can be. Are you sure I won't get on your nerves?"

I chuckled at this. I knew it would be a problem. It had been a problem my entire life.

"You forget about my little stint at your place after I left Stefan. And this last episode with Roman."

"Oh yeah," she said. "But that's different. You know that wasn't a permanent deal. My big mouth on a regular basis might be too much for you."

"I've lived with it this long," I replied. "I guess it'll just be a little more common than I'm already used to. Just do me a favor."

"What?" Reesy asked suspiciously. "Tape my mouth shut?"

"No," I laughed, "but close. Just try to think before you speak sometimes. I've got a soft heart. Sometimes you shoot daggers at it and keep on going. That might get a little hard on me on a day-to-day basis."

"I'll do my best," she smiled, "if you'll do me a favor as well."

"Uh-oh," I asked. "What's that?"

She tossed the paper on the floor beside her and sat up straight on the couch.

"Try to make better choices in men. And don't have no makeshift niggas spending the night and leaving at the crack of dawn waking me up all the time."

That stung a little, but I shouldn't have been surprised she said it.

"I'll do my best," I mumbled.

"Good," she said. "Did you read that book I got you?"

"No," I snapped, pretending to be offended.

I wasn't really, but a funky kind of somber feeling, I don't know what it was, washed over me.

"Well," she said, "I hope you read it before we go."

"Maybe I will. Maybe I won't," I retorted. "Maybe I don't need to. I haven't made that many foolish choices in men in my life."

"I never said you did. But I know a pattern when I spot

one," she laughed. "Reading that book could head it off at the pass."

"Yeah, yeah, yeah, whatever," I said. I was beginning to feel a little depressed.

"So we're still flying up this Friday?"

"Unh-huh."

"Did you order my ticket?" she asked.

"Yep," I replied.

Since the company was paying for me to go up and meet with Bob Blanculowitz, I'd decided to redeem frequent flyer miles to give Reesy a free ticket.

We were flying up for the weekend to play. On Monday I was meeting with Bob. On Tuesday Reesy and I were going to try to find an apartment.

Which Rich, by the way, had arranged for the company to pay for, along with the utilities, for one year as a part of a relocation benefit package.

The company was also paying completely for my move. All expenses, the apartment, the utilities, the movers, hell, even the gum we chewed on the way there, were being charged to Burch Financial.

"So the ticket'll be here by Friday? We can leave after I get off work?" Reesy asked.

"Yep," I said.

"Why are you so tight-lipped all of a sudden?" she asked. "Are you mad at me? I was just playing, sort of, about that book. Read it if you want to. I don't care."

"I'm not mad," I said. "I don't know, I just got kinda weird for a minute. I don't know why."

Reesy rolled her eyes skyward.

"*Oh lord*, a moody bitch." She sighed. "Is this what I have to look forward to?"

"Probably so." I smiled.

"Oh well," she said. "Forewarned is forearmed."

I nodded, still pensive for I didn't know why. Perhaps her allusion to Roman coming and going early in the morning did something to me. I knew the demon of what he had done was still possessing me in a big way. I had to exorcise that demon and confront it. Otherwise it was destined to haunt me for the rest of my life.

"Oh well," I said, rising from the chair. "You wanna go get something to eat? I can't cook, 'cause I've damn near packed up every pot in the place."

"That's fine with me, girl," Reesy said. "Let's go to the Underground. I feel like some Hooters."

"*Hooters?*" I laughed. "Where the *hell* did that come from? You wanna go man-watching or something? You know you can't tell who's straight and who's not in that place. The straight men come to see the women. The gay men come to see the men."

She leaned forward and felt around the floor for her shoes.

"No," she said, "I actually just want some wings and curly fries. Believe it or not, I really do like the food at Hooters."

"I do, too," I agreed, remembering it was the place where I'd first met Roman. "It's just a surprise coming from you."

Reesy looked up from fastening her sandals.

"Why is that?" she asked.

I shrugged.

"You're so hardcore and intolerant when it comes to men. I figured the last place you'd want to be is in a restaurant with men ogling girls gallivanting around in T-tops and butt-outs."

Reesy stood up from the couch and walked over to me.

"I'm not a man-hater, Misty. I love black men."

"Yeah, but do you *like* them?" I asked, slipping on my shoes and picking up my purse.

Reesy put her arm around my shoulders as we walked to the door.

"Not all the time, sistah-girl," she replied. "Not all the time."

I didn't know my ticket to New York was going to be first class. Rich handed it to me just before I left work early Friday afternoon and I was stunned.

"You may as well take your big step in style," he said and smiled.

I didn't know what to say. I took the ticket awkwardly, but I was so happy, I kissed Rich Landey on the cheek.

"Thanks for everything you're doing for me. You're the best mentor a girl could have."

He smiled broadly.

"That's funny, Misty," he said. "I feel the same way, too. Have fun in the Big Apple this weekend. And if there's anything you have a question about Monday after meeting with Bob, give me a call."

"I'll do that, Rich. I certainly will."

We stood in line at the Delta counter. I was trying to upgrade Reesy's ticket to first class.

"I *told* you that man wants to get in them panties," Reesy mumbled. "First class. Yeah, right!"

"Reesy, please! Why don't you just go over there and sit down," I told her. "Here, take my purse and this bag."

The ticket agent upgraded the ticket without a hitch, although she did deduct an additional twenty-five hundred miles from my frequent flyer account.

I went over to Reesy and handed her the ticket. I sat down beside her.

"So how did you manage to get Monday and Tuesday off?" I asked. "Are you taking them as vacation days?"

Reesy had her long legs crossed seductively. Across from her, a brother all geared up in Karl Kani and Timberlands was sloping in his seat trying to take a sneak-peek up her way-too-short dress.

"I told Olivia I had a family emergency," she said.

I think Reesy knew the brother was looking up her dress. She had a wry smile on her face. She eyed him on the sly while she talked to me. I looked over at him. He had a smile on his face, too.

I shook my head. She could rag me all she wanted about my bad choices in men. Maybe I wasn't that smart when it came to the heart, but at least I didn't go around scoping out and picking up bad boys the way she did. Reesy liked roughnecks. The harder the head, the stronger the attraction.

"Hardheads know how to fuck," she told me once. "They ain't worth a damn for a future, but they'll fuck the shit out of your ass."

I looked at her now, casually working her legs up and down, right there in the terminal like a little hoe.

"*Reesy!*" I hissed. "*Reesy!*"

"*What?*" she snapped, turning to look at me. "Why you calling my name all harsh like that?"

"'Cause," I said sharply. "Look at you. You may as well just go ahead and lift your dress up."

She clucked her tongue at me.

"You need to close your legs," I snapped. "This place is full of people and you're sitting here acting like a slut."

"Just because you're uptight sexually, Misty, don't try to transfer that shit on me," she hissed back.

She wasn't looking at me when she said it. She was busy making eyes at the brother.

I was getting pissed.

"If you're not gonna stop, Reesy, I'm going to sit somewhere else. You can make a public display of yourself if you want to. I'm not havin' it."

I stood up abruptly, my purse and bag in hand.

She snatched me down.

"You make me sick sometimes," she griped. "I'm just tryna have a little fun to get in the right mood for the week-end. I can't fuck him or nothing, so what's the big deal?"

I sat there, glaring at her. She made me so furious some-times, especially when she acted like this.

"I think *you* need to read that book you gave me. Cocking your legs open in a full airport terminal is a foolish choice if there ever was one."

"That book is about foolish choices in love, honey, not sex," Reesy gloated. "I don't make foolish choices in love. And there's nothing wrong with a little adventure in sex."

She patted me on the leg.

"You should try it sometime, if you ever learn how to detach your heart."

I was fuming. I turned away from her to cool off. She was messing up the mood for me already, and we weren't even off the ground. What would it be like living with her, I won-dered. Would this be such a good idea?

Reesy leaned over my shoulder.

"Don't be mad at me, Misty," she cooed, her voice barely a whisper. "I'm sorry. I'm a slut; I know it. I'll try to keep it down."

I turned and looked at her.

"You haven't even told your boss you're moving, have you?" I asked, matter-of-factly.

She leaned away from me, surprised.

"N-n-no," she stammered. "There's no point in it."

"So when do you plan on telling her?"

Reesy shrugged.

"Olivia 'Booger-Eater' Bachrodt will have no problem replacing me," she replied, very nonchalant.

"So what were you gonna do, just leave?" I asked.

"Yep."

"What about your night job?"

"They can always replace me. One less set of tits in the house."

"What if you need a reference?" This nonchalance was quite incredible to me.

"From the Magic City?" she asked.

"No, your day job."

"Then I'll get one," Reesy said. "I happen to have a superb recommendation from the head honcho of a big-time firm in downtown Manhattan. She can attest to my positive work ethic, commitment, and reliability."

She looked me squarely in the eyes.

I shook my head in disbelief.

"Where do you come from, Reesy?"

"Same place you do. Venus. 'Cept we come from the black side, where the trees are. Got to have shade where the colored folks live."

I looked at her long and hard. She made a face at me, her cheeks puffed out and her eyes bucked.

Unexpectedly, I began to laugh. Reesy was so damn silly.

"New York City, *here we come!*" she squealed, putting her arm around me. "We gon' bust it out, ain't we?"

She kept talking, not giving me a chance to answer.

"Yep," she nodded, looking around. "We gon' bust that shit out. We gon' take Manhattan like a couple of dicks. Just run up in it like it's one big coochie."

She grinned broadly, turning to me for confirmation.

"We'll have to see, Reesy. We'll have to see."

"*See,* hell," she said. "New York is gon' be my thang, Miss Divine. Watch. I'ma turn that mutha out. It's gon' be one big party."

As she said this, I worried again about the roommate situation. I began to wonder, even after twenty-three years, just how well I knew Teresa Snowden.

Maybe she had some surprises in store for me that I wasn't quite ready for. Maybe she had some things going on underneath that crown of braids that were gonna shock me right back to Venus.

Lolita Files

HER MEMBER PROFILE on *America Online (AOL)* lists Lolita Files' occupations as *"Author of Best-selling Novels; Screenwriter; Actress; SUPERCHICK."*

Sounds a bit audacious, but the woman lives up to her billing. Not only is she the author of Scenes from a Sistah, *from which* "Venus Flygirls" *is excerpted, but she also starred in the recent Broadway production of* Sisters Who Get Everything Without Giving Up Anything *at the Homefront Theatre. She played Rea Montgomery, an over-the-top Southern belle.*

"Ironically," says Files, "Rea is an author who wrote best-sellers about women who get everything from men without having to compromise their morality. The irony is that the men loved them for it." Adds Files, "The women are proud of their femininity."

Scenes from a Sistah *is the first in a trilogy about Misty and Reesy. Her second book,* Getting to the Good Part, *continues the story of these two sisters of the heart from Reesy's point of view and is set in New York.*

Files was born and raised in Fort Lauderdale, Florida. Before becoming a full-time writer, she was national communications director for KinderCare Learning Centers. In keeping with the superchick mode, she is normally on the go, bouncing between New York, Los Angeles, and Florida. Her personal quote in that AOL profile sums it up: "I'm EVERY woman . . . it's ALL in me."

—C. O.

What Have You Done for Me, Lately?

A PERSONAL ESSAY

Paullina Simons

*D*uring an outing to Bear Mountain in New York one September Sunday, I looked at my mother and thought she was wearing a maternity dress.

Now I knew she couldn't be.

One, my mother was thirty-seven years old—in my thirteen-year-old eyes, practically a pensioner.

Two, a maternity dress would imply that my parents were having s—x, and *that* certainly wasn't possible.

And three, I was an only child.

"Do you have any brothers or sisters?" people would ask me. "No," I would say. "I'm an only child."

My mother was obviously wearing a loose dress. What did I know about maternity clothes?

Yet . . .

Oblivious to my thoughts, my mother continued to stroll arm in arm with a woman friend while my dad and I trailed doggedly behind. The day was sunny and warm. Everybody was quite content.

Everybody but me. My mother's tie-dyed blue cotton dress looked *too* loose for my liking.

Eventually we returned home to our apartment in Queens, New York, and I went to sleep. The next day I woke up and went to school. I was in ninth grade and was going to be graduating from junior high school at the end of the year. I was soon going to high school, and in three years, I was going to college. I thought of myself as nearly a grown-up.

Grown-ups didn't get brothers and sisters. Children got brothers and sisters. When I was a child growing up in the Soviet Union, I would have given away one of my parents to have a sibling, and, in fact, thought I had when my dad had suddenly disappeared. My mother had told me he was on an extended business trip, but after a year passed, we finally went to visit him, and I saw he wasn't on a business trip. He was in prison—for political reasons, I would much later learn. When after two long years he had come back to us, my mother and I saw him only every other weekend for two more years.

Then we came to America and settled in Queens. And now, four years later, out of the blue, my mother was wearing a maternity dress.

My parents were still at work when I came home from school that Monday afternoon. I immediately went through my mother's bureau. Nothing, nothing, nothing. Finally I found a bottle of prescription pills, hidden in the back of her makeup drawer. The prescription was in her name. The name of the pills read PRENATAL VITAMINS.

TAKE ONE A DAY, the directions instructed.

PRENATAL.

What did that mean? There was no entry under *prenatal.*

I looked up *natal.*

The dictionary said, "Of, relating to, or accompanying birth." It also said, "Of, or relating to, the time of one's birth."

I read the definition for ten minutes, over and over again.

Just in case, I looked up the prefix *pre-*. "Existing or occurring before," *Webster's* kindly informed me.

I spent until 4:30 in the afternoon trying to wrap my brain around *pre-* and *natal*. I would put the dictionary down, then pick it up again, and look for the word afresh. Maybe I had misspelled it. Maybe I hadn't read the right definition.

At five o'clock, my mother came home, in appropriately tight work clothes. I felt a little better.

At six o'clock, my father came home. We ate dinner. Maybe one of them would say something to me. If it were really true, surely they would say something to me instantly.

They said nothing.

I thought, *Maybe it isn't true.*

That night I tried to come to terms with my feelings. They were all over the place, along with my clothes and school papers and books. They were as disorganized as my room. One thing was clear, however. I was an only child. That was my defining characteristic. All my other traits, every one, stemmed from that one. That was the root of my personality, the very core of my identity. I was my mother and father's only daughter, only *child*. I also knew that my parents were as defined by their one-child-ness, as I was. We were a family for fourteen years. A *one-child family*. Me. I was the child. The *one* child.

When I had been younger, I wanted a brother or a sister, but then I got older. I still asked for a sibling, but more feebly.

Then I started growing breasts.

So here I was, nearly fourteen—with breasts and *everything*—holding a bottle of *prenatal* pills belonging to my thirty-seven-year-old mother.

At fourteen I couldn't have wanted anything less. Maybe a sexually transmitted disease, but that's it.

If my mother really had become pregnant, I knew exactly why she would. She wanted a *child* to love.

Weeks passed. My parents said nothing to me about the existence of the aforementioned pills. I started weakly hoping I misunderstood the dictionary. Maybe *prenatal* meant "to prevent natal." Wouldn't that be nice. I was sure that if my mother were actually pregnant, she would have said something by now. I don't know why I thought that. These were my parents we were talking about. When we were leaving the Soviet Union for good, my father told me a mere three weeks before our departure. When I got my period at twelve, my mother somberly stood before me and said that from now on I was going to bleed for about a week every month. Then she walked out and never spoke of it again. My parents never told me anything.

September turned into October, October into November. In November, it got very cold and I turned fourteen. *The Godfather* premiered on television, I had cavities, friends, and a little romance.

Also, my mother's stomach grew.

Her work clothes got looser, her coats got bigger, the robe she wore around the house didn't tie around her waist anymore.

Still, they said nothing. My father came home and we ate dinner. My mother started coming home earlier and taking unprecedented naps in the late afternoon. Sometimes my father would make dinner when he came home. We would eat late on those nights.

My relationship with my mother deteriorated by the day. She hardly spoke to me, certainly never kindly. She didn't seem at all happy. Every once in a while, she would leave to go to some mysterious doctor, and I'd be blissfully alone in the house.

In December, my mother no longer fit into her coat and had to buy a new one.

Also in December, we had an ice storm and my father photographed it beautifully, with my ever-enlarging mother underneath a splendid ice-covered tree. In those pictures, no one in the family smiled. My mother and I stood next to each other, making sure the sleeves of our coats didn't touch.

I had given up all illusions and grimly waited.

Finally in January, my father came into my bedroom and sat on the edge of my bed. I was reading. I reluctantly put down my book.

"I want to talk to you," he said.

"Yes?" I didn't want to hear it now. What was the point? Still, I sat up and leaned against the pillows.

"Your mother and I—we—all of us—we're expecting a visit from the stork."

"Excuse me?"

"Yes. We're going to have a baby. You're going to have a baby brother." He was smiling out of the corner of his mouth.

"A stork, huh?"

"Yes, a stork."

"I see. When is the stork coming?"

"Sometime in the middle of March." His eyes twinkled.

"And he's bringing a baby brother?"

"Yes, he is."

"I see."

"What? You don't believe me?"

"No."

My father smiled openly. "I'll make you a bet," he said. "If around March twelfth or thirteenth, the stork doesn't knock on your bedroom window and bring you a baby brother, then I will buy you a new pair of shoes."

"Really?" I badly needed a new pair of shoes.

"Yes, really."

"Okay, you got yourself a bet."

He sat there quietly for a few minutes. I could see he was struggling with himself. At last he said haltingly, "Umm . . . do you have any—questions?"

Did I have any questions?

Yes. I wanted to know if having a new child meant we would move to a bigger apartment. If my mother would stay home all the time, if I had to baby-sit, and if so, how much they would pay me. I wanted to know if having a new child meant they would never love me again. I stared at him.

"No," I said.

He squeezed my hand hard and left.

In February, during a particularly ugly fight as my mother screamed at me, she said, "I can't believe you're making me this crazy. You know that I'm expecting a child."

That was the only thing she ever said to me about it.

My mother was miserable. She and my dad fought all the time, about nothing—and everything. Her huge belly heaving, my mother made veiled threats about leaving all of us. I didn't understand any of it and didn't want to. My concern was mostly for me but partly also for my impending sibling. How was my mother going to give the new baby any affection? She seemed to have none for any of us.

February was cold. I had my own problems. The guy I thought I was going out with asked someone else to our junior prom.

I obsessively listened to Fleetwood Mac's "Landslide" and

Carole King's "It's Too Late." I slept badly, lying awake at night, listening to the radio and taping songs.

Already unwelcome changes were upon me. My mother left work; they threw her a big party. That was nice for her, but now she was home all the time. I was not used to having my mother be at home. I thanked God for her long naps.

Our large apartment was apparently too small for a wee infant, so we started contemplating other living options. For now, we moved my parents' bedroom furniture into the living room, which was bigger, and the living room furniture into the bedroom, which was smaller. This did not bode well for the future.

March came.

One Saturday night, March 11, we had Russian pancakes with red caviar and sour cream.

After eating, we cleaned up and sat down in the "living room" to watch TV. It was eleven o'clock at night. Suddenly my mother got up and disappeared into the bathroom. My father went to stand outside the door. I paced in the hall.

Then my mother came out and looked at us—at my father expectantly and at me oddly, as if she was too embarrassed to tell me what was going on.

So she didn't. She just put on her coat. My father procured a bag from somewhere and said to me, smiling, "The stork is coming."

My mother was already heading downstairs.

They left.

I watched TV, I read. Eventually I fell asleep.

At 7:30 in the morning on Sunday, March 12, 1978, the phone rang.

And my definition of myself changed forever.

"I'm coming home," my father said. "You have a sister."

When he returned, he came into my room. I stood up, and my father said, "*Plinochka,* come here."

I came.

He hugged me.

The last time my father hugged me must have been when he came home from prison when I was seven years old.

He said, "*Plinochka*, you have a sister. We have a little girl. I'm so happy. Your mother desperately wanted a boy, desperately, but not I. No, I don't like boys very much. I much prefer girls, and I'm so very happy."

I patted him gently on the back. It surprised me to hear that my mother *desperately* wanted anything except to be left alone.

"But I just want you to know," my dad said to me, "that even though we are going to have a new baby in the house, you will always be my favorite, because the way I loved you when you were a baby, I can love no one."

He said all this in Russian, of course. I continued to pat him on the back.

Later that morning, we went to the hospital to visit my mother and the baby.

"What are we calling her?" I asked in the car.

"Elizabeth," my father said. "Leeza. Elizabeth and Paullina. We have daughters right out of Pushkin." Pushkin was the greatest of the Russian poets.

I waited outside on the hospital playground while my father went to see my mother by himself. I swung and swung and swung, quietly singing "Landslide" to myself.

Finally I was allowed up to the fourth floor to see my mother, who was wearing a hospital gown and looked a little pale but was otherwise in surprisingly good spirits. She asked me how I liked the name Elizabeth. I told her I liked it fine. "Your father wanted to name the girl Axinya," she told me.

I did a double take. "You're joking."

"Axinya is a very nice name," my father defended himself. "Axinya. Axyusha for short."

91

"No," my mother said mock firmly. "We are having an American baby. With an American name. Elizabeth is a beautiful name."

Where is this Elizabeth? I wanted to know.

My mother remained in her room while my father and I walked to the nursery and peered through the hospital glass at cots full of babies.

"There she is!" said my dad, proudly pointing to a swaddled bundle in the middle aisle on the left. "What do you think? She is incredibly beautiful, isn't she?"

She was lying on her side. She was incredibly hairless.

"Look at those cheekbones! Look at those eyes," my father said.

Her face looked round and her eyes were shut.

"She's going to be beautiful like your mother. Thank God she's not going to look like you or me," my father said.

On Tuesday the baby came home.

And my mother came home, too.

Tuesday was a good day because my father came to get me out of school early, and everyone in my homeroom knew why. I was cool that day for two reasons. First, there is something special and enviable about being let out of school early. And second, this must have been a first that year—the mother of a fourteen-and-a-half-year-old having a brand-new baby. It didn't happen very often. In our school, the fourteen-year-olds—not their moms—were having babies.

We drove to the hospital, and my mother was wheeled out to us. She was holding in her hands a bundle of blankets with no sign of human life inside them. My mother was nervous about the cold weather, but it was actually a sunny, warm March day.

We brought the brand-new baby home and laid her on my parents' bed in the "bedroom." I lay down next to her. I was not invited to pick her up, nor did I offer to.

When I lay down next to her, I touched her for the first time. She was soft. My father took some pictures. My mother said, "Stop touching her; you'll wake her up." I stopped and watched her sleep for a while. Then, sure enough, she was awake. My mother and I changed her. We clucked around her, and it was quite something for me to see my mother be unabashedly reverential toward this six-pound squealing bald baby human. "Look at her," my mother said, kissing her. "Isn't she just beautiful? You know, I haven't changed her on my own yet. The nurses helped me in the hospital. I've never used one of these—" she said, pulling out a disposable diaper. "We only had cloth diapers when you were little."

Was I ever little? Little like Elizabeth? And did my mother cluck all around me, too, kissing me, touching me, stroking every part of me? I found it hard to believe.

The diaper changing seemed to take about four hours. I was exhausted afterward.

I went into the "living room" and turned on the TV. I didn't see my parents for the rest of the day. Actually, I didn't see them again for the next 19 years.

My life really had changed. They had completely forgotten me.

It was wonderful.

Sometime in April, my father did take me to the shoe store. I picked out a nice pair of shoes for about forty dollars. I was pleased as punch. It was my first pair of shoes in two years and would be the last for another two.

That summer we got our first-ever case of poison ivy and itched uncontrollably—I the worst of all. Elizabeth was miraculously spared, and my parents proudly stated that it was because she was the first U.S. citizen in the family.

Inspired by Elizabeth's spanking-new and attractive nationality, my parents began proceedings for us to become naturalized citizens of the United States. That was one of the things my sister Elizabeth had done for us. She made us all Americans.

Also that summer, we went on our first vacation together as a *two-child* family. It was the best vacation of my life. My father fished day and night, and my mother sat with my sister outside our little cottage in Perrault Falls, Ontario. I was left to my own teenage devices. A new baby—it was a miracle!

Did I even exist?

Yes—I could tell from the photos. I was the one holding the baby. That was my leg the baby was lying next to. That was my hand propping her up. My hair was in her face. She was sitting smiling against me. I was rocking her carriage. In one photo, I showed the baby her first daffodils.

"She is the most beautiful baby in the whole world," my father proclaimed, and for once I did not disagree, but I harkened back to that Sunday in March when he hugged me and told me I was always going to be his favorite. I realized he had just been trying to make me feel better because he knew how upset I had been.

I *had* been upset once upon a time, but that was before Elizabeth was born. Yes, she was beautiful, and thank God they were busy staring at her and didn't notice what time I would come home.

Though once, they noticed. One warm spring night, instead of baby-sitting, I went to my girlfriend's house. My mother, who *never* called me at my baby-sitting jobs, called the only time I wasn't there. My parents were frantic for four hours, until I finally strolled in at midnight. Understandably, there was a big to-do. I thought, *They care; they still care.* I was so touched. I actually apologized to my mother for not calling her and letting her know where I was. Apology-wise, I think that was a first.

Later that night, when we were sitting in the "living room" as my mother held the sleeping Elizabeth in her arms, she quietly spoke to me. "Once when you were a baby, you got sick—with scarlet fever or pneumonia, I can't remember now. You had a raging fever. . . . I was up all night in a chair by your bed, listening to you breathe."

I thought, *Did you hold the sleeping me in your arms, too, Mom, as you now hold Leeza?* I couldn't speak.

I needn't have worried about my mother—she lavished, drowned my sister with affection. My mother could not take her hands off that baby.

Incredibly, a backwash, an undertow of that love flowed to me. That's another miracle my sister Elizabeth performed. She let my mother touch me again.

For the first year and a half of Elizabeth's life, my mother stayed home. That was odd and strangely unpleasant. I had been a latchkey kid, always alone after school. Now suddenly in the middle of a perfectly nice afternoon, there was my mother, full of conversation just when I wanted to eat and read my book.

Then in the summer of my sixteenth year, my mother decided to go back to work and leave me with the baby. I wanted to be out with my friends, but there was nothing I could do. My mother paid me a dollar an hour, and I had to put away my low-quality, only-child traits—my selfishness, my self-indulgence, my vanity—and become an older sister. It was then that I learned how to take care of a human being. I never had time for myself anymore. There was drool and food—and worse—on my shirts. I had to keep my hair unattractively back so Elizabeth wouldn't pull on it. I had to take her for walks—and what could be better for cramping teenage style than having your classmates see you with a toddler? But in the process, with soiled clothes and ugly hair and exasperation stamped on my forehead, I learned how to become a human being. That was what Elizabeth had done for *me*.

Later that same summer, my grandparents emigrated from

Russia and we all moved to the suburbs. We needed a bigger place to fit my baby sister, so we built a house and my beloved grandma and grandpa lived in it, too, and took care of Elizabeth while my mom and dad worked. Because of Elizabeth, we had our own house for the first time in our lives. Because of Elizabeth, my mother and father's American dream came true.

I graduated from high school when I was seventeen and left for college.

Then I went to England and then to Kansas and then got married young and had my own daughter young. And I knew just what to do with her, astonishingly. Because I had been given a sister late in my adolescence.

Once when I was briefly back home, I observed Elizabeth horsing around with my mom, who was tickling her. My dad was standing nearby, and suddenly he started tickling her, too, and then the three of them just hugged and held on as I stood and watched. Elizabeth was thirteen at the time. I was twenty-seven. And I thought that I'd never had that kind of moment with my parents. That's what she had done for them. As she did for me, she helped them become human beings, too.

And now I have a 20-year-old sister. She is the latest thing in cool. She has a tongue ring and pink hair and hangs out with kids just like her. She is studying art in a New York City college and has changed apartments four times in the last year. At first she lived in a hotel room next to a woman who used to urinate in the public shower. Thank goodness, she doesn't live there anymore. Every once in a while, I send her care packages full of macaroni and cheese, Oodles of Noodles, Pop-Tarts, cereal, and double-chocolate Milanos. "Paullina," Elizabeth says to me on receiving the package, "You told me you were sending me Milanos, but there aren't any Milanos."

"I know. I ate them all," I say. "Next time."

She grunts.

"Leeza," I tell her, "You're my favorite sister."

"Paullina," she says, in a long-suffering tone of someone who's said this a thousand times before, "I'm your only sister."

If I had to do my life over again, I would have preferred a sibling when I was small, when it would have done me the most good. And Elizabeth, too—I wish she hadn't been alone after I left for college. I wish she and I could have been spared the one-child loneliness, though to Elizabeth's advantage, she has had me, and lifelong friends, and a home she has lived in most of her life—three things I had not had.

My sister and I aren't close together in age. Still, we have each other for life.

Paullina Simons

PAULLINA SIMONS'S *father was imprisoned in the Soviet Union from 1968 to 1971 for illegal political activities. Born in Leningrad in 1963, Simons emigrated to the United States with her parents two years after her father's release. Not surprisingly, her degree from the University of Kansas is in political science.*

After college, Simons spent three years as a financial journalist for a news wire agency in London and then returned to the States to work as a producer for the Financial News Network in New York City. When the network folded, Simons struck off in a completely untried direction and wrote her first novel, Tully, a best-seller published in thirteen countries. Red Leaves and the recent Eleven Hours soon followed. She now lives in Dallas, Texas, and is married and has three children.

Having traveled extensively, Simons has noted an interesting deficiency in the questions someone will ask on meeting her for the first time.

Writes Simons, "People ask, 'How many children do you have?' Or 'What number marriage is this for you?' Or 'What do you do?' is a popular one."

Rather, she prefers another question—Do you have any brothers or sisters?—because it "implies a curiosity about the real me that grown-ups are loath to exhibit. Which is precisely why I ask that question first and foremost. I'll know more about people from the answer to that than from any of the standard ones."

How does Simons react to that question herself?

"Invariably I answer, 'I am an only child. And so is my sister.' "

Look for a new novel by Simons, The Bronze Horseman, in the fall of 1999.

—C. O.

Grilled Cheese

Marilyn French

I always felt that fate forced my sister down my throat. Oh, I know family members can't choose each other, but our case felt particularly mean, as if when she came to us, destiny gritted her teeth and wrenched the fatal thread apart with a particularly violent thrust. I don't know why; it wasn't as if we deserved it. We were just a couple of innocent kids. But fate sets many an innocent child in a horrendous life that can't be changed or escaped from.

Our life was not horrendous in any of the usual ways. We were decently sheltered, fed, and clothed, and if punishment was occasionally threatened in our house, it rarely descended. We were more familiar with the sight than the feel of Father's belt. Father was in the air force. A military family, we moved every few years, not just to a new house, but a new culture. Each time we moved, Paulette and I were stuck with each other again. Three years apart, a big gap in childhood, and strangers amid the alien corn, we either had to go out alone—a terrifying proposition if you don't speak the language—or stick together to explore a new base or town. The only alternative was staying home, which was unthinkable.

Everything in our lives changed constantly, even our

economic status. In Panama, Germany, and Saudi Arabia, we were rich enough to have houses with many rooms and servants to clean them. Mother, freed from the domestic labor she loathed, could get all dolled up every afternoon and go to the officers' club to play bridge or watch fashion shows or imported movies—she *loved* movies, as you can tell from our names—and get a little tipsy with the other officers' wives. In such places, there were frequent dances and teas and sometimes even balls. But just as often, we were in Provo, Utah, or Lubbock, Texas, in the middle of a wilderness with nothing in sight for miles except the base, dusty fields, and distant hills. The officers' wives still played bridge, but there were no servants, and the women had to do their own housework. Mother would sulk over the laundry and drink too much. There's a big difference between being tipsy and drinking too much.

Wherever we were, our family was, naturally, our center. But we didn't see much of it. Dad, of course, had a built-in excuse—work; Mother had to invent excuses. The truth was, neither of them much liked kids. Dad was consumed with his work; he loved it: he was a scientist-engineer working on experimental aircraft. When he wasn't at work, he puttered at home. Mother was wrapped up in Dad even when they were apart, obsessed with him or his absence or his most recent sins, whatever they were. She was jealous of his work, resentful that he had that but she had only him.

He was wrapped up in her, too, but his career made an important difference between them, a power difference. He never waited on her like she did him. If by some fluke he should be at home and she out—at the market, say—he wouldn't wait on her; he'd draw mechanical sketches at his basement work table or putter in the garage. But for my Southern mother, "waitin' on Daddy" was one of the miseries of wifedom. I have a whole deck of memories of her, glamorous and made up, her hair waved, wearing something silky and clingy, sitting in an armchair in front of the TV set, waiting for him to come home, her leg waving back and forth impatiently in its black nylon hose, as she sipped a martini and got more and more steamed. Or wearing the sweater, pearls, plaid skirt, and leather pumps more suitable for Lubbock, she'd sit there—still with the martini—glancing at her watch every few minutes, impatient if we approached her to ask something, asking if we couldn't see she was waitin' on Daddy.

We had our own urgencies—a dollar for a school trip, a report card that needed signing, money for a piece of oaktag to make a poster for the fifth-grade elections—but we knew that they weren't urgent for her. She was always waitin' on life to begin, and we weren't part of that life. We weren't part of his, either; we were just two accidents that had happened along, and when he looked at us, his eyebrows often seemed to rise in surprise that we were still there.

Mother's "waitin' on Daddy" was part of the script; it was necessary, along with her growing drunkenness and rage. Her head would start when she heard his key in the door or maybe his car in the driveway, and he'd come in a little tense. He knew how she got when he was late, and he was usually late—his military bearing even stiffer than usual—and he'd stare at her across the room. She'd look up at him, smoldering, and maybe (depending on how late it was) she'd make some nasty crack. Her mascara would be a little smudged, making her eyes even bigger than they were, great dark circles, and her dark hair would be a little disheveled. He'd walk toward her stiffly, his mouth and eyes angry, how dare she question him. Her chin would rise in a defiant tilt, and he'd grab her hair hard, hurting her, and pull her head back and bend and kiss her long, hard. She'd nearly swoon in his arms. When he wasn't late, the script was a little different. She'd still be sitting there, legs crossed, her head leaning back, when he came in, but she'd lean back and smile, a slow, simmering, knowing smile, and when he came to her, she'd melt into his arms.

My sister and I managed to sneak enough looks at this scene that we both knew it by heart and knew there was no role for us in their drama. I know now that we were equally ignored, but when I was little, I thought that Paulette— sweet, pretty Paulette—was inside the charmed circle and only I was left out. Since Paulette had the same impression of me, it is understandable that we viewed each other with cold, hard eyes and spoke to each other with resentful suspicion. I don't know why we took this attitude; we could have joined together against them, created our own children's world. But we didn't.

We lived in our own part of the house. Whatever sort of house we were assigned, however big or small, Mother found a way to separate us from them. She might put us upstairs in a half-finished attic, or give us the two downstairs bedrooms and turn the attic into a Persian pleasure tent for them, or use the Florida room as their bedroom, filling it with greenery. This was easier for her to do when we were rich and had the sprawling houses that are the reward of the rich. But she managed it even when we were poor and lived in the little Cape Cod cottages that were ubiquitous in the Fifties and Sixties.

Except for meals or when we were invited, we had to stay in our part of the house. Mom and Dad inhabited the rest. They had drinks in the living room at night before dinner, and if we had a library or a study, they would sit there after dinner listening to music and reading and talking. They used whatever rooms we had to entertain, but they did that rarely—Mother didn't like to share Dad with anyone. After living in Saudi Arabia (which mother really hated— she was locked on the base and couldn't drive off it) I thought of our quarters as the *harim*.

Like a lot of women in Saudi Arabia, we didn't mind the *harim*. We could mess it up and no one cared; we could jump on the furniture and scrawl on the walls. We had our own television set and the parents never vetoed our TV choices. We didn't fight, because if we did, Father made us turn the TV set off altogether. When we entered the dining or living room, we knew we were on probation.

As kids, Paulette and I rarely talked. The face of the other was, for each of us, the face of our frustration, the visible reminder of our exclusion. We were desperate for friends, kids who did not make us feel separate and different. We could meet other kids only at school—there was always an American school on the base or in town. But the schools were small, and there wasn't always a kid we liked close to our own age. There was a boy named Oliver that I loved in first grade. We rode bikes together—we were in Provo then—and had a hideout in a patch of trees near his house. When we moved back stateside after our tour in Saudi Arabia—a dry, lonely tour for us as well as for Mother—we were sent to Lubbock, another arid place, where I met a girl named Phyllis Runco. We went to fifth grade together. She had long black hair and smart gray eyes and a smart mouth. Her dad was air force, too; she'd lived everywhere, too; and she was really smart—she got A's on all the tests. She had an older brother who gave her the skinny on what was going on around us. He knew all the base politics and dirt. Oh, how I envied Phyllis her brother! I wished Paulette were a boy, or that she knew anything about anything. What use was an older sister if she knew even less about the world than I did? She lived in a dreamworld. Even Mother said so. Such a jerk!

When we reached fourteen, Mother got rid of us for good, sending us to private school in Switzerland. Paulette went first, and for the first time in my life, I missed her. For the next three years, I was all alone in the house, in my part of the house. We were in Germany then, and I didn't have a friend at school. My end of the house was lonely and quiet. The only advantage was I could always watch whatever TV program I wanted, but Paulette and I hadn't disagreed enough to make this a palpable benefit. I found myself wishing she were there, even if she did file her nails or cut split ends off her hair with nail scissors (both of which drove me crazy). I knew she didn't miss me; I figured she was having a fantastic time being away from home. She rarely wrote and never called; Mother rarely called her.

What made this situation even worse was that Paulette changed at boarding school. When she came home for holidays, she looked at me differently, as if I were a stranger and a little bit interesting. Sometimes she smiled at me and I could have sworn she was thinking I was cute. This new attitude made me feel shy around her; she seemed like someone grown up and nice that I wanted to like me. We began to talk for the first time in our lives. But never about anything serious.

But she came home only for Christmas and Easter and one summer, the summer she was fifteen. After that, she worked summers in a resort in the Alps, waiting tables and making beds. All we managed to establish in those years was a sense that if fate had not made us sisters, we might have liked each other.

We were still in Germany when I reached the magic age, and Mother sent me to the same boarding school Paulette attended. She was three years ahead of me, a senior, so we didn't room together or see much of each other. My roommate was a Catholic girl named Anne. She was not smart in school, but she was as savvy as Phyllis had been about living. She had always gone to Catholic schools, which had so many rules that just to maintain their integrity, the Catholic girls became experts in breaking them. By the time they were thirteen, Anne and her pals knew how to get over the walls at night, to forge notes from parents giving permission to go into town, to forge notes giving permission to go somewhere invented for a weekend. I tried a few things with her. As soon as we got off school grounds, we'd both smear lipstick on our mouths and light cigarettes. We each went through a pack of Luckies a week. I learned to talk tough, using dirty words, even if I wasn't always sure just what they meant. Anne, too, was actually pretty innocent, I think. We acted tough and knowing, but I really knew very little and have often questioned how much she knew. I know she was devastated when she had to leave school and get married midway through her junior year—she was as white and dead as a walking zombie; she could hardly speak.

By then, Paulette was gone entirely. She went off to college in Strasbourg when I was a sophomore in high school, and I never saw her much after that. *En principle,* we'd go home for holidays, but we avoided going home whenever we could. We'd go to friends' houses or spend most of our time out. By then, it was embarrassing to be home. The parents were used to being alone by then and didn't bother to conceal anything or even to keep it quiet. They must have grown bored with the same old scenario every night and had embroidered it. The embroideries tended to be noisy: Mother's attacks on Father were screamed or cried; his domination of her was a little more violent. We didn't care to be around.

A year after she started college, Paulette left Strasbourg for London. Somehow, she'd got herself into the Royal College of Dance (we were all amazed at the resourcefulness of the little dreamer), and three or four years later, she landed a job with a French ballet company based in Lyon. It paid barely enough to live, but she didn't care: she lived for her art, she wrote. I thought she was too precious for words.

But in time, I discovered pretentions of my own. I went to college and then to Harvard to study international relations, dreaming of a sophisticated career in the foreign service. It seemed to me ideal—living in world capitals, doing government service, dealing with delicate affairs of state. I was deluded; like my sister imagining herself a star, I imagined a woman could succeed in such a field.

But I did get a job in the foreign service, and I lived another form of my family's hobo existence, assigned to consulates in the wildernesses of Canada and Brazil and embassies in Mexico City and Delhi. I tried to be brilliant, but I never won much praise. I never rose beyond deputy consul for the arts, a middling rank. By that time I understood: no woman did.

By the time I was twenty, it was clear to me that the objects of my desire were not what they should be. I tried to suppress my feelings; I dated men, but only occasionally, my looks not being startling enough to overcome my lack of seductiveness. I knew it would harm my career, if not end it, if the truth about me got out, so when I did finally break down and let myself love someone, we had to hide and pretend. That affair lasted a couple of years, but the fear and guilt were so draining that years went by before I risked it again. The second one was, I guess, the love of my life, but my assignment to Saskatchewan put a strain on it. My lover, Elizabeth, was a psychotherapist, and there wasn't much call for services like hers in Saskatchewan. She could not move there with me, which I understood, and it was hard to maintain a long-distance love affair. Although we still correspond, I know there is someone else in her life.

I had plenty of time alone, time to think. I wasn't miserable, not the way I was at home. I enjoyed my job, even if it was a dead end, and I earned enough to live decently. The worst thing about my life was my disconnectedness, which, it seemed to me, had been with me since childhood. It was almost a condition of my existence. But it felt wrenchingly bad sometimes. I felt like a balloon floating in space and I knew that if I ever landed, wherever I landed wouldn't be home.

Father retired in 1986, and the parents settled down for the first time in their own house—a tract house outside Washington, near an air force base. He went on working as a consultant for government and industry, and he had to be away, sometimes for long periods. Mother complained about it on Christmas cards, but whether she'd been able to make friends, I didn't know. Then, in 1990, Father died of a sudden heart attack.

Paulette and I both flew home. Mother was devastated. She cried continually; we had to make all the funeral arrangements. I was moved by her grief; I knew what it felt like to miss someone. And I was surprised at how bad I felt myself when I looked down at him lying there in his coffin—as though Father had meant something to me. I wondered if there had been a time when I was very tiny, when he had held me or played with me, or been loving to me, to justify these feelings. There was nothing I could remember, but maybe he'd earned points in my heart in the time before memory.

Paulette had had more success as a dancer than our family ever imagined she would. She was hired by a famous Parisian company as *première danseuse*. We sat together having a drink in Mother's living room the night after she arrived. Mother, sedated, had gone to bed. Paulette had changed a lot; she was ultrasophisticated. Well, what else? She was a dancer; she lived in Paris. She walked like a dancer, her carriage as flexible as willow, yet straight as oak. She wore her flaming red hair in a bun at the back of her neck—of course—and had an exquisite sense of clothes. She didn't have many, but she chose them well and wore them beautifully. She broke into French continually, had to catch herself. I found her intimidating.

The first time we talked, she said in a gush, "Ah, Rita, but you've changed."

I hated the way she said that. She sounded so . . . foreign, so superior, so . . . French.

"Really."

"Yes, *chérie*, you are so smart, so competent looking! You look as if you manage a corporation or the government itself! Your suit is so smart. Is it Armani? And what a magnificent haircut! You quite frighten me!"

As airy as ever. The suit was Armani, as a matter of fact, and I was glad she had turned out knowing enough to know a thing like that. And the haircut, a simple cut that allowed me to wash and comb, had cost me eighty dollars. I smiled. "You're pretty smart yourself."

"Ah, I must do everything on a budget. A dancer's wages, oh dear!"

"But you are *première danseuse* now, right?"

"Yes. Things are better. But for years, it was . . . oh well, what does it matter? I was doing what I love!"

Her smile was a beacon in a storm. It was Mother's smile, the one she used when Daddy wasn't late. It could knock your eyes out. But I could see from the wear and tear on her face that she'd had a stormy love life, although she singled out no one in particular.

"And you too, *chérie*. We are a lucky family. But what do you say we take our drinks into one of the bedrooms. I don't know why I feel so uncomfortable here. . . ."

If her overall take on our family was not exactly mine, it was amazing that she felt at that moment exactly how I felt.

In the days that followed, Paulette and I worked very well together; we seemed to think the same way and to have similar responses to things. We made the funeral arrangements with a minimum of fuss and dealt with Mother in exactly the same efficient, kindly, distant way. We shopped and cooked meals for her. I had quite an interesting repertoire from living in India, Brazil, and Mexico, but Paulette cooked French style magnificently, and I felt outclassed.

As soon as Father was buried and Mother had decided to sell her house, Paulette and I extricated ourselves. We had to go back to our lives, and the blessing of it was, Mother didn't really want us there. She bought a two-bedroom condo in a garden apartment not far from where she'd lived before. I imagined that she would stop crying after we left and there was no one to see her. I figured she'd play bridge and go to movies and drink martinis with other air force widows. On the rare occasions when I felt guilty, I told myself that what goes around comes around.

After another six months in D.C., I was promoted—I couldn't believe it!—and sent to Bogotá. As far as I knew, only the big boys went to Colombia; it was full of CIA and DEA. I didn't know what, beyond knowing Spanish well, I'd done to deserve a major assignment—a job in a hot spot—but I took it gratefully. Of course, I was window-dressing: I sat in Bogotá while the guys all went to Antioquia province. I should have guessed. It was 1991. In 1995, I'd have put in twenty years and could retire with a decent pension—much less than if I'd worked thirty years, but enough to maintain me if I could find something more interesting to do. I was so disheartened that I began to plan for it.

Paulette and I corresponded after Father's death. Some tendrils of family feeling seemed to remain in us, enough that I got pleasure from seeing a letter with her handwriting on the envelope. Not that she ever said much in the letters. They were perfunctory, really. But, I suppose, so were mine. Then, around 1992, her letters began to sound the same note of discouragement I felt. She was in her midforties by then; her legs and breath were going. Ballet dancers don't last long—the work is too hard. She still danced, but less—she'd had a couple of falls. She had her face done.

Grilled Cheese

*   *   *

In 1995, Mother had a stroke. My tour in Colombia was just about over anyway, so I stayed a few days to clean things up completely and left the job when I flew to D.C. I went first to the hospital. Mother was completely unaware of my presence. One eye stared straight ahead, the other was closed. One side of her body was paralyzed; the other was not, and her hand twitched and her foot wiggled. But she did not hear or see me. She was still a nice-looking woman, but no one seeing her could imagine the dark, dramatic mysterious love life she'd once created for herself and Father.

Paulette was already there, had been there for a few days. She introduced me to Mother's doctors and some of her nurses; no one could predict anything about her recovery. We drove to her apartment in a complex of identical "garden" apartments, two stories high, set in winding roads adorned with polite greenery.

On the way there, Paulette laughed. "Wait till you see the bedroom."

"Shades of the past?" I inquired.

"Fuck shades. It's the past restored."

"A true *à la recherche du temps perdu?*"

"As if we'd wished for it."

I laughed.

"But smaller than any room we ever shared!"

We shook our heads in comic despair, identically, like twins.

She was silent for a while, then said "Rita . . ." in a tense voice. "Father's insurance covers her, *n'est-ce pas?*"

"Yeah. That's one great thing about the military."

She sighed. "Good. I have a little money saved, but I want to retire soon. I want to come back to the States and open my own business—maybe a little dance academy. I want to come home. I want to find some little town in a

111

pretty, warm place where tree branches hang over the streets and the people all know each other. Maybe in the South. Maybe Mother's hometown. Someday."

I looked at her wistful face. Her hair, which I'd seen only when it was bound in a chignon, was long and wild and, it seemed, redder than ever.

"Really! I'm thinking about retiring myself. . . ."

We looked at each other thoughtfully, then swiftly glanced away.

That night, we had a drink together. Mother was in the hospital, but still we sat in our bedroom, each on her own bed, facing the other. Our knees occasionally knocked each other's.

"I bet you had lots of lovers," I said.

She nodded and examined me. "You?"

"Just a couple. Not as many as you. And women, not men."

Her eyebrows raised. "Yeah?" She reached in her bag and pulled out a pack of cigarettes, shook one out, and lit it.

"You smoking! I can't believe it!"

"Once in a while. I avoided it for the first fifty years of my life, so it probably won't hurt me now."

"You're not fifty."

"Close to it."

I stared at her. "Give me one," I urged.

She held out the pack, mutely. I lit one, then began to cough. We both laughed. I finally calmed down and mastered the damn thing. I exhaled smoke in a great satisfying plume.

"So what's it like, with women?"

"Better than with men," I said.

"Really?"

"Well, in terms of orgasmic satisfaction, yes. I didn't start out gay. I started out the way any girl does, with guys in college. Ugh!"

She laughed, then fell into a musing smile. "But no one special now?" she concluded.

"Saskatchewan did me in," I said bitterly. "It was like being exiled to Siberia."

"Yes. Paris finished me. Funny, how good things bring bad things. And vice versa, I guess."

"Silver linings, they call them."

There was a long silence.

"I'm hungry," I said.

She had lain back against the bed, but now she sat up sharply. "Well, there's nothing to eat in this hellhole. I've been here a couple days, and I can tell you there's nothing but frozen dinners in the fridge, a horrible supermarket in town, and a couple of awful restaurants in the area. France ruined me for American cooking."

"I know what you mean. There must be decent stores somewhere."

"We'll have to explore. But do you think it's worth it? Will we be here that long?"

I shrugged.

We spent the next days mainly at the hospital, outside the ICU. Mother was conscious, but she could not speak or move, and terror shone in her eyes when she looked at us. I kept remembering the time I'd been threatened and then chased by some Panamanian boys who had somehow sneaked onto the base. I'd fallen in the mud and was quite a mess by the time I got home, flushed and dirty, with a torn dress and scuffed knees. The minute I laid eyes on Mother, I broke into sobs, but she stood there with her arms on her hips.

"Rita!" she said sternly, "whatever has got into you?" I sobbed out my story and she gave me an incredulous look. "What boys? How could Panamanian boys get on the base? There are guards! Rita, are you making this up?"

I gave up, limped into my room and lay on the bed, wondering which was worse, the boys or my mother.

Now I looked at her, wondering if she knew how profoundly I disliked her. Paulette and I couldn't sit in the ICU, so we took turns going in every hour; the rest of the time we sat and read in the waiting room. It was uncomfortable and boring, but somehow we both felt we had to do it. We didn't discuss it; we did what we felt we had to. At lunchtime, we would explore, driving to restaurants we'd heard about, for cocktails and shrimp salad or whatever. The first day, we laughed at the coincidence: we'd both ordered shrimp; we'd both ordered martinis. But it happened every day. That night, we both ordered osso buco, again without consulting each other, and the next day at lunch, we both wanted Mexican food.

"We seem to have the same taste in food."

"Yes, but why? I mean, remember Mother's dinners?"

We both grimaced and nodded.

Mother's cooking was uninspired, as one might imagine of a woman who spent all her time acting out a sexual melodrama or dreaming of movie stars. She made meat loaf, of course—everyone did in the Fifties—and minute steaks, tough thin strips of beef that had been hammered into chewability and fried in bacon fat, and dried-out hamburgers with watery green beans and limp yellowed broccoli and lumpy mashed potatoes. She boiled leftover leg of lamb in water and thickened it: I don't know what she called that. It was a dish her mother had made. So much for any mother's home cooking. Sometimes she just opened a can of soup and made grilled cheese sandwiches. They were actually good.

"Grilled cheese," Paulette said, and sighed. "That was good."

"Yes. My favorite, too." Suddenly inundated with feeling, I felt I might cry. What was it? I was remembering a beautiful cocoon of childhood in which I was embraced and loved and safe and fed delicious grilled cheese sandwiches. I longed to go back; I wanted to cry at the agony I felt that I couldn't. Paulette was staring at me.

"Funny how memory tricks you. Saying that, just saying it—grilled cheese—makes me feel I was a beloved little girl, that I had a happy past. . . ."

"I know what you mean," Paulette said, and her eyes filled.

We looked away from each other.

I thought about it late that night, in bed. Paulette's even breathing filled the room, comforting me with her presence. I felt as if all my pores were tiny roots all aching, reaching for a past that held some secret joy. Maybe I retained something deep and hidden from an infancy I did not remember, when I was loved and embraced. Maybe we are imprinted with an ideal family, the one we would have had three million years ago, when we were still close to the animals and loved easily. Because I could feel my love for my mom and dad, and theirs for me, and Sis and I played rough-and-tumble and loved each other fiercely. Maybe all that love was planted in me just as if it had happened. Maybe I would always carry it around with me. I reached over and lightly touched Paulette's hand, which was lying on the edge of her bed. She didn't move.

Marilyn French

⌒

FREDERICA VON STADE inspired this story by Marilyn French. Writes French, "She was speaking on the radio about a piece of music she had commissioned to memorialize her father. She spoke about him with great feeling, although she never met him: he was killed in the war months before she was born. Her emotion reminded me of Emily Dickinson's poem, which I read at my mother's funeral."

> The Bustle in a House
> The Morning After Death
> Is Solemnest of Industries
> Enacted Upon Earth.
>
> The Sweeping up the Heart
> And putting Love away
> We will not want to use again
> Until Eternity.

"Dickinson's implication," French explains, "—that we are heavy with love intended for one specific person, that cannot be transferred to another, or given to a substitute—seems to me profoundly true.

"I also believe we feel this love whether or not that person

116

ever existed. Like von Stade, who never had her father, we carry with us all our lives the love intended for that person. And I think that poor family relationships, that those of the sisters in this story, are intensified by frustration when something thwarts that love, when it cannot be directed at the appropriate person.

"So our rage at our father—or mother or sister or whomever—has a special meanness; like a girl with bound feet whose frustrated bones must grow, but cannot grow straight and agonizingly curve around in a circle. This ideal love, unable to be expressed, curls painfully back in on itself."

A feminist scholar with a Harvard Ph.D., French has written literary criticism, moral analysis, and five novels, including My Summer with George and The Women's Room, which sold over twenty million copies. In 1998, she published a memoir of her bout with cancer, A Season in Hell. She has two children and splits her time between New York City and Singer Island, Florida.

—C. O.

Silver Water

Amy Bloom

My sister's voice was like mountain water in a silver pitcher; the clear blue beauty of it cools you and lifts you up beyond your heat, beyond your body. After we went to see *La Traviata*, when she was fourteen and I was twelve, she elbowed me in the parking lot and said, "Check this out." And she opened her mouth unnaturally wide and her voice came out, so crystalline and bright that all the departing operagoers stood frozen by their cars, unable to take out their keys or open their doors until she had finished, and then they cheered like hell.

That's what I like to remember, and that's the story I told to all of her therapists. I wanted them to know her, to know that who they saw was not all there was to see. That before her constant tinkling of commercials and fast-food jingles there had been Puccini and Mozart and hymns so sweet and mighty you expected Jesus to come down off his cross and clap. That before there was a mountain of Thorazined fat, swaying down the halls in nylon maternity tops and sweatpants, there had been the prettiest girl in Arrandale Elementary School, the belle of Landmark Junior High. Maybe there were other pretty girls, but I didn't see them. To me, Rose, my beautiful blond defender, my guide to Tampax and my mother's moods, was perfect.

She had her first psychotic break when she was fifteen. She had been coming home moody and tearful, then quietly beaming, then she stopped coming home. She would go out into the woods behind our house and not come in until my mother went after her at dusk, and stepped gently into the briars and saplings and pulled her out, blank-faced, her pale blue sweater covered with crumbled leaves, her white jeans smeared with dirt. After three weeks of this, my mother, who is a musician and widely regarded as eccentric, said to my father, who is a psychiatrist and a kind, sad man, "She's going off."

"What is that, your professional opinion?" He picked up the newspaper and put it down again, sighing. "I'm sorry, I didn't mean to snap at you. I know something's bothering her. Have you talked to her?"

"What's there to say? David, she's going crazy. She doesn't need a heart-to-heart talk with Mom, she needs a hospital."

They went back and forth, and my father sat down with Rose for a few hours, and she sat there licking the hairs on her forearm, first one way, then the other. My mother stood in the hallway, dry-eyed and pale, watching the two of them. She had already packed, and when three of my father's friends dropped by to offer free consultations and recommendations, my mother and Rose's suitcase were already in the car. My mother hugged me and told me that they would be back that night, but not with Rose. She also said, divining my worst fear, "It won't happen to you, honey. Some people go crazy and some people never do. You never will." She smiled and stroked my hair. "Not even when you want to."

Rose was in hospitals, great and small, for the next ten years. She had lots of terrible therapists and a few good ones.

One place had no pictures on the walls, no windows, and the patients all wore slippers with the hospital crest on them. My mother didn't even bother to go to Admissions. She turned Rose around and the two of them marched out, my father walking behind them, apologizing to his colleagues. My mother ignored the psychiatrists, the social workers, and the nurses, and played Handel and Bessie Smith for the patients on whatever was available. At some places, she had a Steinway donated by a grateful, or optimistic, family; at others, she banged out "Gimme a Pigfoot and a Bottle of Beer" on an old, scarred box that hadn't been tuned since there'd been English-speaking physicians on the grounds. My father talked in serious, appreciative tones to the administrators and unit chiefs and tried to be friendly with whoever was managing Rose's case. We all hated the family therapists.

The worst family therapist we ever had sat in a pale green room with us, visibly taking stock of my mother's ethereal beauty and her faded blue T-shirt and girl-sized jeans, my father's rumpled suit and stained tie, and my own unreadable seventeen-year-old fashion statement. Rose was beyond fashion that year, in one of her dancing teddybear smocks and extra-extra-large Celtics sweatpants. Mr. Walker read Rose's file in front of us and then watched in alarm as Rose began crooning, beautifully, and slowly massaging her breasts. My mother and I laughed, and even my father started to smile. This was Rose's usual opening salvo for new therapists.

Mr. Walker said, "I wonder why it is that everyone is so entertained by Rose behaving inappropriately."

Rose burped, and then we all laughed. This was the seventh family therapist we had seen, and none of them had lasted very long. Mr. Walker, unfortunately, was determined to do right by us.

"What do you think of Rose's behavior, Violet?" They

did this sometimes. In their manual it must say, If you think the parents are too weird, try talking to the sister.

"I don't know. Maybe she's trying to get you to stop talking about her in the third person."

"Nicely put," my mother said.

"Indeed," my father said.

"Fuckin' A," Rose said.

"Well, this is something that the whole family agrees upon," Mr. Walker said, trying to act as if he understood or even liked us.

"That was not a successful intervention, Ferret Face." Rose tended to function better when she was angry. He did look like a blond ferret, and we all laughed again. Even my father, who tried to give these people a chance, out of some sense of collegiality, had given it up.

After fourteen minutes, Mr. Walker decided that our time was up and walked out, leaving us grinning at each other. Rose was still nuts, but at least we'd all had a little fun.

The day we met our best family therapist started out almost as badly. We scared off a resident and then scared off her supervisor, who sent us Dr. Thorne. Three hundred pounds of Texas chili, cornbread, and Lone Star beer, finished off with big black cowboy boots and a small string tie around the area of his neck.

"O frabjous day, it's Big Nut." Rose was in heaven and stopped massaging her breasts immediately.

"Hey, Little Nut." You have to understand how big a man would have to be to call my sister "little." He christened us all, right away. "And it's the good Doctor Nut, and Madame Hickory Nut, 'cause they are the hardest damn nuts to crack, and over here in the overalls and not much else is No One's Nut"—a name that summed up both my sanity and my loneliness. We all relaxed.

Dr. Thorne was good for us. Rose moved into a halfway

121

house whose director loved Big Nut so much that she kept Rose even when Rose went through a period of having sex with everyone who passed her door. She was in a fever for a while, trying to still the voices by fucking her brains out.

Big Nut said, "Darlin', I can't. I cannot make love to every beautiful woman I meet, and furthermore, I can't do that and be your therapist, too. It's a great shame, but I think you might be able to find a really nice guy, someone who treats you just as sweet and kind as I would if I were lucky enough to be your beau. I don't want you to settle for less." And she stopped propositioning the crack addicts and the alcoholics and the guys at the shelter. We loved Dr. Thorne.

My father went back to seeing rich neurotics and helped out one day a week at Dr. Thorne's Walk-In Clinic. My mother finished a recording of Mozart concerti and played at fund-raisers for Rose's halfway house. I went back to college and found a wonderful linebacker from Texas to sleep with. In the dark, I would make him call me "darlin'." Rose took her meds, lost about fifty pounds, and began singing at the A.M.E. Zion Church, down the street from the halfway house.

At first they didn't know what do to with this big blond lady, dressed funny and hovering wistfully in the doorway during their rehearsals, but she gave them a few bars of "Precious Lord" and the choir director felt God's hand and saw that with the help of His sweet child Rose, the Prospect Street choir was going all the way to the Gospel Olympics.

Amidst a sea of beige, umber, cinnamon, and espresso faces, there was Rose, bigger, blonder, and pinker than any two white women could be. And Rose and the choir's contralto, Addie Robicheaux, laid out their gold and silver voices and wove them together in strands as fine as silk, as strong as steel. And we wept as Rose and Addie, in their billowing garnet robes, swayed together, clasping hands until the last perfect note floated up to God, and then they smiled down at us.

Rose would still go off from time to time and the voices would tell her to do bad things, but Dr. Thorne or Addie or my mother could usually bring her back. After five good years, Big Nut died. Stuffing his face with a chili dog, sitting in his unair-conditioned office in the middle of July, he had one big, Texas-sized aneurysm and died.

Rose held on tight for seven days; she took her meds, went to choir practice, and rearranged her room about a hundred times. His funeral was like a Lourdes for the mentally ill. If you were psychotic, borderline, bad-off neurotic, or just very hard to get along with, you were there. People shaking so bad from years of heavy meds that they fell out of the pews. People holding hands, crying, moaning, talking to themselves. The crazy people and the not-so-crazy people were all huddled together, like puppies at the pound.

Rose stopped taking her meds, and the halfway house wouldn't keep her after she pitched another patient down the stairs. My father called the insurance company and found out that Rose's new, improved psychiatric coverage wouldn't begin for forty-five days. I put all of her stuff in a garbage bag, and we walked out of the halfway house, Rose winking at the poor drooling boy on the couch.

"This is going to be difficult—not all bad, but difficult—for the whole family, and I thought we should discuss everybody's expectations. I know I have some concerns." My father had convened a family meeting as soon as Rose finished putting each one of her thirty stuffed bears in its own special place.

"No meds," Rose said, her eyes lowered, her stubby fingers, those fingers that had braided my hair and painted tulips on my cheeks, pulling hard on the hem of her dirty smock.

My father looked in despair at my mother.

"Rosie, do you want to drive the new car?" my mother asked.

Rose's face lit up. "I'd love to drive that car. I'd drive to California, I'd go see the bears at the San Diego Zoo. I would take you, Violet, but you always hated the zoo. Remember how she cried at the Bronx Zoo when she found out that the animals didn't get to go home at closing?" Rose put her damp hand on mine and squeezed it sympathetically. "Poor Vi."

"If you take your medication, after a while you'll be able to drive the car. That's the deal. Meds, car." My mother sounded accommodating but unenthusiastic, careful not to heat up Rose's paranoia.

"You got yourself a deal, darlin'."

I was living about an hour away then, teaching English during the day, writing poetry at night. I went home every few days for dinner. I called every night.

My father said, quietly, "It's very hard. We're doing all right, I think. Rose has been walking in the mornings with your mother, and she watches a lot of TV. She won't go to the day hospital, and she won't go back to the choir. Her friend Mrs. Robicheaux came by a couple of times. What a sweet woman. Rose wouldn't even talk to her. She just sat there, staring at the wall and humming. We're not doing all that well, actually, but I guess we're getting by. I'm sorry, sweetheart, I don't mean to depress you."

My mother said, emphatically, "We're doing fine. We've got our routine and we stick to it and we're fine. You don't need to come home so often, you know. Wait 'til Sunday, just come for the day. Lead your life, Vi. She's leading hers."

I stayed away all week, afraid to pick up my phone, grateful to my mother for her harsh calm and her reticence, the qualities that had enraged me throughout my childhood.

I came on Sunday, in the early afternoon, to help my father garden, something we had always enjoyed together. We weeded and staked tomatoes and killed aphids while my mother and Rose were down at the lake. I didn't even go into the house until four, when I needed a glass of water.

Someone had broken the piano bench into five neatly stacked pieces and placed them where the piano bench usually was.

"We were having such a nice time, I couldn't bear to bring it up," my father said, standing in the doorway, carefully keeping his gardening boots out of the kitchen.

"What did Mommy say?"

"She said, 'Better the bench than the piano.' And your sister lay down on the floor and just wept. Then your mother took her down to the lake. This can't go on, Vi. We have twenty-seven days left, your mother gets no sleep because Rose doesn't sleep, and if I could just pay twenty-seven thousand dollars to keep her in the hospital until the insurance takes over, I'd do it."

"All right. Do it. Pay the money and take her back to Hartley-Rees. It was the prettiest place, and she liked the art therapy there."

"I would if I could. The policy states that she must be symptom-free for at least forty-five days before her coverage begins. Symptom-free means no hospitalization."

"Jesus, Daddy, how could you get that kind of policy? She hasn't been symptom-free for forty-five minutes."

"It's the only one I could get for long-term psychiatric." He put his hand over his mouth, to block whatever he was about to say, and went back out to the garden. I couldn't see if he was crying.

He stayed outside and I stayed inside until Rose and my mother came home from the lake. Rose's soggy sweatpants were rolled up to her knees, and she had a bucketful of shells and seaweed, which my mother persuaded her to leave on the back porch. My mother kissed me lightly and told Rose to go up to her room and change out of her wet pants.

Rose's eyes grew very wide. "Never. I will never . . ." She knelt down and began banging her head on the kitchen floor with rhythmic intensity, throwing all her weight behind each attack. My mother put her arms around Rose's waist and tried to hold her back. Rose shook her off, not even looking around to see what was slowing her down. My mother lay up against the refrigerator.

"Violet, please . . ."

I threw myself onto the kitchen floor, becoming the spot that Rose was smacking her head against. She stopped a fraction of an inch short of my stomach.

"Oh, Vi, Mommy, I'm sorry. I'm sorry, don't hate me." She staggered to her feet and ran wailing to her room.

My mother got up and washed her face brusquely, rubbing it dry with a dishcloth. My father heard the wailing and came running in, slipping his long bare feet out of his rubber boots.

"Galen, Galen, let me see." He held her head and looked closely for bruises on her pale, small face. "What happened?" My mother looked at me. "Violet, what happened? Where's Rose?"

"Rose got upset, and when she went running upstairs she pushed Mommy out of the way." I've only told three lies in my life, and that was my second.

"She must feel terrible, pushing you, of all people. It would have to be you, but I know she didn't want it to be." He made my mother a cup of tea, and all the love he had for her, despite her silent rages and her vague stares, came pouring through the teapot, warming her cup, filling her small, long-fingered hands. She rested her head against his hip, and I looked away.

"Let's make dinner, then I'll call her. Or you call her, David, maybe she'd rather see your face first."

Dinner was filled with all of our starts and stops and Rose's desperate efforts to control herself. She could barely eat and hummed the McDonald's theme song over and over again, pausing only to spill her juice down the front of her smock and begin weeping. My father looked at my mother and handed Rose his napkin. She dabbed at herself listlessly, but the tears stopped.

"I want to go to bed. I want to go to bed and be in my head. I want to go to bed and be in my bed and in my head and just wear red. For red is the color that my baby wore and once more, it's true, yes, it is, it's true. Please don't wear red tonight, oh, oh, please don't wear red tonight, for red is the color—"

"Okay, okay, Rose. It's okay. I'll go upstairs with you and you can get ready for bed. Then Mommy will come up and say good night, too. It's okay, Rose." My father reached out his hand and Rose grasped it, and they walked out of the dining room together, his long arm around her middle.

My mother sat at the table for a moment, her face in her hands, and then she began clearing the plates. We cleared without talking, my mother humming Schubert's "Schlummerlied," a lullaby about the woods and the river calling to the child to go to sleep. She sang it to us every night when we were small.

My father came into the kitchen and signaled to my mother. They went upstairs and came back down together a few minutes later.

"She's asleep," they said, and we went to sit on the porch and listen to the crickets. I don't remember the rest of the evening, but I remember it as quietly sad, and I remember the rare sight of my parents holding hands, sitting on the picnic table, watching the sunset.

I woke up at three o'clock in the morning, feeling the cool night air through my sheet. I went down the hall for a blanket and looked into Rose's room, for no reason. She wasn't there. I put on my jeans and a sweater and went downstairs. I could feel her absence. I went outside and saw her wide, draggy footprints darkening the wet grass into the woods.

"Rosie," I called, too softly, not wanting to wake my parents, not wanting to startle Rose. "Rosie, it's me. Are you here? Are you all right?"

I almost fell over her. Huge and white in the moonlight, her flowered smock bleached in the light and shadow, her sweatpants now completely wet. Her head was flung back, her white, white neck exposed like a lost Greek column.

"Rosie, Rosie—" Her breathing was very slow, and her lips were not as pink as they usually were. Her eyelids fluttered.

"Closing time," she whispered. I believe that's what she said.

I sat with her, uncovering the bottle of Seconal by her hand, and watched the stars fade.

When the stars were invisible and the sun was warming the air, I went back to the house. My mother was standing on the porch, wrapped in a blanket, watching me. Every step I took overwhelmed me; I could picture my mother slapping me, shooting me for letting her favorite die.

"Warrior queens," she said, wrapping her thin, strong arms around me. "I raised warrior queens." She kissed me fiercely and went into the woods by herself.

Later in the morning she woke my father who could not go into the woods, and still later she called the police and the funeral parlor. She hung up the phone, lay down, and didn't get back out of bed until the day of the funeral. My father fed us both and called the people who needed to be called and picked out Rose's coffin by himself.

My mother played the piano and Addie sang her pure gold notes and I closed my eyes and saw my sister, fourteen years old, lion's mane thrown back and eyes tightly closed against the glare of the parking lot lights. The sweet sound held us tight, flowing around us, eddying through our hearts, rising, still rising.

Amy Bloom

———✦———

COME TO ME, *the short-story collection from which "Silver Water" is taken, was Amy Bloom's debut book and a finalist for the National Book Award in 1993. She had written her first story only two years before. A highly successful psychotherapist living in Connecticut with her husband and three children, she had felt no void in her life that she needed writing to fill. Rather, the occupation came on her as a surprise.*

Explained Bloom to interviewer Janice Lee, "It was like falling in love. . . . I was minding my own business when there was something I thought of, and then I thought of the way I'd like to say it. I didn't think about being a WRITER, in caps."

Come to Me *sold 25,000 copies in the United States, an unusually high number for a collection versus a full-length work of fiction. Bloom's next book, a novel,* Love Invents Us, *appeared in January 1997 and was praised by critics here and abroad.*

Though like "Silver Water" her work often incorporates psychological themes, she fiercely opposes using her patients' lives as a springboard for her work. "It should be illegal," she told Lee. "My patients' stories are their stories."

—C. O.

Seeds

Joy Fielding

I met my sister on the *Sally Jessy Raphael Show*.

Let me explain: It was about four in the afternoon; I was in the middle of doing the laundry, my three-year-old daughter, Tara, at my feet, helping me separate the whites from the colors, her sister Kerry, age six, looming ominously above her, loudly protesting that she was doing it all wrong, when the phone rang. "I'll get it," yelled Kerry, a blur of denim and blond curls as she pushed past Tara, whose round little face was already shrinking into a series of tear-filled wrinkles. "My turn," Tara screeched, unceremoniously dropping my multihued underwear to the tile floor as she waddled after her older sister. By the time I got to the family room, Kerry, her cold-eyed, heart-shaped face flushed with victory, was waving the phone triumphantly above her head while Tara, indignant red blotches staining her chipmunk cheeks, danced helplessly around her. "She hit me," Kerry proclaimed, as I pried the phone from her stubborn fingers. "She hit *me*," came Tara's automatic response. "No hitting," I told them, taking a deep breath and straining for calm, as I lifted the phone to my ear. "Hello."

The man on the other end of the line introduced himself as Tom Anderson, private investigator, then announced he had some startling news for someone named Jan Owen, formerly Jan Greene, originally from Dayton, Ohio, now living in Madison, Wisconsin; was I that Jan Owen? "Your parents were Ronald and Harriet Greene, now deceased?" he continued. "You were an only child?"

Kerry reached over and pinched her sister's arm. Tara started wailing. "No pinching," I hissed toward my older child as I drew Tara toward me.

"What is this about?" I asked Tom Anderson.

"Are you sitting down?" Tom Anderson asked in return.

That's when he told me. Contrary to what I'd believed for thirty-six years, I was not an only child. I had a half sister, seven years my senior. Her name was Brenda, and she was the product of a relationship between my father and a woman, recently deceased, with whom he'd had a brief affair long before he met and married my mother. My father never had an inkling of this child's existence, the private investigator explained, as tears of shock mingled with tears of gratitude streamed down my cheeks. I had a sister.

"You made Mommy cry," Kerry accused Tara, pushing her off my lap and onto the floor.

"*You* made Mommy cry," Tara countered, biting Kerry on her slender calf.

"No pushing, no biting," I responded automatically, as the man on the phone continued spinning his incredible yarn. Apparently, my sister had been searching for me with no success since her mother's death. Finally, after watching an episode of the *Sally Jessy Raphael Show* on which long-lost families were reunited, she approached the show's producers in hopes she might be able to appear on camera to tell her sad tale. The producers did her one better. They hired a private investigator to find me, and now all that was necessary was that I fly to New York, all expenses paid, and surprise the sister I never knew I had on national television. Would I be willing to do that?

Seeds

What would my parents say? I wondered immediately, posing them side by side before the invisible camera of my mind's eye: my father, a tall, balding man whose smiling mouth was oddly out of sync with his perpetually sad gray eyes, one long arm draped protectively around my mother, a full foot shorter than the man she married, her brown wavy hair several inches longer than the style that most flattered her because "your father likes it this way." I recalled my childhood, growing up in a nice house in a comfortable neighborhood, the doted-on only child of a prosperous dentist and his adoring wife. "How are babies made?" I remember asking my mother, my toddler's voice, like chipped glass, cutting through the crowded bus in which we were traveling. "The father plants a seed in the mother's tummy," my mother whispered. "What's the matter with Daddy's seeds?" I demanded indignantly, as laughter broke out around us.

Obviously nothing, I thought as I hung up the phone, having promised Tom Anderson I'd think about the offer and get back to him soon. How I'd hounded my parents about giving me a brother or a sister, as if they were being deliberately stubborn and thoughtless in denying me a sibling, as if this were *my* decision, not theirs, to make.

And now, in a strange way, it was. Fate had presented me with a sister after all. Her name was Brenda, and she was mine for the asking. Sally Jessy Raphael was about to give birth to her on national television. All I had to do was show up and claim her as my own.

"No poking," I warned Kerry as her index finger shot between Tara's ribs. "No kicking," I cautioned Tara as the toe of her red shoe connected with Kerry's shin.

"I hate you," Kerry screamed.

"I hate *you*," came the automatic echo.

In the ensuing weeks, thoughts of Brenda consumed my brain. I tried picturing her. Would she look like me? I wondered, then dismissed this idea. I have my mother's pale complexion and dark blue eyes, her oval face and full upper lip. There is really nothing of my father in my face, and although I have his height, I have little of his natural elegance. This I happily assigned to Brenda, along with his sad gray eyes and smiling mouth. Each passing day brought her image into sharper focus, heightened her reality, bathing her in a Kodachrome glow. We talked, and I heard echoes of my father's voice, deep and resonant. We laughed, and I could feel her breath, sweet and warm, mixing with my own. Though we'd spent our lives apart, we somehow shared the same sense of humor, the same world view.

Brenda walked beside me each morning as I accompanied Kerry to school; she watched over my shoulder as I tucked Tara in bed for her afternoon nap; she gave her smile of approval to each dinner I prepared; she lay in bed beside me at night as I snuggled in my husband's arms. She was the first thing I saw when I opened my eyes, the last thing I saw before I closed them. *I have a sister*, a voice whispered repeatedly inside my head, like a mantra. *I have a sister*.

Of course I went to New York. How could I not?

I remember almost nothing of the plane trip, the hotel, the meetings with the show's producers. Even Sally Jessy herself is little more than an attractive shadow, although, for some reason, the antique silver brooch she was wearing stands out very clearly in my mind. Even now, after I've watched the show several times—the producers were kind enough to provide me with a tape—I find it difficult to concentrate on the details. So, to cut right to the chase: I saw my sister; I met my sister; I didn't like my sister.

The first sign of trouble was my first glimpse of her on the television monitor. I was being kept secluded in a room backstage, so as to maximize the element of surprise. The producers had left me alone with a tray full of doughnuts, a large color monitor, and instructions that they would send someone to get me at the appropriate time. I sat rigid on the green leather sofa, afraid to sample the chocolate doughnut I craved for fear of disturbing my makeup, while a hapless comedian did his best to warm up the audience. I inched forward as a standing ovation greeted the introduction of Sally Jessy herself, then fell back, horrified, as she, in turn, introduced the woman in the chair beside her. "I'd like you to meet Brenda," she began.

I jumped to my feet. *That's not my sister,* I wanted to shout as the camera moved in for a close-up. *You've made a terrible mistake. This aggressively unattractive, middle-aged woman is definitely not my sister.*

Brenda was what is euphemistically referred to as "big boned." Although not exactly fat, she was hardly the lovely, trim figure I'd spent the past several weeks imagining, and her shoulder-length unnaturally blond hair was in dire need of a touch-up. In vain, I searched her square face for signs of my father, but her mouth curled down instead of up, even when she smiled, and her eyes were brown, not gray, cynical as opposed to sad. Obviously, she took after her mother, I thought angrily, even though it was the one thing we seemed to have in common. I was suddenly furious at the poor dead woman, enraged at everything about her daughter, from the way she twisted her unmanicured fingers in her lap to the unflattering beige blouse and brown skirt she wore.

Not that I am any great beauty. My own nails are perpetually chipped; without regular visits to the hairdresser, I would not have the blond highlights that enhance my naturally mousy brown hair; and I could probably stand to lose a few "bones" myself. But hadn't I taken great pains to ensure that my nails were filed and clean, that my hair was washed and stylish, that the new suit I was wearing flattered my figure? This was national television, after all. Didn't Brenda care how she looked? Didn't she know that first impressions are lasting impressions, as my mother used to say? My mother, I reminded myself. The woman my father married. Not *her* mother, the woman he'd left behind. *There but for the grace of God,* I thought. Something our father used to say.

"Tell us why you're here," Sally Jessy said in gentle encouragement, patting Brenda's hand.

Why couldn't Sally Jessy be my sister? I remember thinking, ashamed of the shallowness of my thoughts, the baseness of my emotions. Was I really so vile as to pass judgment on someone because of the way she looked, because she might be a few pounds overweight and in need of a good hairdresser, because her silhouette didn't match the one I'd already drawn?

Shame was quickly overtaken by guilt as I listened to Brenda's story. Her childhood had been miserable. Stigmatized by poverty and illegitimacy, she'd rebelled early and often, with drugs, with booze, with boys. She married the first time at seventeen, and again at twenty-one, both to men decades older than herself, "obviously looking for the father I'd never had," she stated with a resigned shrug. Divorced again, after try number three, and childless by choice—"How could I bring a child into the world, to face life without a father?" Another shrug, this one heavy with defeat. Her mother had done her best, but a woman alone, with no financial support . . . Brenda's voice cracked, trailed off. She shrugged again.

The more she shrugged, the guiltier I felt. The guiltier I felt, the more responsible I felt: for her bad luck, for my good fortune; for everything life had denied her, for all it had given me. As if one was predicated on the other.

Responsibility hardened into resolve. My sister had been robbed of her birthright, and it was up to me, her only living relative, the *fortunate* half sister in her new navy Donna Karan pantsuit, to make things right, to provide Brenda with context, surround her with the loving family she'd never had, bestow on her the legitimacy she craved.

So concentrated was I on my new road to sainthood that I completely missed the part in the story where Brenda's mother, only weeks away from death, finally revealed to Brenda her father's identity, and Brenda began her long, fruitless search. Then I missed the part when Brenda learned her father was dead, but that she had a sister, because that's when a young girl in a brown miniskirt and black tights came to usher me to my correct position offstage, but I did get to hear the part where Brenda lost her job and couldn't afford to continue looking. "What would you like to say to your sister?" I heard Sally asking. "Look into the camera and talk to her."

Whatever Brenda said, once again I missed it, because at the precise moment she started speaking, someone began hooking me up to a microphone. Even later, when I watched the tape, I found myself distracted during her speech by the memory of several sets of hands reaching up under my jacket in an effort to attach a small microphone to my lapel. "I love you, sis" is what reverberates loudest in my brain. "If you, or anyone who knows you, is out there watching . . ."

I almost missed my entrance.

"We have a surprise for you," Sally Jessy was saying. "We've located your sister. She's backstage now, waiting to meet you. Jan, come on out and meet your sister, Brenda."

That was my cue, but my feet wouldn't move. I stood there, as if mired in molasses. Brenda gasped, jumped out of her chair, looked anxiously toward the wings. Still, I didn't move. Suddenly I felt forceful hands on my back, pushing me forward. Someone thrust a large arrangement of spring flowers into my arms, and I tripped onto the stage to thunderous applause. "Oh, my God," Brenda sobbed, stepping forward to embrace me, crushing the flowers against the jacket of my new suit. *What's happening?* I remember thinking. *Who is this stranger? Who am I?*

"This must be quite a moment for the two of you," Sally said, growing misty eyed, as both Brenda and I cried openly. Except I wasn't sure why exactly I was crying. I knew I was supposed to be happy, but the truth was that my overriding emotion was fear, fear that Brenda wasn't the person I wanted her to be, fear that I wasn't the person I'd always thought I was. "What are you two going to do now?" I heard Sally ask, as if she were speaking from the far end of a long tunnel.

Brenda squeezed my hand. A jolt of pain shot from my palm to my elbow. "Make up for lost time," my sister said.

Brenda returned with me to Wisconsin the next day. Now that we were off the air, our lives were once again our own, however altered they might be. Since Brenda was currently unemployed and had nothing to rush home to, it was decided she would spend the next several weeks in Madison, getting to know me and my family. I insisted on paying for her ticket, and she put up no resistance. My husband, Fred, picked us up at the airport, pumping Brenda's hand enthusiastically in greeting, ignoring the seeming indifference of her response. "Nice car," Brenda said, as Fred held open the door of our new black Camry. "Nice house," she said, as we pulled into the driveway of our redbrick, Georgian-style home. "Nice kids," she said, as Kerry and Tara fought over who would be the first to give their aunt a hug.

"Is she always so effusive?" Fred asked after Brenda retired to the guest room to rest before dinner.

"She's been like that since the cameras stopped rolling," I told him, recounting our strained dinner of the night before, compliments of the Sally show. "I tried talking to her. I told her all about you, the kids, why I gave up teaching to be a stay-at-home mom, stuff like that. My life, basically. She wasn't interested. I asked about her, what kind of job she was looking for, if she liked movies, politics, books. She gave me one-word answers, and lit one cigarette after another. I decided she must be shy, so I just kept babbling on. I told her about my childhood, my mother, my father. "*Our* father," I immediately corrected. "You'd think she'd be interested in him! She just smoked her cigarettes and looked bored. I think she hates me."

"She doesn't hate you," Fred said. "She's just 'making strange.' "

"She's strange, all right," I said, then bit my tongue. I was being judgmental, hasty, unfair. Brenda had appeared on the Sally show in hopes of one day meeting her sister; she hadn't expected that sister to be hiding backstage, waiting to ambush her. She simply hadn't been prepared. Fred was right: this was all new to Brenda. We'd thrown a lot at her at once. She was probably feeling a bit overwhelmed. We couldn't expect her to fit right in.

Why can't we? I wondered later, as I was setting the table for dinner. Hadn't Brenda longed for a family all her life? Hadn't she spent a lot of time and money trying to find us? Hadn't she gone on national television with her heartfelt plea? *I love you, sis.* Weren't those her exact words? So why wasn't she down here with the rest of us, helping with dinner and getting to know her new nieces? Why had she spent the entire afternoon holed up in her room? "Who wants to tell their Aunt Brenda that supper's ready?" I asked.

"I do," Kerry said, quickly pushing past her younger sister.

"Me, too!" Tara shouted, following close on her sister's heels.

"No running," I cautioned, stirring the large pot of spaghetti sauce bubbling on the stove while Fred finished setting the table.

Kerry and Tara were back seconds later, enthusiasm drained from once eager faces. "She says she's not hungry," Kerry announced.

"She was smoking a cigarette," Tara whispered, large hazel eyes wide with alarm.

I made no attempt to hide my dismay. I'd already asked Brenda not to smoke in the house. "I'll talk to her later," I said, ushering everyone to the kitchen table.

"Pisgetti!" Tara squealed with obvious delight, as I spooned the steaming pasta onto her plate.

"Not *pis*getti," Kerry corrected. "Pis*getti*."

"That's what I said—pisgetti!"

"Maybe Aunt Brenda doesn't like pisgetti," Kerry offered, a line of bright red sauce winding down her chin.

She was right. Brenda didn't like pisgetti. "I ate so much of it as a child. It was one of the few things we could afford," she explained the next day. The same held true of the meat loaf I prepared the following night. Nor did she like the salmon I grilled several nights after that. "We didn't have the money for fresh fish," she said, "so I never acquired a taste." Chicken was all right, but "chicken is chicken." About the only thing that brought a smile to her lips was when Fred suggested taking us all out for a steak dinner, although her enthusiasm was tempered by the realization that Kerry and Tara would be coming along. ("Don't you ever do anything without them?") She ordered the most expensive item on the menu, barely said a word between bites, and flirted with the waiter, who was young enough to be her son. She lingered over coffee and repeated cigarettes—"Well, you won't let me smoke at your house"—and became testy at the first sign the girls were growing restless. ("Really, you're not doing them any favors by letting them get away with murder.") Once back home, she went directly to her room to watch television. "There's something kind of obscene about one house and three TV's," she'd commented when I'd first shown her around our tidy four-bedroom house, although she obviously found nothing obscene about watching one every waking minute.

Not that she spent much time awake. Brenda slept till noon every day, then filled her afternoons watching soap operas. She wasn't interested in sightseeing or meeting any of my friends. When I asked if she wanted to go shopping, she snapped, "With what? Not everybody can afford expensive silk scarves like you can." Guiltily, I'd slipped the butterfly-print scarf from around my neck and returned it to its drawer.

Brenda never smiled, lifted a finger, or offered to pay for anything. She expected to be waited on, accepting it as her due. Nor was she grateful for anything we did for her. She rarely said please, never said thank you. Still, I persisted. She was my sister, after all, my older sister at that, and she'd had an undeniably hard life. With enough patience and love . . .

"Kerry, stop that," I said.

"Stop what?" Kerry asked innocently.

"I saw you getting ready to kick your sister."

We were sitting at the kitchen table, working on a giant Sesame Street jigsaw puzzle. Tara was trying to squeeze one of the larger pieces into a space for which it clearly didn't belong.

"She's going to wreck it," Kerry protested.

"*You're* going to wreck it," Tara shot back.

"You're an idiot," Kerry said.

"*You're* an idiot," Tara told her.

"No name calling," I cautioned.

Kerry jumped to her feet. "I hate you," she yelled at Tara, grabbing the top of the puzzle box and whacking it across her sister's head before running from the room. Tara started wailing. Directly above us in the guest room, I heard Brenda raise the volume on the TV.

"It's okay, sweetie," I said, comforting my younger child and kissing the top of her sweet-smelling head. I held her until she stopped crying, then we continued working on the puzzle until she suddenly stopped, looked around, and said,

"Where's Kerry?" as if noticing for the first time that her sister wasn't there.

"I'm not sure," I told her. "Shall we have a look?"

Tara took my hand and led me up the stairs to Kerry's room. Kerry was on the floor, playing with her Barbie dolls. "I don't like Tara," she announced, defiantly unapologetic, as we entered the room. "I don't like her, and I don't love her. And you can't make me."

I sat down on the floor beside my older child. "You don't have to love her," I told her gently. "And you don't have to like her." Kerry stared at me as if I'd taken complete leave of my senses. "But you can't hurt her. Do you understand?"

"I don't have to love her?" Kerry repeated.

"You just can't hurt her."

"Do you love *your* sister?" she asked suddenly.

"Well, that's a little more complicated," I began, then stopped.

You don't have to love her.

"No," I answered, after a lengthy pause. "No, I don't love her."

"Do you like her?"

You don't have to like her.

"No. No, I don't like her," I admitted.

"I don't like her either," Kerry whispered.

"I don't like her either," echoed Tara.

Then I did something I hadn't done in over a week. I threw my head back and laughed out loud.

The next morning, I asked Brenda to leave. She looked more irritated than surprised, but since her normal look was one of mild irritation, it was hard to tell exactly what she was feeling. "I was wondering if you could spare me some money to help me get back on my feet," she said, as if this were a perfectly natural request to be making at this time. "After all, I never got to share in Daddy's inheritance."

So, it was all about money, I realized, disappointment overtaking anger, as I wrote her a check for two thousand dollars, all the money I'd managed to save in the last year. It was easier than trying to explain that any money my father had left had been eaten up by my mother's subsequent medical bills. Besides, I knew Brenda wouldn't be interested. She took the check, then went upstairs to pack her suitcase. She left an hour later without saying good-bye.

I saw her again approximately six months later. It was an accident. Normally, I don't watch TV in the morning, but Kerry had the sniffles and I'd kept her home from school. She and Tara were playing in Tara's room—"Liar!" Kerry shouted. "Liar, liar, pants on fire!" came the embellished retort—and I plopped down on my freshly made bed and absently began fiddling with the remote control. Suddenly, there she was, cynical brown eyes filling with fresh tears, square jaw quivering into the butterfly-print scarf at her throat. "It was awful," she was whispering, as Sally Jessy Raphael leaned forward in her chair.

"It didn't work out?"

Brenda shook her head, clearly too overcome with emotion to speak.

Sally patted her hand and looked directly into the camera. "We're talking today with people whose family reunions didn't work out quite the way they'd hoped. Can you tell us what went wrong?" she asked Brenda.

"I wish I knew," Brenda said. "My sister seemed like a nice woman. She even invited me to her home for a few weeks. But then she left me alone all day. Just ignored me completely. We never went anywhere. Her kids were always fighting. If I said anything, anything at all, she took it the wrong way. Clearly, I wasn't welcome. Finally, I couldn't take it anymore, and I left."

"Liar!" I shouted at the TV screen.

Liar, liar, pants on fire.

"That's my toy!" Kerry raged from the other room.

"My toy!" came Tara's immediate response.

"That's my scarf!" I gasped, jumping off the bed, waving my index finger wildly at the screen. As if she'd heard me, Brenda patted the beautiful butterfly-print scarf tied lazily around her neck. I'd been looking for that scarf for months. "Damn you," I cried helplessly. "That's *my* scarf." I collapsed back on the bed, my head in my hands, not sure whether to laugh or cry.

"Mommy?" said a small voice. "Are you all right?"

I lifted my head. Kerry and Tara stood in the doorway, hand in hand, their beauty, warmer than sunlight, filling the room. *Two good little seeds*, I thought, *waiting to flower*.

"Would you like to play with us, Mommy?" Tara asked.

I took one last look at the TV. Sally had moved on to another guest. Brenda was nowhere to be seen. I reached for the remote control unit, pressed the appropriate button, watched the screen go blank. Then I smiled at the two young sisters waiting for me in the doorway. "I would love to play with you," I said.

Joy Fielding

"I HAVE LONG been fascinated by what happens after the cameras stop rolling on shows like Sally Jessy Raphael's," says Joy Fielding, "especially in cases where families are reunited, and I thought it could provide an interesting backdrop for exploring the often complicated relationship between sisters."

One of Canada's foremost authors, Fielding has published twelve novels worldwide, beginning with The Best of Friends, which she penned after a career as an actress—including one episode of Gunsmoke—and writer for television. Other novels include See Jane Run, Don't Cry Now, The Other Woman, and her most recent, Missing Pieces.

Like other authors in this anthology, she began writing at an early age, bravely sending off her first short story to a magazine at age eight, and first television script to the Canadian Broadcasting Corporation at age twelve. Both were rejected, but in the spirit of the true writer, she went back for more.

Persistence has paid its dividends. In 1996, See Jane Run was adapted into a major network television movie in Canada and the United States.

Fielding is a graduate of the University of Toronto. She and

145

her family split their year between Toronto and Palm Beach. She has one sister.

How does she get along with her? you may wonder.

Says Fielding, "I have a wonderful relationship with my sister, who is six years my junior and one of my closest friends, and I hope that one day the same will hold true for my daughters."

—C. O.

A
Red Sweater

Fae Myenne Ng

I chose red for my sister. Fierce, dark red. Made in Hong Kong. Hand Wash Only because it's got that skin of fuzz. She'll look happy. That's good. Everything's perfect, for a minute. That seems enough.

Red. For Good Luck. Of course. This fire-red sweater is swollen with good cheer. Wear it, I will tell her. You'll look lucky.

We're a family of three girls. By Chinese standards, that's not lucky. "Too bad," outsiders whisper, ". . . nothing but daughters. A failed family."

First, Middle, and End girl. Our order of birth marked us. That came to tell more than our given names.

My eldest sister, Lisa, lives at home. She quit San Francisco State, one semester short of a psychology degree. One day she said, "Forget about it; I'm tired." She's working full time at Pacific Bell now. Nine hundred a month with benefits. Mah and Deh think it's a great deal. They tell everybody, "Yes, our Number One makes good pay, but that's not even counting the discount. If we call Hong Kong,

China even, there's forty percent off!" As if anyone in their part of China had a telephone.

Number Two, the in-between, jumped off the "M" floor three years ago. Not true! What happened? Why? Too sad! All we say about that is, "It was her choice."

We sent Mah to Hong Kong. When she left Hong Kong thirty years ago, she was the envy of all: "Lucky girl! You'll never have to work." To marry a sojourner was to have a future. Thirty years in the land of gold and good fortune, and then she returned to tell the story: three daughters, one dead, one unmarried, another who-cares-where, the thirty years in sweatshops, and the prince of the Golden Mountain turned into a toad. I'm glad I didn't have to go with her. I felt her shame and regret. To return, seeking solace and comfort, instead of offering banquets and stories of the good life.

I'm the youngest. I started flying with American Airlines the year Mah returned to Hong Kong, so I got her a good discount. She thought I was good for something then. But when she returned, I was pregnant.

"Get an abortion," she said. "Drop the baby," she screamed.

"No."

"Then get married."

"No. I don't want to."

I was going to get an abortion all along. I just didn't like the way they talked about the whole thing. They made me feel like dirt, that I was a disgrace. Now I can see how I used it as an opportunity. Sometimes I wonder if there wasn't another way. Everything about those years was so steamy and angry. There didn't seem to be any answers.

"I have no eyes for you," Mah said.

"Don't call us," Deh said.

They wouldn't talk to me. They ranted idioms to each other for days. The apartment was filled with images and curses I couldn't perceive. I got the general idea: I was a rotten, no-good, dead thing. I would die in a gutter without rice in my belly. My spirit—if I had one—wouldn't be fed. I wouldn't see good days in this life or the next.

My parents always had a special way of saying things.

Now I'm based in Honolulu. When our middle sister jumped, she kind of closed the world. The family just sort of fell apart. I left. Now, I try to make up for it, but the folks still won't see me, but I try to keep in touch with them through Lisa. Flying cuts up your life, hits hardest during the holidays. I'm always sensitive then. I feel like I'm missing something, that people are doing something really important while I'm up in the sky, flying through time zones.

So I like to see Lisa around the beginning of the year. January, New Year's, and February, New Year's again, double luckiness with our birthdays in between. With so much going on, there's always something to talk about.

"You pick the place this year," I tell her.

"Around here?"

"No," I say. "Around here" means the food is good and the living hard. You eat a steaming rice plate, and then you feel like rushing home to sew garments or assemble radio parts or something. We eat together only once a year, so I feel we should splurge. Besides, at the Chinatown places, you have nothing to talk about except the bare issues. In American restaurants, the atmosphere helps you along. I want nice light and a view and handsome waiters.

"Let's go somewhere with a view," I say.

We decide to go to Following Sea, a new place on the Pier 39 track. We're early, the restaurant isn't crowded. It's been clear all day, so I think the sunset will be nice. I ask for a window table. I turn to talk to my sister, but she's already talking to a waiter. He's got that dark island tone that she likes. He's looking her up and down. My sister does not blink at it. She holds his look and orders two Johnny Walkers. I

pick up a fork, turn it around in my hand. I seldom use chopsticks now. At home, I eat my rice in a plate, with a fork.
The only chopsticks I own, I wear in my hair. For a moment,
I feel strange sitting here at this unfamiliar table. I don't
know this tablecloth, this linen, these candles. Everything
seems foreign. It feels like we should be different people. But
each time I look up, she's the same. I know this person. She's
my sister. We sat together with chopsticks, mismatched
bowls, braids, and braces, across the Formica tabletop.

"I like three-pronged forks," I say, pressing my thumb
against the sharp points.

My sister rolls her eyes. She lights a cigarette.

I ask for one.

I finally say, "So, what's new?"

"Not much." Her voice is sullen. She doesn't look at me.
Once a year, I come in, asking questions. She's got the
answers, but she hates them. For me, I think she's got the
peace of heart, knowing that she's done her share for Mah
and Deh. She thinks I have the peace, not caring. Her life is
full of questions, too, but I have no answers.

I look around the restaurant. The sunset is not spectacular and we don't comment on it. The waiters are lighting
candles. Ours is bringing the drinks. He stops very close to
my sister, seems to breathe her in. She raises her face toward
him. "Ready?" he asks. My sister orders for us. The waiter
struts off.

"Tight ass," I say.

"The best," she says.

My scotch tastes good. It reminds me of Deh. Johnny
Walker or Seagrams 7, that's what they served at Chinese
banquets. Nine courses and a bottle. No ice. We learned to
drink it Chinese style, in teacups. Deh drank from his rice
bowl, sipping it like hot soup. By the end of the meal, he
took it like cool tea, in bold mouthfuls. We sat watching,
our teacups of scotch in our laps, his three giggly girls.

150

Relaxed, I'm thinking there's a connection. Johnny Walker then and Johnny Walker now. I ask for another cigarette and this one I enjoy. Now my Johnny Walker pops with ice. I twirl the glass to make the ice tinkle.

We clink glasses. Three times for good luck. She giggles. I feel better.

"Nice sweater," I say.

"Michael Owyang," she says. She laughs. The light from the candle makes her eyes shimmer. She's got Mah's eyes. Eyes that make you want to talk. Lisa is reed-thin and tall. She's got a body that clothes look good on. My sister slips something on and it wraps her like skin. Fabric has pulse on her.

"Happy birthday, soon," I say.

"Thanks, and to yours, too, just as soon."

"Here's to Johnny Walker in shark's fin soup," I say.

"And squab dinners."

"*I Love Lucy,*" I say.

We laugh. It makes us feel like children again. We remember how to be sisters.

I raise my glass. "To *I Love Lucy,* squab dinners, and brown bags."

"To bones," she says.

"Bones," I repeat. This is a funny that gets sad, and knowing it, I keep laughing. I am surprised how much memory there is in one word. Pigeons. Only recently did I learn they're called squab. Our word for them was pigeon—on a plate or flying over Portsmouth Square. A good meal at 40 cents a bird. In line by dawn, we waited at the butcher's, listening for the slow, churning motor of the trucks. We watched the live fish flushing out of the tanks into the garbage pails. We smelled the honey-brushed cha sui bows baking. When the white laundry truck turned onto Wentworth, there was a puffing trail of feathers following it. A stench filled the alley. The crowd squeezed in around the truck. Old ladies reached into the crates, squeezing and tugging for the plumpest pigeons.

My sister and I picked the white ones, those with the most expressive eyes. Dove birds, we called them. We fed them leftover rice in water, and as long as they stayed plump, they were our pets, our baby dove birds. And then one day we'd come home from school and find them cooked. They were a special, nutritious treat. Mah let us fill our bowls high with little pigeon parts: legs, breasts, and wings, and take them out to the front room to watch *I Love Lucy*. We took brown bags for the bones. We balanced our bowls on our laps and laughed at Lucy. We leaned forward, our chopsticks crossed in midair, and called out, "Mah! Mah! Come watch! Watch Lucy cry!"

But she always sat alone in the kitchen sucking out the sweetness of the lesser parts: necks, backs, and the head. "Bones are sweeter than you know," she always said. She came out to check the bags. "Clean bones." She shook the bags. "No waste," she said.

Our dinners come with a warning. "Plate's hot. Don't touch." My sister orders a carafe of house white. "Enjoy," he says, smiling at my sister. She doesn't look up.

I can't remember how to say *scallops* in Chinese. I ask my sister; she doesn't know either. The food isn't great. Or maybe we just don't have the taste buds in us to go crazy over it. Sometimes I get very hungry for Chinese flavors: black beans, garlic and ginger, shrimp paste and sesame oil. These are tastes we grew up with, still dream about. Crave. Run around town after. Duck liver sausage, beancurd, jook, salted fish, and fried dace with black beans. Western flavors don't stand out; the surroundings do. Three-pronged forks. Pink tablecloths. Fresh flowers. Cute waiters. An odd difference.

"Maybe we should have gone to Sun Hung Heung. At least the vegetables are real," I say.

"*Hung toh-yee-foo-won-tun!*" she says.

"Yeah, yum!" I say.

I remember Deh teaching us how to pick bak-choy, his favorite vegetable. "Stick your fingernail into the stem. Juicy and firm, good. Limp and tough, no good." The three of us followed Deh, punching our thumbnails into every stem of bak-choy we saw.

"Deh still eating bak-choy?"

"Breakfast, lunch and dinner." My sister throws her head back and laughs. It is Deh's motion. She recites in a mimic tone. "Your Deh, all he needs is a good hot bowl of rice and a plate full of greens. A good monk."

There was always bak-choy. Even though it was nonstop for Mah—rushing to the sweatshop in the morning, out to shop on break, and then home to cook by evening—she did this for him. A plate of bak-choy, steaming with the taste of ginger and garlic. He said she made good rice. Timed full-fire until the first boil, medium until the grains formed a crust along the sides of the pot, and then low-flamed to let the rice steam. Firm, that's how Deh liked his rice.

The waiter brings the wine, asks if everything is all right.

"Everything," my sister says.

There's something else about this meeting. I can hear it in the edge of her voice. She doesn't say anything and I don't ask. Her lips make a contorting line; her face looks sour. She lets out a breath. It sounds like she's been holding it in too long.

"Another fight. The bank line," she says. "He waited four times in the bank line. Mah ran around outside shopping. He was doing her a favor. She was doing him a favor. Mah wouldn't stop yelling. 'Get out and go die! Useless Thing! Stinking Corpse!' "

I know he answered. His voice must have had that fortune teller's tone to it. You listened because you knew it was a warning.

He always threatened to disappear, jump off the Golden Gate. His thousand-year-old threat. I've heard it all before. "I will go. Even when dead, I won't be far enough away. Curse the good will that blinded me into taking you as wife!"

I give Lisa some of my scallops. "Eat," I tell her.

She keeps talking. "Of course, you know how Mah thinks, that nobody should complain because she's been the one working all these years."

I nod. I start eating, hoping she'll follow.

One bite and she's talking again. "You know what shopping with Mah is like, either you stand outside with the bags like a servant, or inside like a marker, holding a place in line. You know how she gets into being frugal—saving time because it's the one free thing in her life. Well, they're at the bank and she had him hold her place in line while she runs up and down Stockton doing her quick shopping maneuvers. So he's in line, and it's his turn, but she's not back. So he has to start all over at the back again. Then it's his turn but she's still not back. When she finally comes in, she's got bags in both hands, and he's going through the line for the fourth time. Of course she doesn't say sorry or anything."

I interrupt. "How do you know all this?" I tell myself not to come back next year. I tell myself to apply for another transfer, to the East Coast.

"She told me. Word for word." Lisa spears the scallop, puts it in her mouth. I know it's cold by now. "Word for word," she repeats. She cuts a piece of chicken. "Try," she says.

I think about how we're sisters. We eat slowly, chewing carefully, like old people. A way to make things last, to fool the stomach.

Mah and Deh both worked too hard; it's as if their marriage was a marriage of toil—of toiling together. The idea is that the next generation can marry for love.

In the old country, matches were made, strangers were wedded, and that was fate. Those days, sojourners like Deh were considered princes. To become the wife to such a man was to be saved from the war-torn villages.

Saved to work. After dinner, with the rice still in between her teeth, Mah sat down at her Singer. When we pulled out the wallbed, she was still there, sewing. The street noises stopped long before she did. The hot lamp made all the stitches blur together. And in the mornings, long before any of us awoke, she was already there, sewing again.

His work was hard, too. He ran a laundry on Polk Street. He sailed with the American President Lines. Things started to look up when he owned the take-out place in Vallejo, and then his partner ran off. So he went to Alaska and worked the canneries.

She was good to him, too. We remember. How else would we have known him all those years he worked in Guam, in the Fiji Islands, in Alaska? Mah always gave him majestic welcomes home. It was her excitement that made us remember him.

I look around. The restaurant is full. The waiters move quickly.

I know Deh. His words are ugly. I've heard him. I've listened. And I've always wished for the street noises, as if in the traffic of sound, I believe I can escape. I know the hard color of his eyes and the tightness in his jaw. I can almost hear his teeth grind. I know this. Years of it.

Their lives weren't easy. So is their discontent without reason?

What about the first one? You didn't even think to come to the hospital. The first one, I say! Son or daughter, dead or alive, you didn't even come!

What about living or dying? Which did you want for me

that time you pushed me back to work before my back brace was off?

Money! Money!! Money to eat with, to buy clothes with, to pass this life with!

Don't start that again! Everything I make at that dead place I hand . . .

How come . . .

What about . . .

So . . .

It was obvious. The stories themselves meant little. It was how hot and furious they could become.

Is there no end to it? What makes their ugliness so alive, so thick and impossible to let go of?

"I don't want to think about it anymore." The way she says it surprises me. This time I listen. I imagine what it would be like to take her place. It will be my turn one day.

"Ron," she says, wiggling her fingers above the candle. "A fun thing."

The opal flickers above the flame. I tell her that I want to get her something special for her birthday, ". . . next trip I get abroad." She looks up at me, smiles.

For a minute, my sister seems happy. But she won't be able to hold onto it. She grabs at things out of despair, out of fear. Gifts grow old for her. Emotions never ripen, they sour. Everything slips away from her. Nothing sustains her. Her beauty has made her fragile.

We should have eaten in Chinatown. We could have gone for coffee in North Beach, then for jook at Sam Wo's.

"No work; it's been like that for months, just odd jobs," she says.

I'm thinking, It's not like I haven't done my share. I was a kid once, I did things because I felt I should. I helped fill out forms at the Chinatown employment agencies. I went

with him to the Seaman's Union. I waited too, listening and
hoping for those calls: "Busboy! Presser! Prep Man!" His
bags were packed, he was always ready to go. "On standby,"
he said.

Every week. All the same. Quitting and looking to start
all over again. In the end, it was like never having gone anywhere. It was like the bank line, waiting for nothing.

How many times did my sister and I have to hold them
apart? The flat *ting!* sound as the blade slapped onto the
linoleum floors, the wooden handle of the knife slamming
into the corner. Was it she or I who screamed, repeating all
their ugliest words? Who shook them? Who made them
stop?

The waiter comes to take the plates. He stands by my sister for a moment. I raise my glass to the waiter.

"You two Chinese?" he asks.

"No," I say, finishing off my wine. I roll my eyes. I wish I
had another Johnny Walker. Suddenly I don't care.

"We're two sisters," I say. I laugh. I ask for the check,
leave a good tip. I see him slip my sister a box of matches.

Outside, the air is cool and brisk. My sister links her arm
into mine. We walk up Bay onto Chestnut. We pass Galileo
High School and then turn down Van Ness to head toward
the pier. The bay is black. The foghorns sound far away. We
walk the whole length of the pier without talking.

The water is white where it slaps against the wooden
stakes. For a long time Lisa's wanted out. She can stay at
that point of endurance forever. Desire that becomes old
feels too good, it's seductive. I know how hard it is to go.

The heart never travels. You have to be heartless. My sister holds that heart, too close and for too long. This is her
weakness, and I like to think, used to be mine. Lisa endures
too much.

We're lucky, not like the bondmaids growing up in service, or the newborn daughters whose mouths were stuffed with ashes. Courtesans with the three-inch foot, beardless, soft-shouldered eunuchs and the frightened child-brides, they're all stories to us. We're the lucky generation. Our parents forced themselves to live through the humiliation in this country so that we could have it better. We know so little of the old country. We repeat the names of grandmothers and uncles, but they will always be strangers to us. Family exists only because somebody has a story, and knowing the story connects us to a history. To us, the deformed man is oddly compelling, the forgotten man is a good story. A beautiful woman suffers.

I want her beauty to buy her out.

The sweater cost two weeks' pay. Like the 40-cent birds that are now a delicacy, this is a special treat. The money doesn't mean anything. It is, if anything, time. Time is what I would like to give her.

A red sweater. 100% angora. The skin of fuzz will be a fierce rouge on her naked breasts.

Red. Lucky. Wear it. Find that man. The new one. Wrap yourself around him. Feel the pulsing between you. Fuck him and think about it. 100%. Hand Wash Only. Worn Once.

Fae Myenne Ng

CALLED ON TO SPEAK to literature classes across the country, Fae Myenne Ng is author of the PEN/Faulkner Award–nominated novel Bone. It was a book written, as she has said, to honor the older generations of Chinese Americans whose struggles and hard work made it possible for the following generations—women such as the sisters in "A Red Sweater"—to do better than the last.

In illustration of this, although today Ng is a successful writer, her mother was a seamstress in the sweatshops of San Francisco's Chinatown. Ng herself was born and raised in San Francisco. First-generation Chinese Americans have long been her inspiration and Ng cites as an early influence "listening to old-timers in Portsmouth Square reciting classical poetry in Cantonese."

Ng has received many awards and fellowships, among them the PEN/Nelson Algren Fiction Award, a Pushcart Prize, National Endowment for the Arts award, McDowell Fellowship. Lila Wallace–Reader's Digest Literary Fellowship, and, more recently, a fellowship in literature from the American Academy of Arts and Letters, which took her to Rome.

Her fiction, published in Harper's, American Voice, and the City Lights Review, is often anthologized and has appeared in Calyx and Granta magazine's 20 Under 40: Best Young American Novelists.

—C. O.

Traffic

Tracy Robert

My mother is on the sauce again, dangerously. She's missed a week of work—one of many medical front-office jobs she's lied to get and is destined to lose—and complains that the ulcer no doctor can find is acting up. In her valise-size purse, there's a bottle of green mouthwash and a bottle emptied of mouthwash and filled with chablis, and on the nightstand, a book called *Making Anger Your Ally*. My mother snores. The drapes are pulled on a magnificent morning panorama of Dana Point Harbor and the Pacific. She bought this condominium for its view.

"Might as well let her sleep," says Carson, my younger sister. When our parents split up ten years ago, my mother decided her life was over, all but the view, and at age thirteen Carson became her nurse, housekeeper, and confidante. More than once Mom has said, "Oh Carse, if you leave home, I'll do myself in." Carson has an attractive olive-skinned face without the help of makeup, but she's around forty pounds overweight. In high school, she had a boyfriend who rinsed his hair a different shade of blond every month and played piano in a beach restaurant bar. Our mother suddenly managed to stock the cupboard with an assortment of Carson's favorite chips and crackers, and jars of peanut butter, chunk style. In the freezer, pizza bread, lasagna, French fries and Rocky Road ice cream. As Carson got larger, her boyfriend developed an eye for cocktail waitresses and their outfits, which, Carson said, resembled *Swan Lake* in bondage.

My sister and I are embarking on an end of summer weekend to see relatives in Los Angeles: our father, our paternal grandparents, and Meemaw, our mother's mother. We take this trip out of a sense of duty to these removed people who always remember our birthdays, and also because we like to assure ourselves that most of our relatives are quirky but physically intact. I have a new car to show off, a Honda Civic wagon that looks like a space exploration vehicle, and I'm making better than thirty thousand a year for the first time in my life, on account of political measures for teacher salaries. Carson keyboards at a micrographics firm and has a used Toyota Celica, metallic gold, but it's in the shop awaiting body repairs. A motorcycle slammed into the right rear of her car. "I sat there looking at this guy," she says, "sprawled out on the asphalt, no helmet, and I thought, 'Hey, when they throw me in jail for manslaughter, maybe I'll lose weight and for sure I won't have to live with Mom.' " She won't be thrown in jail because although she was completing a left turn, the motorcyclist, who broke two ribs, was doing over fifty in a thirty-five zone. The insurance companies called it a draw.

I don't seek out my mother when she's drinking. Something close to reflex tells me to flare like a cornered animal, then run. The last time I spoke with her, I was ecstatic about my raise. "Swell," she said. "I'll come to you when I need a loan." I told her not to bother and hung up. Her condo is worth thousands more than the fixer-upper I have a second mortgage on. "How bad is she?" I ask.

"Pretty bad," Carson says. "She almost ate carpet lint on the stairs the other night, but the banister caught her."

"She hurt herself?"

"Too drunk for that. Superflex Gumby, bends in all directions." Carson pulls the reclining lever on the bucket seat and goes into an imitation of my mother's supplicant fetal position. " 'Carse, baby, I'm frightened, so alone, so all alone. Please try to understand.' I'm so bored with that routine I've actually blown it a couple times."

"How?"

"By bellowing at her like you do, asking her just what catastrophe she's expecting that's worse than what she's done to herself. Also by telling her I've been more sympathetic than any AA convert she'll ever lean on, so she'd better ease off."

Apparently, my mother is losing her grip on her greatest banister.

When we reach our father's hillside Pasadena home, he says our mother's phoned. "I could tell by her voice she's off-center," he adds. She claimed Carson left the house with her car keys.

"What keys?" Carson says. "I don't even have my own goddamn keys." She tromps into the house.

My father helps me unload the Honda. "What do you think?" I say. "I mean, you know your oldest child has arrived when she doesn't ask for help on the down payment."

"Fantastic, Char," he says. "I'll let you know how I like it after I've driven it. You will let me drive it, won't you?"

My father is a congenial, dapper man. He's never missed an alimony payment; he vigilantly avoids speaking ill of our mother. But he's also the most oblivious driver I've ever had the misfortune to ride with. He swerves, he speeds, he creeps, he straddles lanes, he faces passengers for moments at a time, long moments, while he converses with them. The only explanation for his survival on LA freeways is that other drivers spot him at once and keep their distance.

"Sure I will," I say sheepishly. "You're my father, aren't you?"

A nylon flight bag in each hand, he stands motionless, then sets them down. "Charlotte," he says. "Bonnie and I are going to get married in about a year. I thought I should let you know." Bonnie is a tiny, exquisite Asian woman who runs an interior decorating business. My father and she have gone together seven years; the announcement is no surprise.

"I think that's wonderful, Dad. And it may force Mom to accept that you're not going to charge in on a white steed to raise her up from the mud."

"That's not my reason for doing it, of course," he says.

"Of course. Just that's she's on my mind. I do think it's great about you and Bonnie."

"Well, I'm not so sure," he says. His heavy-lidded eyes look resigned yet somewhat terrified. There'd be no place left in my father to bury the guilt if he shattered someone else's expectations. My mother was a tall, delicate, blue-eyed beauty when they married. She in fact was a singer-starlet who put him through law school on her earnings. I have a snapshot in my wallet to remind me of how she was. She wears a cotton floral sundress and gazes expectantly at the foothills beyond a wishing well.

My father trudges away with the bags.

Carson returns. "Another episode," she says, "brought to you by the unquenchable Vivian Rioux. She called Bonnie a Chink."

"Three guesses who wants to drive my car, and I wish it were Bonnie."

"Holy fucking pile-up. You're not going to let him, are you?"

"What else can I do? If my car comes through this unscathed, I'll definitely believe there's a Supreme Being."

"I'll believe there's immortality," my sister says.

In my father's study, where Carson and I tonight will sleep on futons, is a book called *Love Is Saying No to Fear*.

Meemaw lives in a cluster of Sunland apartments for the elderly. Carson calls it Heart-Rate Hotel. Air conditioners hum and click like life-support systems. Meemaw stands at the railing in front of her second-story cubbyhole. "Phew," she says. "Damn heat makes my skin curl up. The car's absolutely adorable, Charlotte." She wears a housecoat of a fabric printed to look like a crazy quilt. I give her a hug, my fingers barely interlocked around her middle.

"So, how are you, Meemaw?"

"Same as usual. Fat and sassy." Her hair, cut in the Dutch-boy style she's worn the three decades I've known her, is whiter than last year, eyes clear and deep brown behind her wire rims. Both Carson and I take after her. I've learned to control the weight by eating less than I want to.

Meemaw puts buttermilk bread, bologna, and cellophane-wrapped American cheese slices out for sandwiches. Carson reacts automatically to the food; I have a diet soda and nibble on a cheese corner. I mention to my grandmother that I'm nervous about my father's driving my car. She drops her sandwich and runs for a paper towel to cover her mouth with. She's laughing, and Meemaw never laughs demurely.

"I haven't thought of Frank's driving for ages," she sputters. "One time we were coming home from Foster's Freeze, he took a corner like a bat out of hell. You were just a baby, still in your car seat, no more than two years old. And you jerked yourself back up straight and said, 'Geez Christ, Dad. Slow down!' " She laughs some more. " 'Geez Christ, Dad,' you said. Your little eyes were round as quarters, black as coal tar." She dabs at her eyes with the paper towel. "I'm going to have to go to the bathroom before I wet my pants."

Carson chuckles as she finishes her sandwich and I shake

my head. At the start of the hallway, I notice a grouping of pictures, four teenage girls: my grandmother, mother, sister, and me. My mother's portrait is central to the arrangement. She's the fair-haired princess, but she looks wan and lonely in this gathering of dark eyes.

"What's your mom been up to?" Meemaw asks. She depends on us for news. Owing to Meemaw's rigid views on liquor, she and my mother go at it worse than Mom and I do.

"You might say she's catapulted off the wagon," Carson says.

"Lord," Meemaw says with a wince. "Sounds more like her father every time I hear." Meemaw divorced her husband, an alcoholic who occasionally beat her, after twenty years of marriage. "So spoiled, so self-important. He thought entire creation should kowtow and kiss his lily-white butt." There were suitors after the divorce, but Meemaw chose to live in peace with her ceramic animals, her photographs, her wealth of stories that make her laugh or wince. Not all of them concern our family; she worked thirty years as an aide in the psychiatric ward of a veterans' hospital.

"I know a thing or two about drunks," she says. "All this rigmarole about it being a disease. Alcoholism is not a disease. Now, the addiction may be a disease, but you can't bottle a disease. You make the decision to put the bottle to your lips. It's a weakness of character. Never known a drunk who didn't lie to himself and believe it. And I've never known a drunk who knew the joy of giving love as opposed to taking and taking and taking it."

Sometimes when I talk to my mother on the phone, she says, "I love you," then pauses oppressively, waiting to hear me return the endearment. I oblige her but resent having to.

Meemaw's last words to us are, "Don't grieve too much over your mother. Don't let her stomp on your lives. You've got to go on living."

When we get into the car, my sister slaps her ample

thigh and says, "I can always depend on Meemaw for a good time," but her chin crinkles into the texture of orange peel. "If Mom would literally stomp on my life, maybe I could leave her."

My father doesn't ask to drive to my grandparents', so I'm spared the dreaded ride at least until tomorrow. Grandpa Claude and Grandma Eloise shuffle out to examine my car. She wears an indigo batik caftan and he wears a matching sport coat. The toothbrush touchups don't hide all the gray in my grandfather's sparse hair, which he combs from his neck over the crown of his head. His shoulders have diminished, and Grandma is working on a sizable dowager's hump. "You come to see me only when you have a new car," Grandpa says in his persistent French accent. "If I buy you a new car every month, will I see you then each month?"

"Claude, you know we're delighted to see our granddaughters whenever our paths cross," says Grandma, one of those rare people to whom the word *serene* applies. She belongs to a nondenominational church and has taught interpretive dance as long as I can recall. She doesn't simply pray the Lord's Prayer—she dances it. Grandpa's an atheist. My mother once informed me they divorced around the time I was born. Grandpa, an opera singer and voice teacher, had an affair with a German coloratura. Shortly thereafter, Grandma inherited hundreds of thousands from a rich aunt, and Grandpa came hotfooting back. He has a passion for costly Far Eastern antiques. My mother unveiled this story because she hates them both. She says they're pretentious, since they don't discuss their tawdry past, but I think she hates them mostly because they're blithely eccentric and are no longer part of her life.

Grandpa nearly scurries to show me his latest acquisition, a roomful of carved mahogany furniture, inlaid profusely with mother-of-pearl. There are mother-of-pearl trees, flowers, benches, bridges, pagodas, lovers, clumps of grass, even tiny rabbits. *"Splendide, n'est-ce pas?"* my grandfather says. I nod in silent awe of the artists who must have devoted their lives to carving these pieces, then populating them with creatures, plants, and sanctuaries. I'd love to command such tender patience.

In the kitchen, Grandma prepares a snack of Gouda, dry-roasted peanuts, marinated artichoke hearts, and ginger ale. "Let us eat, drink and be merry," she says, toddling out with the tray. She frequently takes a poetic turn. One Thanksgiving, she read an original poem called "I Am Thankful" in which the title clause was repeated so many times I lost track.

"Tell me, Carson dear, about your mama." She puts the accent on the second syllable of *mama*.

Carson falls to the floor in a mock collapse. This is no small achievement, surrounded as she is by pedestals supporting jade icons and ivory geishas. Grandma looks as though the joke has eluded her, but our grandfather claps his manicured hands and cackles until the veins stand out on his neck.

"This one, she missed her calling," he says. "A comedienne." He doesn't understand Carson's humor is more necessity than avocation.

"You know," Grandma says. "I belong to a metaphysical prayer ensemble. I dance with all my heart for your mother."

"She's beyond metaphysics," I say, arching an eyebrow.

"Smile," Grandpa says. "You are so pretty when you smile."

"We mustn't give up hope," Grandma says.

"To live in this world," Grandpa says, "you must be strong like me, like the ox." He then tells a story of how he trained a recalcitrant, spitting camel in Tunisia.

The day I graduated from college, my grandfather came to me and said, "I want so much for you to be strong and happy." His eyes were bloodshot. I left the reception area, went behind an oak tree and cried. Thanks to my embittered mother, I'd thought him a cold son of a bitch, and the discovery he wasn't seemed as important as my impending career.

Sunday my father drives my car to Bonnie's, a short trip on surface streets. We're picking her up for brunch. She greets us in a white gauze shirtdress and purple belt with a cloisonné buckle. Her fingers spread wide apart and she flaps her hands in the air. "Just did my nails," she says. They are long, squared off, polished vermilion. "My hands were a mess from painting." Because she's so energetically meticulous, I could easily hate her. She lives in a restored brick cottage with rounded ceilings and leaded glass cabinets. Her house plants are huge and gathered on the sunporch. Their leaves look lacquered.

My father has to take the freeway to the restaurant. At first he forgets to shift into fifth, and, when he remembers, hits third instead. Finding fifth, he checks the car back to forty miles per hour. Cars blur past us. Minimal damage at slow speeds, I rationalize. My sister briskly taps her foot on a plastic floor mat, and Bonnie clutches the handle above the passenger door, forgetting her fresh polish. I rather like her for that.

"Do we want Lincoln?" my father says.

"If possible," Bonnie says. My father then wedges my car between a bottled water truck and a convertible Cadillac in the right-hand lane. I look behind to see the driver of the convertible rip his sunglasses off, twist his middle finger like a corkscrew above the windshield, and lean his whole torso into the horn.

"Anything's possible," my father says. Carson holds my left wrist, her coloring faintly yellow.

Coasting down the off ramp, my father cranks his head

around at me. "I wouldn't mind having this jewel for myself, Charlotte," he says, about to rear-end a LeMans stopped at the light. I brace myself for impact. There's an awful screech of rubber on asphalt, and my car, so new there's still tape from the factory sticker on the window, shudders and halts inches behind the Pontiac. Bonnie's nails gouge her palm. "Brakes not as tight as they should be," my father says. "You might have them looked at." My eyes clamp shut until we park at the restaurant, which is called Casablanca.

As Bonnie and our father scramble to confirm reservations, Carson takes me aside. "The Lord hath made a miracle," she pronounces. "We shall live to eternity."

Casablanca teems with tropical plants, movie memorabilia, and ceiling fans. The waiters wear short white jackets and Moroccan hats. One of them brings us a pitcher of margaritas and a basket of tortilla chips. In the middle of the dining area, a stooped woman with a fine Mayan profile smacks flour tortillas onto a grill over an open fire. "*Salud,*" my father says, raising his glass.

"Cheers," I say. "Here's to your marriage and your future."

Bonnie grabs for her drink, misses, and knocks it over. A pale green slush cascades off the tablecloth into my lap. In sympathy and respect for Bonnie's clumsiness, I stare at the puddle forming in the folds of my khaki bermudas.

"Are we going to play statue, or what?" Carson says.

"I feel like an utter imbecile," Bonnie says.

"No problem," I say. "The heat from the tortilla pit was beginning to get to me." I drizzle my way to the ladies' room door, on which the sign says INGRID BERGMAN. Down the hall, the men's says HUMPHREY BOGART.

When I return, Carson eats a triple-decker seafood torte while my father and Bonnie munch on calamari crepes. I have the plain salsa omelette. My father waves a troupe of mariachis, sweating in their ornate costumes, over to our table: two guitars, a bass, a trumpet, a harp. The harp player arrives last with a thud.

"You do '*De Colores*'?" my father asks.

"Uh huh, *si*," the harp player says. He plucks a few notes, yodels perfunctorily like a jungle bird, and they launch into song. I know very little Spanish—all I can decipher are the title and a couple of lines about springtime and the clucking of chickens, young and old. It's a pleasant, sprightly number, but I never know whether I should eat and ignore or pay reverent attention when people perform at tableside. Something about the situation makes my eyes feel dry and wonder where to glance, and my feet shift, not certain if they should keep time. I end up studying my plate, moving radishes around with my fork.

"*Gracias*," my father says, handing the harp player a dollar bill. He says to me, "You can bet it's an authentic Mexican restaurant if they play '*De Colores*.'"

I'm tempted to suggest to my father that if he's after authenticity, he could try a restaurant where the waiters don't wear fezzes, where the menus aren't pasted onto film cans, and where they don't serve Italian squid in French pancakes, but I don't. Instead I ask, "Why?"

"Because, Char, it's not just another fiesta tune. It's a song that makes grown men and women break down in public and cry."

"Fancy that," I say. He shoots me a face I haven't seen since I wobbled home from a college party reeking of beer and marijuana—an expression of reticent belief that any platelets of his flow through my veins. I think of the book on love and fear in his study. If I told my mother the divorce had tainted his life as much as it had hers, she would phone him, drunk, to commiserate, and he would eventually hang up on her with the same relief that I do.

* * *

I walk Carson into the condo to make sure she'll be all right when I leave. She goes upstairs to investigate. "I can't find her," she yells. "You suppose she spontaneously combusted?" I answer the kitchen phone. There's lipstick on it, the toned-down mauve my mother's worn since her starlet days.

"Carson?" a raspy female voice says.

"No, Charlotte."

"Charlotte, this is Monica, one of Viv's friends from the program. We've admitted her to Mission Hospital. We were afraid she'd hit her head and bleed to death."

"That's understandable," I say.

"Your mom's real sick. Her lungs are shot. She has to dry out."

"Again," I say.

"Yes, again. She needs some deodorant and a robe. Don't be too hard on her."

"She'll get them," I say.

Upstairs, Carson packs an overnight case. "I'm an expert at this," she says. "Don't worry about it."

"Carse, you know if I go I'll work myself into a primal fury. She doesn't need that. I'll send a plant or something."

"The queen of low drama will appreciate it, I'm sure." Caustic, but there's a backbone to her charity. Mine, however, is invertebrate. I can't abide a sparkling hospital room where people retch and quake and watch soap operas while they recover from slow, deliberate poisoning. I feel immobilized and activated at the same time. It's akin to my response when someone sings while I'm trying to eat. I hug my sister, who doesn't stop packing the case to hug me back. She knows what she has to do.

For many years, I thought my mother was insane, that she drank to loosen the pull of her insanity. She lay in bed, stunned by what I thought and she said was fear, though of what, specifically, she couldn't or wouldn't say.

Wishing she'd quickly be cured, I made an appointment for her to see a therapist, promised I'd accompany her because she was afraid to go alone. The morning I came for her, she sat primly on the bed. She wore a double-breasted navy pantsuit, white leather pumps, a pearl stickpin in her lapel, pearl earrings. Her hair was done in a chignon, her face impeccably made up. She moved to rise but sat back down on the bed. She tried again with the same result. I saw the neck of a bottle poking from under the dust ruffle.

"You're drunk, Mom. It's nine-thirty in the morning and you're drunk. You're so drunk you can't stand up. How did you manage to get dressed? How did you do your makeup?"

"I wanted you to be proud of me. I wouldn't embarrass you, Char . . . wanted to look nice." She began to sob dryly.

"I can't carry you up and down stairs, Mother. This is your fault. No more rescue missions from this daughter."

Her face became strangely controlled. "Well, fine. I don't need someone looking at me like I'm shit. You think I'm shit, don't you? That's what you think I am."

"'Bye, Mom."

"Don't you? Don't you?"

Drunk as my mother was, she saw through my act of kindness.

Carson and I have dinner out to celebrate the return of her Toyota. "To mobility," I say, toasting her iced-tea glass with mine. As if she might transport herself to another country, Carson looks toward a painting of a whitewashed villa.

"So," I say. "Mom's detoxing. How are you doing?"

She arches her body once, violently, as if it conducted a jolt of electric current. Her napkin sallies off her lap to the floor by me. As I bend to retrieve it, I glimpse her feet in rubber thongs. They're my feet: broad, flat, callused. They're our mother's feet and Meemaw's also, built to carry a substantial load for many miles. But feet as big as snowshoes won't support a drunk.

"So, how are your new classes?" Carson mimics my matter-of-factness.

"My classes. I kicked a kid out of fourth period for wearing a T-shirt that said HAPPINESS IS A TIGHT PUSSY. I'm not sure what offended me more, the sexual pun or the picture of the boozed-up kitten. I was supposed to think both were cute and funny."

"A scream," Carson says, distracted by the arrival of her chicken tostada. She wanted the burrito but deferred to her diet, the fifth she's tried in as many years.

I sample my tostada and survey this restaurant, which, I'm confident, is authentic. In addition to the villa landscapes, there are paintings of matadors and bulls, red roses dripping blood, and the Mona Lisa as a skull on a black velvet background. There are fluorescent Day of the Dead tableaus on slabs of bark.

"Seriously, Carse, why don't you leave? Why are you always tending her at home, in the hospital . . ."

"The hospital keeps her alive, you may recall, and while she's alive there's the chance she'll improve."

"What about your chances? Your life?"

"Maybe my umbilical cord wasn't lopped off quite as neatly as yours. And while we're on the subject of chopping, why don't you cut me some slack, Charlotte? I have a smidgen of time left—I'm only twenty three."

Right, I say mentally with a sigh. And next year you'll be twenty-four, then twenty-five, then before you can say *immortality*, you'll slip into the land of the eternally ancient, those stranded faces who care too much and get too little from caring.

A single mariachi enters through the back hallway. With him, he brings the odors of storage and pomade. He wears a brown caballero outfit and takes a guitar from a case that's well acquainted with a car trunk. His eyes are animated by a sad, resilient wisdom. "Any requests, *señoritas?*"

"How about '*De Colores*'?" I say, and bat my eyes at my sister, who shows me the whites of hers.

In slow motion, the man seems to smile and lose the smile. His vibrato is not quite natural, but his tenor is achingly pure. I put my fork down to listen. I can't translate any more of the lyrics than I could the first time, but the man's voice, its clarity, draws me into the song and I begin to understand it on my own terms. I see my mother wearing the sundress of my wallet picture. She balances a large basket on her hip, her head thrown back in laughter, and she flings feed to some chickens. Clothes blow like flags on a rope line behind her and her joy is infectious: the chickens follow her around as if in gratitude. How strange, I think, my mother doesn't use a clothesline, nor has she kept chickens. Then I realize I don't remember the last time my mother laughed, or did anything but drink and feel miserable, with abandon. I have only the photograph. I think also of the obligatory gifts I sent her: a nightshirt, the gray-blue color of her eyes, to wear in the hospital; a frosted amethyst scarf to wear when she gets out. Both colors are like her, really—like flowers out of focus.

"Earth to Alpha Charlotte," says Carson, snapping her fingers before me. My eyes are not dry in their sockets, and my feet rest side by side on the floor. I've been staring directly into the face of the lone singer, and into his absence after he leaves our table.

"Hey," Carson whispers. "Why'd you pick that song?"

Feebly, I offer, "Because Dad wasn't here to foist it on us?" and instead of crying, I laugh so hysterically my sister has to lead me out to the car.

In the moment the restaurant door opens and the heat and highway noise assail us, I barely hear the singer begin again.

Tracy Robert

GIVEN THIS STORY'S *theme of one sister observing the enabling behavior of another, I asked Tracy Robert how much of a responsibility she personally feels a sister bears in pointing out unhealthy situations to her siblings.*

"I have often mused that my brother and sister and I are pieces of a whole person," says Robert; "that if we fuse our individual gifts, together we would make the healthiest, happiest being on the planet, perhaps in the cosmos. Instead, we are partial and almost always aware of our shortcomings because we see what we aren't in each other.

"Though contemporary psychology would view Carson as an 'enabler,' to do so is unfair to both her and her sister, the narrator of the story. I consider them parts of a whole person: Carson has the gift of stopping to help; Charlotte, the gift of movement. While Carson doesn't have much of a life of her own, Charlotte essentially has no mother, and who's to say which void is more crippling?"

A teacher of college English, Robert lives in Southern California. Her novella, Flashcards, *won the Pirate's Alley Faulkner Prize for Literature, and she has recently completed a novel about the adventures of a middle-aged woman starting from scratch.*

—C. O.

175

Pyroclastic Flow

Fay Weldon

"*Pyroclastic flow*, Miss Jacobs, is the vulcanologist's term for what we loosely call lava. *Pyro* from the Greek for 'fire'; *clastic* from the Greek *klastos*, 'broken'; *lava* from the Latin *labes*, 'to fall,' though that seems one of those rather desperately arrived at derivations to me. 'Pyroclastic flow' gets used a lot in Montserrat these days, or what's left of Montserrat, because of the useful way it rhymes with *vol-can-o* in the many reggae songs now devoted to the subject. But that's by the by. What I am offering you now, Miss Jacobs, is my own pyroclastic flow, the stream of words issuing from my mouth, in free association. Blow the top, relieve pressure, and the stuff pours out. You told me to free associate: you're the therapist: I suppose you know what you're doing. My doctor thinks you do, trusting as he does that a few sessions with you will relieve me of a pain in the neck with no observable physical cause. Like those who claim *lava* is derived from *labes*, he is searching for unavailable answers to unimportant questions.

"The pyroclastic flow of Mount Montserrat, or what's left of it, travels at one hundred twenty miles an hour, at a temperature of between six hundred and eight hundred degrees Celsius. You'd better watch out, if it's coming your way. Run your hardest; it will still catch you up. Jump over the harbor wall into the blue Caribbean and the lava still comes after you, sizzling and bubbling, hardening like toffee in cold water when you test it, and that's you, boiled to death by bits and pieces of accumulated past.

"In the first session, I gave you my mother, in the second, my father; and my neck still twinges terribly when I turn suddenly. I can't look over my shoulder when I'm driving. Today I shall give up my sister. Such generosity!

"My sister Edy is married to a vulcanologist: this is her life's work. He flew off to Montserrat on Monday, charged by the government to find out if the volcano is going to blow the rest of its top and pyroclastic flow pour down into the 'safe' side of the island, or whether it's worth 'redeveloping,' as the remaining inhabitants demand. Once, the rich holidayed in Montserrat; now only the poor and the stubborn remain. George Martin's studio, where once the Rolling Stones and The Who recorded, is to all accounts now gaunt, hollow, and silent, shrouded in ash.

"Edy's husband Rolo says the answer is 'Don't know.' No one knows what a volcano is going to do next until it does it. The worldwide sample of active volcanoes simply isn't large enough for sensible deductions to be made. Ruapeho did this, St. Helens did that, Krakatoa was altogether different: so what. I suggested to Edy that her husband was misappropriating public money in flying out to Montserrat to bring back an answer he knew already. I was half joking, but she put the phone down on me. Edy has no sense of humor, which I believe to be a character trait of elder siblings. She flew with Rolo to Montserrat on Monday morning, though I believe she paid for her own ticket.

"Edy is two and a half years older than me, and not yet at any age when this is a disadvantage. I don't think it will ever be, in fact; I can see my time will never come. Perhaps to be thirty-seven and a half when one's sister turns forty might be seen as a good thing; but any number with a zero feels like a new beginning, while seven and a half feels like protesting too much. And to be eighty-six when one's sister is eighty-eight is nothing like the advantage eight has over six. I'll never get those years back, ever. I feel she deprived me of them. Edy could walk, talk, learn her tables before me. All I did ahead of her was menstruate, and grow breasts and a bum, which were an embarrassment to me. I was 'big for my age': she was small. She was neat and composed and competent, while I fumbled and stumbled from lack of years, and too much growth.

"Ouch. I moved my head too fast. This is what happens. When I talked to you about my father I could detect no memories of abuse. When I talked about my mother's death I failed to pierce the wall of indifference with which, according to you, I protect myself. When I speak about my sister, I get a pain in the neck. Well, there's the answer. She's to blame.

"Yes, my sister Edy is a pain in the neck. She is so much better than me. She is brave, noble and sensitive, slender, beautiful; she moves gracefully where I clump-clump. I am younger, plumper, bigger, slipperier than she and could no more stand at my husband's side at the foot of an active volcano with ash whirling all around, bits of burning forest hurtling through the air, in the possible path of a pyroclastic flow traveling at one hundred miles an hour, and helicopters swarming in and out of smoke, than I could fly. What a pain!

"Edy phoned me from Montserrat in the middle of last night to ask if I was okay, to say they'd arrived safely, and to apologize for putting the phone down. Oh yes, we're close: divided only by two and a half years and the fact that since her marriage to Rolo she seems to have no public or personal morality left. I put it to her again on the phone last night that Rolo had no business accepting money from the government to find out an answer he already knew; she said but these days governments had to have the backing of scientists and experts before they did a thing—everything has to be re-found-out, to keep up to date. I said I thought that was a specious argument, the least she could have done was not condone her husband's actions by flying with him, and we lost the connection in a lot of crackle, which I hope was not the terminal pyro-clastic flow arriving, accompanied as it is by bursts of gas along the periphery. Edy's way of getting out of an ideolog-ical fix.

"Edy always maintains I suffer from sibling envy. Personally, I think I suffer from rage. Terminal rage. Edy likes to diminish the severity of my condition by applying the jargon of family therapy. It ought to be, she pointed out to me on the day of our great row, the other way 'round. She is meant to be jealous of me, because I came along and stole my parents' attention. But she's not jealous of me. There is, as she delighted in telling me that day, nothing to be jealous of. Edy is a truth teller of a wounding kind.

" 'I only say it because it's true,' she'll say, having pointed out my zits or my too tight skirt, or whatever. To which I say, 'Telling the truth is just an excuse for hurting people,' and she'll come back, if I'm not careful, with 'Mum told me on her deathbed to tell you a home truth or two—someone had to.' I don't believe Mum said this, any more than I believe in Diana's last words to Al Fayed. But Edy likes to say them: they hurt. You know how it is; those mysterious words people say to you so you think there's something wrong with what you are, not just what you do, and there's no mending it.

"What happened was that three years back Mum had a

stroke, and Edy and I were meant to be traveling up north together to be at her side, and were to meet on the train, but I waited on the wrong platform, had to get a later train, and by the time I got there, Mum had just died, and I was in no position to check out what her last words, if any, actually were. Edy was impatient and called the undertaker because Dad couldn't find his glasses, and in the end ran the whole funeral. No one else had a look-in. I'm Daddy's girl. Edy's Mummy's girl. I haven't cried over her death. The grief counselors don't know what to do with me.

" 'Face it, Sally,' said Edy on the day of the great row. 'You didn't love Mother and she didn't love you. How could she? You were unlovable.'

"A lot of pyroclastic flow came out of Edy that day. I couldn't dodge. It overwhelmed me. 'You're not even a real artist,' said Edy. 'You've sold out. All you do is dress shop windows for money. A nine-to-five person.' I have a good job designing display windows for Liberty's. It's one of the most sought-after jobs in London, but what does she care? Edy and I both went to Goldsmith's. She said I was copying her, as usual, but all I was doing was going to the best place around. I got a better degree than her, but of course she got hers first. Edy is now a fine artist—she does morally superior, semifigurative pictures that have frames around them, and every now and then sells one. She can afford to be so grand: she has Rolo's salary to live on. I'm on my own: I have to support myself.

"My mother was a painter. She died at her easel, staring into a space that wasn't even there anymore. She seldom looked at me, though she'd sometimes sketch Edy, who inherited her pre-Raphaelite hair and looks—quantities of crinkled red hair; a high, pale forehead; and hooded eyes. It wasn't that I was ugly; I'm perfectly personable. I just looked too much like my beetle-browed father, whose role in life was to support and admire my mother, to be seen to exist in my own right.

"I hope the ground in Montserrat rocks under my sister's feet. How dare she say these things to me! She who accompanies her husband on illicit outings at the taxpayers' expense. I hope she is smothered by ash and dies terrified. She put a pillow over my face when I was two and tried to suffocate me but I struggled free. She was jealous, in spite of what she claims. On the day of the row, she said she wasn't punished for trying to kill me—my mother wanted me dead, too. I was such an ugly, whiny, spoilsport—a party-pooper from the day I was born.

"Bits and pieces, bits and pieces; the pyroclastic flow of the past hot off the press.

"All I'd done to upset her was try to demonstrate to Edy that Rolo, like so many men, had no moral fiber. That he wasn't worthy of her, that she shouldn't marry him. I did my best to seduce him and almost succeeded—he likes a bit of bosom—and then he went and told her, to salve his own conscience. What an idiot! But I was only doing it for her sake: she had no business losing her temper and saying all those horrible things to me. His accepting the freebie to Montserrat proves I was right to do what I did. I had to at least try. She knows I love her. I pleaded drunkenness, and we're all still friends, but there is a pressure there in her, waiting to blow.

"You raise your eyebrows at me, Miss Jacobs. Oh, all right; I know when I'm defeated, when my own words betray me. The pain in my neck is not Edy. I am the pain in her neck. The little sister who hangs around it like an albatross and won't let go. She puts down the phone; I tell a home truth; she tells a home truth. She's right; I'm in the wrong. I get the pain. It is natural justice. The pyroclastic flow grows cool and slows. I'm lucky Edy phones me at all. The volcano is quiescent. Perhaps.

"I can't say the pain in my neck is gone; no such luck. Miracle cures are not so easy. But I suppose understanding what goes on is a step forward. Thank you. I shan't make another appointment now, but there's no knowing what's going to happen next. There she blows! I'll just take a rain check, if that's okay."

Fay Weldon

HAVING BEEN RAISED *among a family of women, Fay Weldon no doubt knows the subtle little tricks that we sometimes employ to—how shall I put this?—destroy our sisters' day. With this biting yet humorous short story, however, she puts a different spin on the world of sisterly infighting.*

"The motivation behind 'Pyroclastic Flow'?" Weldon writes. "The idea that perhaps the persecuted sister is the one who's doing the persecuting. The ease with which we all, in family relationships, see ourselves as victims."

Though Weldon was born in England and lives there today, she grew up in New Zealand and earned degrees in economics and psychology at the University of St. Andrews. Choosing to follow her mother's example and become a writer, she is the author of twenty-one novels, including Down Among the Women, Female Friends, Praxis, Puffball, The Hearts and Lives of Men, The Cloning of Joanna May, *and the more recent* Worst Fears. *Dozens of her short stories have appeared in periodicals and are collected in four volumes,* Watching Me, Watching You; Polaris; Moon Over Minneapolis; *and* Wicked Women.

Those unfamiliar with her work until now might recognize her delightful wit in the story for the movie She-Devil, which starred Meryl Streep and Roseanne and was originally adapted for British television before moving on to Hollywood.

Married for the second time, Ms. Weldon is the mother of four sons.

—C. O.

GI Jesus

Susan Palwick

$\mathcal{I}$ don't know if it was a miracle or not, what happened at the hospital. I can't make up my mind about that. I always thought those headlines about "Instant Miracle Cures" in the trashy supermarket newspapers were a crock. You know the ones: THALIDOMIDE BOY GROWS ARMS TO PROTECT MOM FROM RAPIST! "I had to save her, and it was the only way!" BARNEY PERFORMS CPR ON SEARS SANTA CLAUS! "I was walking through the TV department and all of a sudden I couldn't breathe, and this little purple guy jumps straight out of the set and starts pounding on my chest!" SIAMESE TWINS SEPARATE WHEN THE MEN THEY LOVE MOVE TO OPPOSITE COASTS! "The doctors said it could never be done because we shared a brain, but love conquers all!"

I never believed any of that stuff, but what happened at the hospital would sound just like that, if I let it. So I don't know anymore. Maybe my story's a crock, too, or maybe those trashy ones are truer than anybody ever thought. One thing I can tell you, though: if there are miracles, they don't happen in an instant. Whatever a miracle is, it takes its own sweet time growing. When I see those newspapers now, I wonder what stories those people would tell if they had more than two square inches of the *Weekly World News* to do it in.

Because if anything real happened to them, they do have stories—trust me on that—and probably long ones, too.

Mine started months ago, the day I went to church with Mandy. I'm not religious, never have been—nobody in my family ever has been, so far as I know—but Mandy's been my best friend for thirty years, and when your best friend calls you up crying and asks you to go to church with her, you do it, even if you've never been too sure you even believe in God, even if you're very sure that you don't believe in anything the priest in that church has to say. The last time I'd been in that church was when Mandy and Bill got married. I was their maid of honor, and I shouldn't have been. Cindy should have been. So I guess the story really started back then, twenty years ago, because when Mandy asked me to be maid of honor I said, "Now wait a minute, how come you aren't asking your sister that? That's a sister's job."

We were sitting in Sam's Soda Shop, where we always went to have important conversations. Mandy had called me and told me to meet her there, and I figured she needed to tell me about some fight she'd had with Bill, or fret about how his mother still didn't like her. We'd ordered what we always did, a root beer float for me and a vanilla shake for her, and then she came out with the maid of honor thing and I choked and started spurting root beer out my nose. There are certain ways of doing things, in a little town like this. I don't know how it works other places, but if you get married in Innocence, Indiana, and you don't ask your sister to hold the bouquet, that has to mean you don't love her. What's worse, it means you want everybody to know you don't love her, because even sisters who can't stand each other do what's right at weddings. And I knew Mandy loved Cindy. She was the only person in her family who did. "You have to ask Cindy," I said. "She's your *sister*."

Mandy hadn't touched her shake. She hadn't even taken

the paper wrapper off the straw. "I can't ask her. My parents would kill me."

"Your parents?" I'd never liked Mandy's parents, and I wasn't very good at hiding it. I knew they must be mad at Cindy about something, but they were always mad at Cindy about something: smoking or drinking or having too many boyfriends or having the wrong boyfriends or having boyfriends at all. Plenty of other girls in town did all the same things Cindy did, but they lied about it and Cindy never would. Mr. and Mrs. Mincing were ashamed of her: not because of what she did, but because everybody knew about it. They cared about their reputation more than they cared about Cindy, and Mandy knew that as well as I did, and she hated it, too. So I shook my head at her and said, "Mandy, your parents are *already* married, aren't they? What business is it of theirs? Whose wedding is this, anyway?"

"They're paying for it," Mandy said, in this tiny voice she gets when she's really upset, and then, all in a rush, "She's pregnant. She's starting to show: that's how we found out. And she won't say who the father is and she won't say she's sorry and I'm not supposed to tell anybody, Cece, not even you, so you have to *promise* to keep it a secret."

"Oh," I said, thinking a lot of things even I knew better than to say, like if she's showing already it's not going to be a secret for long, like if your mother's so happy about the lovely grandchildren you and Bill are going to give her, why can't she love this grandchild, too? But I saw right away that Mandy's parents would never let Cindy be in the wedding, and I knew Mandy would do whatever they wanted, because she always did. She never could talk back to them. That's why she was the favorite daughter.

Mandy was my best friend, but sometimes I got just plain disgusted with her. She never stuck up for herself at all, and somehow she got everything she wanted. Here she was marrying Bill and planning this big wedding, while Hank Heywood, who made me dizzier than anybody I'd ever met, hadn't even kissed me yet. And if I ever did get married, my dad couldn't afford to pay for a fancy wedding, and my mother had died when I was a baby, so there wouldn't even be anybody to fuss over the dress and stand there crying during the ceremony. It wasn't fair.

I wanted to say something really mean to Mandy, right then, but I knew I was just feeling sorry for myself when I should have been feeling sorry for Cindy. So I took a swig of root beer float to calm myself down and tried to say something useful instead. "What does Bill say about this?"

"Bill's staying out of it."

Bill stayed out of a lot of things, mainly debt and drugs and trouble, which was why Mandy's parents liked him so much. A fine upstanding young man, they said. I could have told them a few things about what he got into and what stood up when he did it. I'd had a scare myself, about a year before Mandy and Bill started going together, but nobody knew about that except Bill and I wasn't about to tell a soul, and neither was he. I'll say this much for Bill: he knew how to keep a secret. He knew how to keep promises, too, mostly. Turned out I was just late, but we had a few nervous weeks there, and the whole time he said, "Now don't you worry about anything, Cece. I'll get the money for a good doctor if that's what has to happen, I promise." He'd have done it, too. Funny, I never doubted that, even though I knew full well I didn't love him and he didn't love me. I don't doubt it now. He was a better man when he was seventeen and scared than when he was thirty-five and broke his big promise, the one he'd made to Mandy at the altar, in front of the priest and all those people and God, if you believe in God.

But I'm getting way ahead of myself. So I said to Mandy, "Well now, look, if I'm not your maid of honor, who will be?" Because I still didn't like the idea, not one bit. A brides-maid, fine, but maid of honor? Standing at the altar next to Mandy and Bill, knowing that Cindy should have been the one up there and that I wasn't any better than her, just luck-ier? Knowing that Bill knew all this, too, and that Mandy didn't know any of it and now I'd never be able to tell her? Even back then I watched enough soap operas to know that once you get into a tangle like that, you don't get out. You're in it for life. Your kids are in it, probably, and their kids, too. It doesn't end.

"I guess I'd have to ask my cousin Sandra," Mandy said, looking at me like I'd just drowned the last puppy in the world. She still hadn't touched her shake, and I gave up. First of all, Sandra was the snootiest bitch in the county; I didn't know anybody who liked her, not even Mandy, and Mandy liked everybody. Secondly, there was the cousin thing. If you don't ask your sister to be your maid of honor and ask your best friend instead, maybe you can get away with it. "We're so close." "We're just like sisters." Something like that. But not to ask your own sister, and then to ask *another* relative, some cousin you don't even like? That's ten times more of an insult all around, and there's no way of hid-ing it.

"Okay," I said. "I'll do it." I guess I didn't sound very honored, but I've never been good at lying about things like that. Mandy smiled at me and let out a big sigh of relief and finally reached for her shake.

So I was the maid of honor, and Sandra and our friends Christy and Diane were the bridesmaids. We carried pink sweetheart roses and white carnations, and wore pink satin dresses with big bunches of tulle at the shoulders. I still have that dress hanging in my closet—not that I'll ever be able to fit into it again; not that I've been able to for years now. I always thought I'd give it to my daughter, when I had one.

That's never going to happen now, I guess, even if I ever do get married. You hear stories on the news about women having babies after forty, but that always smacks of "Instant Miracle Cure" to me. And going through the Change is enough work, without having to chase a toddler around while you're doing it. I guess I could give the dress to one of Mandy's girls, but what would I say? "This is the dress I wore when your mother married the man who ran off with his secretary fifteen years later"? The girls are real bitter about Bill. The oldest was only thirteen when it happened, and when you're that age everything's easy: black and white, right and wrong. And the other three believed whatever their big sister told them.

So no one will ever get to wear that dress again, which is too bad, really. It's still the fanciest dress I've ever owned, and I was excited about wearing it in the wedding, even if it should have been Cindy's dress. I squared my conscience about that by promising myself that if I had to be maid of honor I was going to do it my way: I was going to be real nice to Cindy, so that maybe Mandy would be brave enough to be nice to her, too, and then when Mr. and Mrs. Mincing saw the two of us being nice their hearts would soften and they'd take Cindy back into the family. I was going to fix everything, oh yes I was. I had it all planned out.

That's the kind of plan you can only come up with when you're nineteen and don't know how anything works yet. I'd never been in a wedding before: I didn't know how scared I'd be, in front of all those people. I didn't know that Cindy would sneak into the church late and sit in the very back pew, rows and rows behind the rest of the family, cowering there trying to hide. Cindy'd always been so bold about everything that I thought she'd be bold about the wedding, too—especially since by then everybody in town knew she was expecting, it wasn't like it was a secret at all—but maybe the church made her lose her nerve. Who could blame her?

The priest had been saying something boring but pretty nice, and then all of a sudden he gets going on how we're there to bless the joining of two souls, to make a marriage that will last until death, longer than youth and longer than beauty, longer than the sinful desires of the body. He wasn't looking at Mandy and Bill anymore by the time he said that; he was glaring over their heads, practically yelling at the back of the church. And then all three of us knew what must have happened, even though we hadn't seen Cindy come in. You could feel everybody else in the church fighting not to turn around and stare at that back pew. Some of them did, mostly kids, before their parents yanked them back around again. I couldn't see that from where I was, of course, but Hank told me about it after the ceremony. That was only about a week before he got shipped out to Vietnam: he was one of the last ones to get sent over. He never did kiss me before he left—he was so shy, Hank—but he wrote me letters until he disappeared. He just vanished into the jungle; nobody ever found out what happened to him. I wore one of those silver POW/MIA bracelets for a while—you know, back when everybody was wearing them. After a while it stopped being the thing to do; people would give you funny looks when they saw it, ask what it was. Some people thought it was a Medic Alert bracelet, thought I was diabetic or something. And it was ugly, to tell you the truth, so finally I took it off. But I've never stopped wondering what happened to Hank. A lot of my nightmares are about jungles, even now.

So. Anyway. I'm standing up there at Mandy's wedding, I can't see anything but the altar and the priest—he was young then, handsome, like that guy in *The Exorcist*—and he's thundering along about the transience of youth and beauty and the body like we're not at a wedding at all, more like we're at a funeral, and Mandy's making little choking noises and Bill's clutching her hand and all three of us are glaring at that guy. Shut up, shut up, *shut up*. Well, he didn't. Never so much as looked down at us. I should have said something. Maybe I would, now, but I was too scared then, especially since it wasn't my church and who was I to challenge somebody else's priest? I tried to catch his eye, I did, I'll say that much for myself, but he wouldn't look at me, so I was left staring at the statue on the wall behind him, the one of Jesus nailed to the cross. If you want to feel lousy about having a body, all you have to do is look at that thing. Ouch. Every nail. Every drop of blood, I swear, and that poor man in so much pain he must have been out of his mind with it, just praying to die soon so it would be over. You can tell all that, from that statue. I guess that makes it good art. I tried to talk to Mandy about it once, but Mrs. Mincing was there and she gave me a lecture about how Jesus wasn't suffering on the cross, he was at peace, he was happy to be doing the Lord's will, and if I'd been a godly person I would have known that. Well, religious or not, you'd never know it from looking at that statue. Even now, whenever I think about what might have happened to Hank in the jungle, I wonder if he wound up looking like that. It's what my father looked like, when he was dying of cancer.

So I'm standing there looking at that statue, figuring that's what Cindy feels like, too—like she's nailed to a piece of wood with everybody staring at her and nobody doing a thing to help—and I'm thinking, well, I'll talk to her at the reception, I *will*, even if the whole town cuts me dead for it. I'll go up to her and say something friendly. Better yet, I'll go up and give her a big hug. Except that I never got my chance, because Cindy didn't go to the reception. Of course she didn't: I should have known she wouldn't. She walked out of that church and she disappeared. For years. Like Hank.

Well, it ate at Mandy like you wouldn't believe. She

thought it was her fault, because if she'd included Cindy in the wedding maybe everything would have happened differently. "You were right," she kept saying. "You were right all along. I should have asked her." Which made me feel like dirt, of course. I kept telling her I hadn't been right, I'd just been self-righteous, and that's not the same thing. Her parents paid for that wedding and it was their show all along, not hers and Bill's, and they sure didn't want any spotlights on Cindy. Mandy couldn't have done anything.

"Blame the priest," I kept telling her. "Blame your parents, if you have to blame somebody." Mr. and Mrs. Mincing didn't even look for Cindy: just said good riddance, as if you can wash a daughter off your hands as easily as a speck of dust. Mandy and Bill looked, got the police to put out a missing-person report, checked with bus stations and lying-in homes and hospitals, everyplace they could think of. They printed up flyers with Cindy's picture, and every year on Cindy's birthday they put ads in papers all over the country: "Happy Birthday, Cindy, We Love and Miss You, Please Call Your Sister Mandy Collect." They did all that stuff for six or seven years, I don't even remember how long it went on, and they couldn't find a clue. It wasn't cheap, either, taking out all those ads. Bill was a prince about it, he really was, and it can't have been easy on him. I used to wonder if maybe he was the father of Cindy's baby, especially after what had happened to me, but I decided that no, he couldn't be, because Cindy has to have gotten pregnant while Bill and Mandy were a steady couple—practically engaged already—and I just couldn't believe that Bill would do such a thing. I still can't, even with what he did later. And there were plenty of other guys who could have been the father. So I think he was so good about the search because he was a decent man, not because he felt guilty.

But finally, after years of not finding anything, Bill told Cindy that their marriage was haunted and that she had to choose between looking for Cindy and living with him. She and I had a long talk at Sam's Sodas over that one, believe me. She didn't touch her vanilla shake at all that time, and we talked and talked and finally I told her I thought Bill was right. "You've done everything you can," I told her. "You'd have found her by now if she wanted to be found. Wherever she is, she wants you to be happy, Mandy." I don't know if I believed that even while I was saying it, but Mandy did, and she said it made her feel better, and she prayed for Cindy every night and settled down to loving Bill and her kids the rest of the time.

You can't forget a lost sister, though. Mandy and I still talked about Cindy, how she'd probably gone to some big city—Chicago, Houston—and gotten a good office job, because Cindy could type like nobody's business. We decided Cindy was happy. We knew it. We had her life all planned out for her. Except that we didn't know anything, of course, and we knew *that*, even though we never admitted it. We told each other that she'd probably had her baby and then gotten married to some nice young lawyer or doctor who wanted kids, in a church with a *nice* priest this time. Mandy always insisted on that, that this new priest would be kind, he'd forgive Cindy her past the way her husband forgave her her past, the way priests are supposed to forgive, because that's what Christ did. That's what Mandy said; I didn't know, not being religious. The only priest I'd ever met was the one who married Mandy and Bill, and I'd heard so many different things about Christ from so many different people that I didn't know what to think. Seems to me you can make anything you want to out of Christ; he's like a politician that way.

After Mandy and Bill stopped looking for Cindy they seemed happy for a long time. Bill was going great guns with his CPA business—even in a little town like Innocence, everybody needs their taxes done—and Mandy kept busy taking care of the kids, which would have been a full-time job for anybody. They looked like the perfect family, and I was jealous again. Thinking back on it, I guess I should have known better. There was plenty of tension there, like the way Bill always talked about how his girls were going to go to college, not just get married right out of high school and have babies like all the other women in town. The girls were smart enough to know that every time he talked that way he was putting down their mother, and they didn't like it. Mandy didn't mind that so much—she wished she'd been able to go to college, too—but whenever Bill talked about teenagers having babies she remembered Cindy, and the old wound opened all over again. So really, that family was in an awful mess even before Bill fell for his secretary.

That was the first time Mandy ever called me crying, when she found out about Bill and Genevieve. That was the girl's name, a movie-star kind of a name, the sort of name most wives around here wouldn't trust even if she hadn't been twenty-two and blond, with the kind of figure you usually only see on swimsuit calendars. She said the whole thing, too, Genn-eh-vee-ehve, didn't shorten it to Jean or Jenny, so everybody thought she gave herself airs. God only knows what she thought she was doing in a little town like this, aside from making trouble. Somebody said she came here after college—of *course* Bill would fall for a college girl, even if she only majored in phys-ed—to work and save enough money to go to California and be an actress. Seems to me like if she'd really wanted to be an actress she wouldn't have settled down in Muncie with Bill after the divorce, but what do I know? Maybe she really loved him. He was handsome, Bill was, even then. He'd kept himself fit all those years when Mandy and I were getting bigger and bigger, Mandy from having four kids and me from sitting around Yodel's Yarns, eating candy bars and dreaming about the day when Hank would come home from 'Nam and walk through the door and ask me to help him pick out a nice wool blend for a cable sweater because it's cold back here, away from the jungle, and what are you doing tonight, Cece? Want to help me stay warm?

I'd been dreaming about Hank all those years, and Mandy had been dreaming about Cindy, and Bill, it turned out, had been dreaming about platinum-blond secretaries with 38C cups and twenty-four-inch waists who took *Penthouse* letters in the nude at the hot sheets hotel on the highway. The kid who worked the front desk told his girl-friend, who told her cousin, whose hairdresser gave Mandy's godmother her monthly perm. It made it a lot harder on Mandy, that all those people had known before she did, and of course she was beside herself. Who wouldn't be? But when she called me crying and started ranting about Genevieve, calling her a slut and a bitch and a little whore, I still thought, *This isn't the Mandy I know.* Because she never used words like that, and they were the kinds of words her parents had used about Cindy, the words that priest would have used if he hadn't been in a church. "I hope she rots and dies," Mandy hissed at me. "I hope she gets hit by a truck. I hope she burns in hell."

Mandy wanted me to be angry, too, to keep her com-pany, and of course I felt sick about the whole thing. But mostly I was sad, listening to her, because I felt like every-one I knew had died somehow, changed into other people when I wasn't looking, people I didn't like very much. The Mandy who'd cared about people even when they got into trouble had turned into her mean mother and into that horrible priest both, and the Bill who made promises turned into the Bill who broke them, and the Cece who was smart and pretty and deadset on marrying Hank turned into—well, what I am now. Not pretty, except maybe in the face, and not married, and not much of anything, really, except somebody who runs on at the mouth and runs a yarn store, helping people who still know how to knit pick out patterns for baby blankets. I'd turned into Aunt Cece—that's what Mandy's four girls always called me—just like I really was Mandy's sister, just like Cindy really had never existed.

I couldn't spend a lot of time being sad, though, because there was too much else to do. First of all, I was mad myself, mainly at Bill. Mandy wanted Genevieve to rot and die and I wanted Bill to rot and die—or part of him, anyway, the upstanding part. And I knew I had to stop hating Bill and concentrate on loving Mandy and the girls instead, because that's what they needed now. That's what Bill had taken away from them: knowing that they were loved, the way you know the sun will always come up, the way you know there will always be air to breathe whether you've done anything to deserve it or not. And right then, I had to keep Mandy from doing anything that would make her hate herself later on. So I said, "Mandy, honey, I know you want that woman to die right now, but when you calm down you won't feel so good about saying so, I know you won't, and you have to think about that. You have to be careful now, because you're so upset. You have enough to feel bad about, without adding anything that doesn't have to be there. I don't care a fig about that woman, or Bill either. All I care about is you and the kids. You just sit tight, Mandy. I'll be there in ten minutes."

So I went over and stayed there, shut down Yodel's Yarns for a solid week and did what Mandy needed me to do: cooked, did laundry, answered the phone and the door. News got around fast, the way it always does about something like that. I kept the people Mandy didn't want to see away from her and made coffee for the ones who were welcome. I looked after the kids and tried to help them make some kind of sense out of what had happened. I helped Mandy find a lawyer and went with her to talk to him, because I knew I'd hear more of what he was saying than she could. I did the same kinds of things that Mandy had done for me when my father died. But that makes sense, because when a marriage dies it's pretty much like a person has, anyway.

Mandy's parents had moved to Albuquerque for their arthritis years before that—and good riddance, if you ask me—so I was really the only person around who could do all those things for her. I did whatever I could to help, but the whole time I felt like I didn't know Mandy at all anymore, like there was this new person where my best friend had been and I just had to keep pretending she was the person she was supposed to be, because otherwise what would I do? There I was, in this house I knew as well as I knew my own, better maybe—it was the house where Mandy'd grown up; she and Bill had taken it when her folks left—doing all the things I'd known how to do my whole life, like making sandwiches and telling the kids stories, and I felt completely lost.

So now maybe you can understand a little bit how I felt the second time Mandy called me crying. That was four months ago, about five years after Bill left, and I'd gotten used to the new Mandy by then but sometimes I still missed the old one, the one who loved everybody and never cursed anybody out, even the people who'd hurt her. The new one was a lot tougher, I've got to give her credit for that, but she was colder, too, more selfish, less able to be nice to people just for the sake of being nice. I guess she had to be that way. Maybe she missed that earlier part of herself, too. People who didn't like Mandy, before Bill left, always said that she'd never grown up, that she was just a little girl inside, and that's what they meant, I guess: that she was so sweet to everybody, that she always tried to think the best of people. Mandy grew up fast, after Bill and Genevieve, and the people who hadn't liked her before started to like her better. They said she'd finally found her backbone. Seemed to me she'd lost her heart, or thrown it away because it hurt her too much, and I wasn't sure she'd made such a good trade.

So I was almost glad, when she called me crying again, because it meant she'd gotten her heart back, whatever else had happened. Oh, I was scared, too, and guilty about that first flash of gladness. All three of those feelings went through my head in the minute between the time when I picked up the phone and the time when I could understand what she was saying. Because she was crying so hard I couldn't, at first. I thought something must have happened to one of the kids, or Bill had come back—I didn't know what. It was 9:45 on a Sunday morning, and I'd just started a donut and my first cup of coffee. I was standing in the kitchen in my robe, holding the phone in one hand and my coffee mug in the other, saying, "Mandy, what's wrong? Mandy, you have to slow down, I can't understand you. What happened?"

"Cindy's come home," she said finally, in a great gasp, and my knees went weak and the coffee mug shattered on the floor—my favorite mug, too, it was the one my father always used, all the way from Hawaii. It had bright fish and flowers all over it. I don't know where Dad got it; he'd never been to Hawaii. I always meant to ask him, and a few months after he died I was drinking coffee out of that mug and I realized that I never had asked, that I'd forgotten to ask, and that now I never could. And I started bawling like a baby, just like I was bawling now, with the mug in a zillion pieces on the floor and hot coffee everywhere.

"Oh, Mandy," I said. "Oh Mandy. I'll be right there. Just let me get dressed. Is she—is she—"

Is she happy, I wanted to know, does she have the life we made up for her? But Mandy said, "No, no, don't come here, meet me at the church."

"*What?*" I said. Mandy hadn't been in that church since her wedding, because of the priest. She said she never could believe that Father Anselm knew any more about God than the tomatoes in her garden did, probably less. She said she'd go back when the church got a new priest, but the last I'd heard Father Antsy was still there, even though Catholics usually rotate priests every five years. Bill always made it into a joke and said the church had forgotten about Innocence, but Mandy thought we were stuck with Antsy because the bishop couldn't find anybody else who wanted him. So it seemed to me that church was the last place she'd want to go.

"There?" I said. "Why? I don't—"

"Ten o'clock Mass," Mandy said, still crying. "Hurry."

Then she hung up. I looked at the clock; it was 9:50. "Oh, Lord," I said, and ran to get ready.

Well, you can imagine how fast I drove to get there. If I was ever going to get a speeding ticket in my life, it would have been then, and I don't know what I would have said if I'd been stopped. "I'm late for church, Officer." But nobody stopped me, even though I was zooming along at about seventy miles an hour. I thought Cindy would be at the church, too. I kept wondering what she'd look like, after all this time.

I got there after the service started, of course, and had to sneak in those big doors, feeling like some kind of thief, thinking about Cindy sneaking into the wedding so long ago. It was dark inside, except for the stained glass and the candles. I didn't think it was pretty today. The place stank of incense and the organ howled and rumbled and wheezed like something out of some old movie, probably one with Vincent Price. There weren't many people there: two or three families, some old ladies, and Mandy. I saw her right away, sitting in the third pew.

By herself. I hustled up and slid in beside her. "Mandy! Where—"

"Shhhh," she said, and reached out and grabbed my hand and squeezed, hard. "She wants us to pray for her."

"Us?" I said. "Who, us?" Mandy knows I'm not religious. "Where *is* she?"

People were glaring at us, by then. "Home," Mandy whispered. In the candlelight I could see that she was crying again. "Hush, Cece. Just pray. Pray for her to be well."

Which meant she wasn't, which meant, as far as I was concerned, that we had no business sitting there in that stink, that we should have been with Cindy, taking care of her or taking her to a doctor or doing something that would do some good. I couldn't see how this was going to do any good, sitting in this cave listening to Father Antsy droning about the temptations of television. When he got going on Teenage Mutant Ninja Turtles as the four reptiles of the apocalypse, I whispered to Mandy, "Look, I can't stand this. I'm leaving, I'll go to your house—"

"No," she whispered back, and grabbed my hand again. "She asked for you to be here. Because I told her—how we used to talk. How we used to tell ourselves she was happy. It meant a lot to her, that you did that. She wants you here, Cece. She asked us to come to Mass because she couldn't. Please."

Well, I didn't feel I could leave, after that, but I sure couldn't pray, either. I just sat there, fuming, wondering what was wrong with Cindy, trying not to listen to Antsy— he'd started in on soap operas—staring at that horrible cross up front, with that Jesus looking like he was going to open his mouth and scream in agony any second. Which was pretty much how I felt, just then. I heard Antsy saying something about body and blood and thought, *Well, now he's talking about TV movies,* and then everybody stood up and filed out into the aisle and I did too. I just followed Mandy, I was

so distracted I couldn't think straight, and I took the stale
biscuit and the sip of wine and then I remembered, when we
sat back down again, that I wasn't supposed to do that, that
at Mandy's wedding she'd said you were only supposed to
take the communion if you were Catholic. I couldn't see
that it mattered. Father Antsy wouldn't know the difference—I hadn't been in that church for twenty years and he
wasn't exactly a big yarn buyer, so for all he knew I was a
Catholic cousin visiting from another state—and anyhow I
hadn't had much breakfast, not that a tiny little stale biscuit
helped much. Mandy had said the wine and biscuit were
supposed to be Christ's body and blood, I remembered that
now, and the whole thing made me a little sick to my stomach, and even angrier. This priest lectures about the sinful-
ness of the body and then he makes people eat stale biscuits
that are supposed to be pieces of a body—what kind of sense
does that make? It's no better than those mountain climbers
who eat each other when they run out of food, in my opinion. I don't see how anybody can believe that about Jesus'
body anyway. The biscuit's just a cracker; it's not even meat.
If they fed you hamburger, well, maybe that would be different, but they don't, and thank goodness, too.

So anyway, finally the Mass was over and we drove back
to Mandy's house, with me shooting questions at her the
whole way. Cindy'd shown up at five in the morning, just
knocked on the door and there she was, standing on the
porch, said she'd taken Greyhound from New York, said she
didn't know where her baby was, it had been a boy and she'd
left it in a train station where somebody would be sure to
find it, said she'd done a bunch of things since then, in New
York and Florida, wouldn't say what they'd been, but from
the sound of it they hadn't been anything good. She hadn't
been doing anything like what we'd imagined for her, that
much was sure. "She's very thin," Mandy said, trying not to
cry, "and she looks very tired, and she has a terrible cough.

She wanted to know if I thought I could still love her. I told her, of *course*, Cindy, do you have any idea how much time I spent looking for you? And she said, but you didn't know I'd look like this, and then she asked me if I thought God could still love her."

God's too busy watching television, I thought, but I didn't say that. Antsy was the one watching television, and if there was a God, he probably didn't like Antsy any better than I did. So I just said, "She's home. She's home now. She's come home to get better. It's going to be all right, Mandy."

But when I saw her—lying in bed upstairs, with Mandy's oldest girl feeding her soup and the younger ones standing there looking scared—I knew it wasn't going to be all right, and that getting better wasn't what Cindy had come home for. She looked like the Christ hanging in that church, the same way I always pictured Hank looking in the jungle, the way my father had looked at the end: like somebody who's dying by inches and can't even think of what to hope for anymore, except for the pain to be over.

That was the beginning of the darkest time I've ever known. Mandy kept saying that Cindy was going to get better, she was, of course she was, she had to, and even when Cindy got worse instead, Mandy wouldn't take her to a doctor. I think she knew the truth, deep down, and was afraid to hear it from someone else. I was over there as much as I could, helping to take care of Cindy, but most of the time I'm not sure she knew where she was or who we were, or who she was herself. And finally even Mandy had to see that, and she took Cindy to the doctor and the doctor said Cindy should go into the hospital right away, right now, and Mandy said nonsense and took Cindy home again. And she screamed at me when I said the doctor was right. And in the meantime the girls had gotten more and more sullen and angry and confused, and the oldest one's boyfriend had gotten killed on his motorcycle, and the youngest one had started staying out way too late and getting bad grades in school. And it seemed to me like Mandy'd gotten her heart back only to have it broken again, for good this time, and maybe her mind too. I was afraid for her.

I was afraid for myself. A few days after Cindy came back I'd started having belly pains and the runs, and I told myself it was just the excitement, just worry and stress, it would get better in a little while. It didn't, though. It got a little worse each day, and each day I got a little more scared, because intestinal cancer was what had killed my father, and this was how it had started. I was afraid to go to the doctor and I was afraid not to go to the doctor, and I was too embarrassed to talk to anybody except Mandy about it. Too many times when I've been sick, even with a cold, people have blamed me for it, because I'm overweight. I don't know if those extra fifty pounds are my fault or not, but being sick isn't. Mandy knows that.

But I couldn't talk to Mandy, because she had too many problems of her own, and I knew she was counting on having me there, and how could I tell her I was afraid I might be going away, too? Half the time she was so distracted she couldn't understand what you were saying even if it was about something simple, like buying milk. How could I tell her I was afraid I had cancer?

I couldn't. And if I couldn't talk to her I couldn't talk to anybody, and that hurt almost as much as my belly did. I lay awake for hours at night, worrying, and I looked worse and worse all the time, more and more exhausted, and nobody at Mandy's house even noticed. All of them were looking more and more exhausted, too, and I guess it was silly of me to feel like they didn't care about me anymore, but that's how I felt anyway.

The morning after Mandy refused to put Cindy in the hospital, I woke up and thought, I'd better go to the doctor today.

Don't ask me why I decided to do it then: because Mandy's pig-headedness made me see my own, maybe, or because the pain had woken me up in the middle of the night—that had never happened before—or because there was so little hope left that what did it matter? I'd already decided I had cancer. What could the doctor say that would be any worse than that? He'd just be telling me what I already knew.

So I called the doctor's office and told them what was going on and made an emergency appointment—they were mad at me for making them find a space that day, you could tell—and I closed the store for a few hours and went over there. It was Dr. Gallingway, the same one who'd treated my father. I'd never much liked him, but he was the best doctor around for that kind of thing. The nurse came and asked me a bunch of questions and took a bunch of blood and had me get undressed and get into one of those ridiculous paper gowns, and then Dr. G. came in.

"You've let yourself go," he said, looking at me. "You used to be an attractive woman, Cece."

You see what I mean? No hello, Cece, how are you, what are you doing these days? Just an insult, and then he starts lecturing me on how I have to watch my diet, I'm ruining my health the way I live—as if he has any idea how I live when he hasn't even seen me for ten years—and I'm already at risk for cancer because of my family history. As if I didn't know that.

I just sat there and looked at him. Later I thought of lots of things I should have said—"You've let yourself go, Dr. Gallingway. You used to have manners. You used to have hair"—but of course none of that occurred to me when it would have been useful. I just sat there feeling ashamed, and when he finally wound down I said, "Well, I guess the question's whether you want to make any money off my unhealthy lifestyle or not. Because if you don't stop talking to me that way I'm walking out of here."

Dr. Gallingway shut up, goggling at me like his stethoscope had just demanded a raise, and I swallowed hard and told him why I was there. When I was done he shook his head and said, "You shouldn't have waited so long to come in. First thing tomorrow morning I want you to go over to the hospital for an upper GI."

"Sounds like a soldier," I said. It was supposed to be a joke, even though when I said it I thought of Hank, dying in the jungle somewhere.

He didn't laugh. He looked at me and said, "It stands for *gastrointestinal*," a little more slowly than he'd been talking before.

"I know," I told him. You pronounce that very well, Dr. Gallingway. How many years of medical school did it take for you to learn such a long word? I thought about saying that, I swear, but I'm glad I didn't. It was like Mandy's saying she wanted Genevieve to die: one of those mean things you'll probably regret later, when it's too late.

I remembered when my father had his upper GI. He'd called it Upper Guts, Inner, because he couldn't remember all those syllables. I teased him about it, on the way to the test. I think that was the last time Dad and I laughed about anything, because when they did the test they saw something growing in there and they told me they had to keep him in the hospital and then they told me they had to operate and then they told me it was cancer. I drove home from Dr. Gallingway's office wishing I could just die in my sleep.

The upper GI was at eight in the morning in a room that looked like the inside of a rocketship, all metal and huge machines. I'm not a morning person, especially when I'm not allowed to have my coffee and donut, especially when I haven't gotten any sleep because I spent all night crying, and I never much liked science fiction movies. The last one

I saw was *Alien*, and I didn't exactly want to think about that right now, with my own gut feeling just like something was about to come busting out of my belly. I sat there in another smock—cotton, this time, and at least they'd let me keep my underwear on—hoping the doctor who did the test wouldn't have too many tentacles and wouldn't look at me like he thought I did. At least I'd never met him before, so he couldn't tell me I used to be an attractive woman.

When he came in I saw that he was real young and handsome, and wearing, I swear, a collar that made him look just like a priest. Later he told me that it was a lead shield to protect his neck from radiation, but when I first saw him it didn't incline me to be friendly. I hadn't been too impressed with doctors and priests lately, and here was somebody who looked like both.

He smiled at me and held out his hand and said, "Good morning, Ms. Yodel. I'm Dr. Stephenson," and I thought, well, at least he has manners. He asked me how I was feeling and I told him, and I told him about Dad, and I thought, well, here comes the lecture.

He didn't lecture me, though. He just looked serious and said, "I'm sorry. You must be very frightened," which made me feel better right away, because I hadn't been able to tell anybody about being scared, not even Mandy, and you'd think Dr. Gallingway could have said something nice like that, with all the money I was paying him, but of course he didn't. Then Dr. Stephenson said, "Your symptoms could be caused by a lot of other things, you know."

Well, I didn't know that. Dr. Gallingway sure hadn't bothered to say anything like that. So I decided I liked Dr. Stephenson, even if he did look like a priest. He knew his job was to make people feel better, not worse. You'd think every doctor would know that—and every priest, for that matter—but as far as I could tell not too many of them had figured it out. It made the entire world seem a little bit friendlier, meeting someone like that. The way I felt then, it was almost worth having to have the upper GI.

"So what we're going to do," he said, "is have you drink a glass of this barium"—he held up this big paper cup of white stuff, looked like one of Mandy's vanilla milk shakes, with a big plastic straw in it—"and I'm going to watch it on the fluoroscope, this screen over here, as it travels down your esophagus into your stomach and your small intestines. The barium tastes chalky, kind of like Mylanta, and the test doesn't hurt. It's boring, more than anything, because it takes a long time. Sometimes I'll have you roll over onto your sides and onto your stomach, so I can see things more clearly on the screen, and during part of the test I'll have to press on your abdomen with that balloon paddle over there." He pointed at this weird plastic and rubber thing hanging on the wall, looked like a plastic tennis racket with a rubber middle, had a bulb dangling from it, like one of the ones they use to inflate blood pressure cuffs. "That's to make the barium move around to the places I want to look at. Do you have any questions, before we start?"

"Yes," I said. "Barium's radioactive, right? How do I get it out of me?" I was worried that even if the barium didn't find any cancer, it could cause cancer if it stayed in there.

He nodded and said, "It comes out the way anything else you eat comes out, and the barium's not all that radioactive, actually. After you leave here, make sure to drink a lot of fluids for the rest of the day, to flush the barium out of your system. Prune juice is good; it moves things along."

"How about coffee?" I said.

He laughed. "That's fine. That moves things along too."

The test wasn't bad, really. It was interesting even at the beginning, because I could look at the screen, so I could watch the barium traveling down my throat and into my stomach. It looked just like those pictures of the inside of the body you see in books, only in black and white. The bar-

208

ium was white in the cup, but on the screen the barium was black and my innards were white, like a negative.

Dr. Stephenson said my throat looked fine and my stomach looked fine, and we'd have to wait awhile for the barium to move through the small intestine. I should move around, he said. I'd have wanted to move around anyway, because it was cold in there. So he went away for a while and I walked around and read the labels on the machines and wondered how my father had felt, pacing in a little room like this, in the last minutes when he didn't know yet that something was growing in his gut.

So, of course, I'd gotten myself pretty scared again by the time Dr. Stephenson came back, especially since the pain was acting up. He took the balloon paddle off the wall and had me lie down again, and I craned my head back so I could see the screen, and he turned on the machine. And the face of Jesus stared out at me from the fluoroscope, just the same way he looked on that cross in Mandy's church, like *he* was in so much pain he could hardly stand it.

"Oh my God," I said. "Look at that!"

"What's wrong?" said Dr. Stephenson. He didn't act like he'd noticed anything, and I thought maybe I was crazy. When I looked at the screen again I could see that Jesus' face was made up of all the curls and folds of my gut, but it still looked like Jesus' face, with the thorny crown and everything. It was just like one of those pictures you see on the cover of the *National Enquirer*: Jesus in somebody's fingerprints, the Devil in somebody's cornflakes. Elvis everyplace. I always thought all that stuff was nonsense, even worse than "Instant Miracle Cures," and here it was happening to me.

"Doesn't that," I said, "doesn't it look to you like, well, like a face?" I didn't want to say whose face. Dr. Stephenson would think I was a religious fanatic.

He cocked his head sideways and squinted at it and said,

"Why, so it does. I see what you mean. Isn't that interesting. I'm going to press on your stomach with the balloon now, Ms. Yodel." And he did, and I watched Jesus' face kind of roll around on the screen. He must have been seasick in there. He looked about as green as I felt. And Dr. Stephenson worked away with his balloon and told me about how fluoroscope images are like Rorschach blots—you can see anything in them if you look hard enough. Once he did an upper GI on a little boy who swore he saw Big Bird.

The place where Dr. Stephenson was pressing now made Jesus' mouth open and close, like he was trying to say something. "Get me out of here," probably. And I wondered how he'd gotten in there to begin with and then I realized, of course: it was that stupid biscuit, the one I'd eaten by mistake when I went to church with Mandy. The pain had started right after that, come to think of it. So there must have been something to its being Christ's body, although if that was true I didn't see how Catholics walked around without bellyaches all the time. Maybe it didn't hurt, if you were Catholic. Maybe that's why you weren't supposed to eat the biscuit unless you were. I mean, you'd think they'd *tell* people something like that, honestly, there should be a Surgeon General's warning. Here I was, I'd been in pain for months, I'd thought I was dying. I was paying all this money for this upper GI—which wasn't cheap, believe me—and the whole time the problem was nothing but a piece of stale biscuit.

Well, I got pretty mad when I started thinking like that, let me tell you. I was fuming by the time the test was over. Dr. Stephenson squeezed my hand and grinned at me and said, "I have good news for you, Ms. Yodel: I see no evidence of a Mass," and I just looked at him like he'd lost his mind.

"A mass," he said gently after a minute, "a lump—that means I don't see anything that could be cancer."

You're damn right there's no cancer, I thought, furious, and then I thought I'd had to drink this stuff that could cause cancer, maybe, to find out I didn't have any, and I got even madder. But none of that was Dr. Stephenson's fault and he'd been real nice to me, so I had to try to be polite. "Thank you," I said, "I'm very glad to hear that." And then I realized that must sound very cold to him, so I said, "You're a very nice man. Most doctors don't explain things as well as you did. Thank you," and that made him look happy and I felt a little better, about him, anyhow.

Not that I felt better about anything else. How was I going to get Jesus out of there? With prune juice? He'd been in there for months and plenty of other things had come out, but he hadn't. Who do you talk to about something like that? Any doctor would think I was crazy, and I couldn't see myself going to Father Antsy. He'd just tell me everyone should have Jesus inside them, and that's fine if you're a believer, but I didn't feel much more religious than I had before I ate the biscuit. Jesus hurt, and that's the truth, and I wanted my intestines back to myself. If it had been the Devil inside me, maybe a priest would have been some help. I wondered if Jesus could make your head turn all the way around, like Linda Blair's.

I thought about all of this when I was getting dressed, and I walked through the hospital lobby still thinking about it, so mad I wasn't even looking where I was going, and I practically walked straight into Mandy.

"Cece!" she said, and grabbed me and started crying. She didn't even ask me what I was doing there, which shows you how upset she was. "Cece. I finally decided the doctor was right. Cindy's upstairs now, I brought her here two hours ago and went home to get her toothbrush because I'd forgotten it and I was just heading out the door again when they called me to say she's dying, she'll only last another few hours, and she knows it, too. She's asked for Father Anselm."

"She asked for *him?*" I said. We were already heading for

the elevators. "Why in the world would she do that? He's the one who drove her away from here in the first place!"

"She wants last rites," Mandy said. "He's the only Catholic priest in town. It has to be him. Last rites are a formula: how badly can he do? She's dying and she wants forgiveness, Cece."

"She won't get it from him," I said. A wedding's a formula too, and we both knew what Antsy had done with that. "That man wouldn't forgive his own grandmother if she took too long crossing the street. He'd blame it on her sinful body." It's a good thing Mr. and Mrs. Mincing were in New Mexico, baking their joints, or Cindy probably would have wanted them there, too. All three of those people should have been asking Cindy's forgiveness, as far as I was concerned, but I guess Cindy was too sick to see it that way. Or maybe if she'd been able to see it that way she wouldn't have wound up where she was in the first place.

It seemed like that elevator took forever to come, and when we finally got upstairs we found Cindy pretty much looking like a corpse already, lying there just barely able to blink with about five tubes in each arm, and old Antsy standing next to her bed, holding his Bible and yammering away. I don't know if he'd done the rites yet or not; he was halfway into a rip-roaring sermon from what I could tell. "Cynthia Marie, let us pray that the Lord will see fit to wash clean your heinous sins," that kind of thing, as if the Lord might think about it and decide not to after all, with that poor woman dying and wanting just this one thing before she went. It made me crazy, and I guess the Jesus in my belly must have felt the same way, because my stomach started hurting something awful. I could just picture the little guy squirming around down there, just wishing he could set this idiot straight, and I decided I'd help him out.

"Oh, *shut up*," I said—exactly what I'd been wanting to say to that man for twenty years now, ever since the wedding—and Mandy actually giggled and Father Antsy glared at me like I'd just committed a really world-class sin. But my belly quieted down, so I figured Jesus approved. "You want to talk about heinous sins?" I asked Antsy. "Before you start in on Cindy's, why don't you think about your own?" He glared even harder when I said that, but I kept talking anyway. The Jesus in my belly must have given me confidence, or maybe I was a little loopy with being so tired. "Listen to yourself," I said. "When's the last time you said anything nice to anybody? I know all the things you hate, Father Anselm. You hate bodies and you hate TV and you hate people who make mistakes. Why don't you talk about what you love, for a change? Isn't that part of your job?"

"I love God," he said, looking down his long skinny nose at me, and my belly panged and I thought, GI *Jesus doesn't think so*.

"If you love God," I said—as if I was some kind of authority on God, what a joke!—"it seems to me you've got to love people too, since God's supposed to love them. I don't think you've gotten that part down yet. Why don't you practice? Tell Cindy something you love about her. Go on."

He looked down at her, down at the bed, and wrinkled that nose like Cindy was some piece of meat that had fallen behind the refrigerator and stayed there way too long, and he said in the coldest voice I've ever heard, a voice that would turn antifreeze into icicles, a voice that would give the Grinch nightmares, "God loves you, my daughter."

"And you don't?" Mandy said. She was shaking. "No, of course you don't. How could you? Get out of this room, Father Anselm."

Antsy got, in a hurry, and I gaped like an idiot. I'd never heard Mandy talk that way to anybody. Even when she wanted Genevieve to die, she never sounded like that. She practically had sparks coming out of her ears, she was so mad. At first I couldn't believe it and then I thought, well,

why not? Here's the old Mandy who cares about people joining forces with the new Mandy, the one who sticks up for
herself, and they make a pretty good pair after all, don't
they? "Good for you," I said softly. I'd never been so proud of
her.

She didn't answer, just went over to the bed and took
one of Cindy's hands in hers and started rubbing it, and I
went over too. Cindy just stared up at the ceiling. There was
no way to tell if she'd even heard anything that had just
happened, or if she'd hear anything we said now, but I knew
I had to say something to her, because I'd never have
another chance. And it occurred to me that I'd said a lot of
things to Cindy, all those months she'd been at Mandy's
house, but they'd always been about the present, not the
past. "How are you feeling today, Cindy? Can I get you some
water? Do you want another blanket?" I'd never said anything about how we'd all gotten to where we were, and I'd
never told her anything about how I felt.

"I'm so sad you're so sick," I told her, and then, all in a
rush, "It isn't fair, you know, it isn't, not one little bit. I
know you think you're being punished for something, but
what happened to you could have happened to just about
any girl in this town, Cindy. It could have happened to me.
I had a pregnancy scare when I was seventeen years old—I
never even told Mandy that—and when she and Bill got
married and I was standing up in front of the altar I felt just
awful, because I wasn't any better than you were and by
rights you should have been the one up there, if your
mother and daddy hadn't been so mean about what had
happened to you. I know Mandy thought so too, she did. I
wanted to tell you all of that, but you left before I could. I
don't blame you for leaving; I'd have done the same thing
in your place. And whatever else you did, after you left,
well, I'm not in any position to judge. All I can say is I
wish you hadn't suffered so much, Cindy." We still didn't

know much about what had happened to her, or where, but we'd seen things when we were taking care of her. Scars, from needles it looked like—and from other things too, things I didn't want to think about. It looked like people had hurt her, and not by accident either, and it looked like she'd tried to hurt herself. "You were just a little girl, Cindy, no worse than anybody else, and more than I wish anything I wish you hadn't had to go through your life thinking you were bad."

It was the truth, that's all. She hadn't so much as twitched the whole time I was talking, and I still couldn't tell if she'd heard a word I'd said. I bent and I kissed her forehead and I said, "God bless you, Cindy," because I knew she believed in God, even if I wasn't sure I did, and I knew she'd wanted some kind of blessing from Father Antsy and she hadn't gotten one. Mine probably wouldn't do her much good, but at least I'd tried. And when I'd straightened up from kissing her I realized that the pain in my belly was gone, completely gone, for the first time in months, and I thought, well, GI Jesus must have liked it, whether Cindy did or not.

Mandy hadn't said anything. She just stood there, holding Cindy's hand and looking at me, and I could see she was about to start crying again and I didn't think I could take it. "I'm going home now," I said, "so you can say your good-byes in private. Call me—later. All right?"

She nodded, and I left. It wasn't even that I wanted to give her privacy, because I knew Mandy wouldn't have minded if I'd stayed, but it was just too sad in that room. Whenever I looked at Cindy I thought about my father, and Hank in the jungle, and that poor wooden Christ on his cross, and I just couldn't stand it, not after a sleepless night and no breakfast. I wouldn't have been any good to Mandy if I'd stayed, and I had things I had to do for myself. On my way home I bought a gallon of prune juice, and as soon as I got home I started drinking it. I didn't like the idea of that barium spending one more second sloshing around my insides than it absolutely had to.

I drank prune juice for the next two hours, and then I drank water for two hours after that, and nothing was happening except that I had to pee every two seconds. All that liquid was coming out, but the barium wasn't. I was starting to get pretty worried about it when the phone rang, and I thought, Oh, Lord, that'll be Mandy, crying her head off, and it was and she was. I kept saying over and over, "I'm so sorry, Mandy," and finally I realized that she was trying to say something herself.

"Cece, listen to me, it's not what you think, she's not dead, she's better."

"She can't be better," I said, as gently as I could, and I thought, well, it's over. Cindy's dead and Mandy's gone clean out of her mind, and now I'm going to have to bring up those four girls all by myself. And then I remembered that Mandy was religious, and I thought, maybe this is just church talk. Maybe she's trying to comfort herself. "You mean—she's in heaven now, Mandy?" It felt weird even saying the word, but if it helped her that was what counted. "With the—angels?" Like I said, I was really tired.

"*Angels?*" Mandy said. "I don't believe in angels any more than you do, Cece Yodel! I mean she's better, right here in the hospital, every bit as alive as I am!"

I nearly groaned. If Cindy was still alive that meant they'd put her on some kind of machine, and people could keep breathing for years on those things, sucking money into the hospital faster than a drowning man gulps seawater. "Mandy, I really truly don't think she'll ever be better—"

"But she *is*," Mandy said, babbling. "It's a miracle, that's all, that's the only word for it, she's so much better the doctors can't believe it, *they* say it's a miracle even, her fever's gone and she knows who I am and they did some blood tests and they're *normal* now, Cece, they were all haywire before and they've just gone back to plumb normal, Cece, I swear to God I'm not crazy and I'm not making this up—"

"I know you aren't," I said. All of a sudden I knew what had happened. "Mandy, honey, I can't tell you how happy I am and I'll be there just as soon as I can but I have to go now, all right?"

I did, too. The prune juice was finally working. I rushed into the bathroom and got there just in time, and sat there, just being happy, while the prune juice did what it was supposed to do. So there, Father Antsy. Even Jesus needs a body to work miracles with, and he picked mine, how do you like that? I know religious people think pride is a sin and most of the time I agree with them, but this time I felt like I hadn't had anything to feel proud of in so long that maybe I deserved it, and anyway I was mainly happy for Mandy and Cindy. And I sat there thinking about miracles, and I thought, Well, GI Jesus, how about one more miracle, how about letting us know where Hank is? How about bringing him home, happy and healthy?

I figured Jesus wouldn't have enough time for that, though, because he was probably on his way out of my body, now that Cindy was better. I wondered what he'd look like when he left, if maybe he'd look happy too, finally. When the juice had finished its work I looked down wondering if I'd see a tiny cross in there, or a little guy in a beard and loincloth, or what.

Well, that was just silliness, of course. What came out was white, whiter even than the barium had been when I drank it, white as freshly bleached sheets or new snow or any of the other things people talk about when they're trying to describe whiteness—so white it looked almost like it glowed, but maybe that's because it was radioactive, I don't know. It didn't look like anything to do with Jesus, though.

It looked like a big fish, and then when I flushed and it was whirling around it changed shape and looked like a bird, and then it was gone. Which just goes to show you that Dr. Stephenson was right: if you look at a shape that isn't much like anything in particular, you can see anything you want.

So I had to laugh at myself, the way I'd given myself all those airs about pulling off a miracle. Oh, Cindy's been getting a little stronger every day since then: the next day she drank some Sprite and the day after that she sat up in bed and then she started going to the bathroom by herself and watching game shows and asking for cheeseburgers. She's coming home from the hospital tomorrow. So it sure looks like an Instant Miracle Cure, but even if it is, it probably has nothing to do with me or my intestines. Cindy just decided she wasn't ready to die, that's all—you hear stories about that all the time—or the blood tests were all wrong to begin with. You hear stories about that, too. So I'm still not going to say I'm religious. But I have been putting in a few prayers for Hank, just in case there's a God after all.

Susan Palwick

~

"GI JESUS," which was nominated for the World Fantasy Award, was written while Susan Palwick was running a 102-degree fever, the week after she herself had had an upper GI. "Alas," says Palwick, the test "turned up nothing nearly as interesting as the one in the story does."

An assistant professor of English at the University of Nevada, Reno, Palwick received her undergraduate degree from Princeton in 1982 and a Ph.D. from Yale in 1996. Fifteen of her short stories have been published, as well as the novel Flying in Place, which won the Crawford Award. She is currently working on a second novel, Shelter.

Considering the adroit way "GI Jesus" handles the subject of separation between sisters, I asked her what she believes a woman misses out on most when she divorces herself from a relationship with her sister.

"Shared history," says Palwick, "which is why Cindy's return in the novelette is so poignant, because she's returning after all those years and won't tell anyone what's happened to her."

—C. O.

Under the Rose

Rita Dove

I The Eldest
was the battering ram; my looks attest to it. Every freedom was wrung by action: I endured the wails of a frightened
mother when I came home disheveled after dark; the rage of
an ineffectual father stiffened my shoulders and narrowed
my eyes. I tried it all. If I could not be doted upon, I could be
worried about; I would get out into the world. Can't you
imagine? Can you blame me? Three years later came my first
sister, and then the baby, the darling.

At first we loved her too, and sometimes called her
Cookie, she was so round and perfectly baked. She was a
hoarder. Weaned from the breast too late, she would tuck a
spoonful of pablum in the pouch of her cheek like a hamster.
For how long had we thought those cheeks were naturally
puffed, the round face of a cherub! But one afternoon she
stumbled over a ripple in the hall rug and with a thud her
chin hit the parquet; a clump of masticated banana spurted
from between her lips and lay before us, mother and two
older sisters, like the indecent gelatinous workings of a snail
scraped from its shell. Alerted, every evening Mother would
check Babs's mouth for signs of hoarded food, and each
evening found packed between gums and cheek the soggy
remains of bread, or green beans blackened from saliva. In

time those baby teeth, soft pearls, began to decay; despairing, Mother brushed them after every meal with a mixture of salt and baking soda. Oh, the screams when that bracing paste met raw gums! And yet this did not cure her. One by one the teeth dropped out until there was no retaining wall for the hoarded food, and she was forced to swallow. By the time her adult teeth came in, strong, straight, and white, she had forgotten the old habit.

What could prompt a toddler to store up nourishment like a chipmunk sniffing winter? What could she know already of life, how it whittles? Or was she no more than an animal following instincts, proclamations of Enlightenment, delayed gratification and propriety notwithstanding? Hasn't she been this way always—continually stocking the cave with nuts against the impending frost?

This last daughter was the first one to Get Out. This was my disgrace. Even if she left against her will, even if the Turn of Events spelled Tragedy to our House . . . I was the one destined to break out of the nest, I was my parents' heartache. All my life I had been practicing to disappoint them, and then nothing—no scandal, no hairy groom nor inappropriate lover—could outshine Beauty's contract. What neat upstaging! What sabotage!

After much thought, I decided on a course of action nobody would have expected of one so flamboyant, so carefree: I decided to stay put. Never to marry but to wither into old maidhood. I simply refused to participate in the ancient games: I abandoned my jewels and silks, I put away the hankies scented with dried violets and the talcs laced with thin curls of tangerine peel. Each morning I scrubbed my body with a hunk of brown soap such as the farmers use; I eschewed the wooden tub and stood in the courtyard before the pump, betraying not so much as a gasp as ice water shot up from the bowels of the earth to rinse me squeaky clean.

It was easier than I had imagined; it was hardly denial at

all. How little the soul needs, finally! If there are no plums it will feed on the pits, or on the dream of pits or, finally, on itself. And it eats so slowly; it grows faster than it can be consumed.

The Middle One

No one watched me. No one Paid Attention. The first time I understood this, observed the never-changing scene at the dinner table and saw how clearly I didn't count, I felt as if the carpet under me had opened with a terrifying wave of pity, whispering, *Let go,* but I took off, let loose, cast my flaking soul on the waters—what a freedom to be the ampersand.

The Mother

Yes, I spoiled her. She was the youngest: she ruined my body, she kicked away the scaffolding and stood by, cooing as the last of prewar grandeur, my flaking gold, came crumbling down. I spoiled her because she was all there was left; I wanted her to have it, Beauty, all the things that were free for the asking. Because I had grown away from all that; my Youthful Adventure was over. I suppose I hated her just a little, I can see that; but mostly I was giving her an education.

When she grew old enough to read, I told her stories; I made her the heroine. This was a mistake, because she grew up believing all endings would be, if not happy, then at least neatly turned. She grew up confident that life could be conducted with grace.

I had married my husband because he was malleable. That I loved him is beside the point—Love, too, is a matter of education. I balanced my desire for the things of the world with the house he built; I compared the clamorous sighs of other suitors with his good smile above the merchant's waistcoat; I thought of the trips he would make while I baked pies in the kitchen, gazing out into the clearing; I imagined the gilt mirrors he would bring back, accepted in trade but utterly useless to the few tired wives in the region; I thought a *mirror in every room* and when he proposed I did not hesitate.

I have not regretted that decision, although my buoyant, fecund life has become a magnificent mulch. Just consider my daughters, each a product of my horticulture and each so remarkably different. Martha bloomed faster than I could complete the trellis; unsupported, she ran wild and burst early. Her bold brain grew too heavy for its spine; I could see the strain in her face as she struggled to defy us—and of course the first disappointment chilled her. *Nipped in the bud,* she did not wither so much as freeze, rigidly accepting the stasis of the present, refusing the uncertainties of anticipation. She simply stopped, arrested all growth, and in time began imperceptibly to shrink, darkening around the edges like an arrangement of dried wildflowers.

Then Megan, who never understood the battle for sunlight. Content to be marginal, she valued above all her capacity to be innocuous and made a virtue out of small, efficient movements. Even her name was a compression: not as robust as *Martha,* more arid than *Mother.* I did not realize the pattern I had fallen into, the progression of M-words humming through our house, until Megan was three. Then came Beauty.

Barbara, Babs, Baby—a wild attempt to start again, to break the chain. After all, my real name, before Wife and Mother, had been Beatrice; but none of the names I gave her would stick. My husband called her Beauty, her sisters dubbed her Cookie—and the sisters were right; she *was* a cookie, the kind you nibbled with a glass of milk; a sweetness that fired the blood, only to produce a drop in energy minutes afterward: to gorge oneself on this delicacy meant to come out much weaker than before.

Beauty

As for my looks—I was lucky. Looks are a matter of fashion, and my complexion, my figure, happen to be in accordance with the age. A mere generation ago in the great cities beyond the lake, women were delicious when they bore a pale countenance on a precarious stalk, heads like peeled eggs. They plucked their eyebrows, even shaved back their hairline to accommodate the illusion of a regal brow. The stark white facial powder contained a lead base, so that the more they applied, the more their skin was eaten away. And the two spots of rouge imitating china dolls in a toymaker's window—these, too, carried their weight in lead. Beneath the bald-eyed countenance of Elizabethan beauties, the virginal flesh rotted like pears.

Roses? I'm rather afraid of them, though nobody has guessed; men will believe anything. Even when I told him to stop he piled them at my feet, in my lap; their fiery heads sprawled across white tablecloths or tucked under my pillow like a bloodstain, a tubercular dribble in the night. They weren't really for me. After all, he was the one who had squandered an entire garden plot on them, a brute in search of Romance way before I came along. I see him stumbling through the rows with his pruning shears, trimming back growth, or gently lifting the flushed lip of a petal with a sweaty paw to get at the aphids in their cunning green industry, humming "I'm in the Mood for Love." When he discovered my father, he found another sentimental fool; the two hearts gushed in recognition. I was merely the expedient: legal tender.

It was never the rose; that's the biggest irony. I prefer silks. Thousands of tiny worms spinning week upon week in order to produce one handkerchief's worth of glimmering breath: That's the kind of dedication I appreciate.

It was never the rose but the idea of a rose, the sort of thing expected from fair young maidens. I made my request in January, in the dead of winter, so my wish was more than charming or frivolous—it was impossible. I had mocked my father. He did not fail me.

My sisters asked for the easy pleasures, but I was the youngest; I stood flat-chested and scrawny under a flannel nightshirt and watched them frowning into their mirrors; I knew how little the stuffs of the world satisfy. As a child I had caught my mother crying over the stove and when I asked her why she was crying she would make up yet another gooey story starring the Invincible Princess Rose, stories guaranteed to put me to sleep within five minutes. How could I tell her I was more interested in the pungent taste of millet soup?

Those weeks I lay in terror of his approach; his stench was insupportable. The merest brush of his cheek against mine left angry red welts. Nothing in my life had prepared me for this abandonment. His touch was discreet, but his eyes! Liquid with sex, they held me in their glistening fever until I lost all appetite, even for my favorite *pâté de foie gras*; one wet glance and I began to regurgitate effortlessly, all that gluttonous liver loosening. The sight of a golden plate made my jaws ache.

So I ran back to Mama who wept openly this time, pressing her soggy cheek to mine. My sisters looked on, silent. That I had not yet been defiled was of no consequence; it was only a matter of time. As a sister I no longer existed. I had preempted them, but someday they might have to follow, and so they watched for clues. When, in the mirror, I first saw him stagger, I packed my bags. I had driven him mad, and like the thief fatally proud of the perfect execution of a crime, I felt compelled to return to the scene.

By the time I arrived, I found him aswoon between rows of new hybrids. Flies were already collecting in the frothy corners of his lips. I was moved by pity but also the desire to avoid Ugliness; although to die for love is not in bad taste, to be the lethal perpetrator of longing is always unsavory.

How gloriously my tormentor had staged my return! By bending over the dim rosebeds I could see that he had just shaven; he was languishing but nowhere near the demise promised so ravishingly.

Yes, that was it: he merely looked ravished; laid out for my delectation, awaiting my kiss. He allowed me to lead him through the crowds of scents to the villa, past corridor upon corridor of doors shut and bolted against the wind that was rising, an evening wind that swept through the hallways and guttered the candles.

Crazed by my extended absence, he had made of my sleeping chamber a garden as well, filling the very pillow-cases with petals, installing a fountain on the balcony so that all night the liquid veil sizzled. In this madhouse of desire he had slept, ordering meals brought up by the eunuchs, the most exquisite delicacies, each and every one flavored with the essence of attar: rose gelée on white toast, rose wine and rose-petal bouillon, golden curry studded with rose hips.

All this he whispered into my shoulder, the quenched wicks smoking; the air smelled heavy and burned, like incense. Where was the Moment of Transformation? When would the beast melt, harden into a prince? Did I really yearn for a prince? Which is more likely to have a soul, an animal or a rose? And when I was opened—*deflowered*—what glutted mass would spew out, and how could I ever hope to stopper that scent?

And yet my chest kept rising and falling. I wrenched the casements wide till moonlight poured over my hands, the silken parquet, the glacial bedsheets forming a fervid cocoon. *Now*, I thought, moving into his furred arms. *Now, at last, I am anonymous.*

Rita Dove

WHEN SHE SERVED as poet laureate of the United States from 1993 to 1995, she was the nation's youngest, and also the first African-American to fill that post. She was born in Akron, Ohio, in 1952, the daughter of the first African-American research chemist in the history of the American rubber tire industry. It was her father's insistence that, at an early age, she study and learn that started her on the road to an embarrassment of accolades, beginning shortly before her eighteenth birthday, when she was ranked one of the top hundred high school students in the country and invited to the White House as a presidential scholar.

After graduating from Miami University of Ohio summa cum laude, she received a Fulbright Fellowship and attended the University of Tü, West Germany, earned a master of fine arts degree from the University of Iowa Writers' Workshop, and now holds the title of Commonwealth Professor of English at the University of Virginia in Charlottesville.

Her collection of forty-four poems, Thomas and Beulah, inspired by the lives of her maternal grandparents, won her the Pulitzer in 1997. Among her other awards are the 1996 Heinz Award; the 1996 Charles Frankel Prize, which is the U.S. government's highest recognition for achievement in the humanities;

the 1997 Sara Lee Frontrunner Award; and most recently, the 1997 Barnes & Noble Writers for Writers Award.

Despite the awards and national recognition, it is the one-on-one connection with her readers that Dove loves best.

"I can tell you that the moments which have thrilled me the most, in the deepest way," she said in a 1994 interview, "have been those times when I have received letters from people I don't even know who tell me exactly how something of mine moved them. That's a bigger thrill than the Pulitzer or the poet laureateship."

Dove's work includes the novel Through the Ivory Gate, a book of short stories, Fifth Sunday, a collection of essays entitled The Poet's World, and the play The Darker Face of the Earth, which had its world premiere in 1996 at the Oregon Shakespeare Festival.

Dove lives in Charlottesville with her husband, German writer Fred Viebahn, and their daughter Aviva.

—C. O.

The Summer Before the Summer of Love

Marly Swick

The three of us were sitting on the muggy screen porch pushing the food around on our plates in silence. Meat loaf, Rice-A-Roni, and frozen peas. My older sister and I had just returned from spending the weekend at our father's small brown apartment in a huge new complex on the other side of town. It had only been a couple of months since he moved out, but it already seemed as if we had never lived any other way. Johanna and I were still full from the butterscotch beanies our father had bought for us at the Dairy Queen on the way back home. It was a muggy August night and the little girls next door were galloping back and forth through the sprinkler in matching pink polka dot bathing suits that had once belonged to my sister and me. The DiBernard girls were four years apart, like Johanna and I, so my mother gave Mrs. DiBernard all our old clothes. It was like watching old home movies of ourselves, of some dumber and happier time, and as we sat there pretending to eat our dinner in the steamy heat, I wished that Johanna and I were back inside those hideous bathing suits, splashing and shouting away.

"You're not eating anything," our mother reproached us, although she wasn't eating anything herself. She seemed twitchy and impatient.

"We had a big lunch," I said. "At China Palace."

Our mother frowned and pursed her lips. She thought our father was trying to buy our loyalty with Chinese food, Big Macs, and ice cream. I had heard them arguing about this on the phone the week before.

"Good meat loaf," I said, dutifully shoving a forkful into my mouth.

Johanna sighed and pelted peas at a couple of birds in the backyard.

Before the separation our mother had been a lazy, absentminded cook. Our father would come home from work and the still-frozen roast would be sitting there on the counter. He would jab a fork into it, then sigh and frown down at it, as if all of our mother's sins and flaws were neatly consolidated in this icy lump. "So what's the big deal?" our mother would say, picking up the telephone. "No one's going to starve." Half an hour later a pizza would arrive. The neighborhood kids always envied us when they spied the large indestructible pizza box sitting on the curb by the trash.

In those days, at least in Ohio where we lived, divorce was still something mostly associated with other people—movie stars or trashy types, people with winter tans or criminal records. All of our friends had two parents, and after our father moved out, the same kids who used to drool with envy at our empty pizza boxes suddenly looked down on us, as if we'd had to sell one of our cars or something.

Our mother seemed to take to the kitchen in a desperate attempt to salvage our respectability. For the past two months, she had been serving us these dull, well-balanced meals. "You are what you eat," she'd say, smiling her new fake Betty Crocker smile. As if eating these boring all-American meals would make us just another boring all-American family.

"Are you finished, Suzanne honey?" She hovered over

me and when I nodded, my mouth full of Rice-A-Roni, she whisked my plate away, whistling.

"What's her problem?" Johanna said as soon as the kitchen doors swung shut. "She's acting like a weirdo."

I shrugged.

A second later, our mother returned with three bowls of sliced strawberries and bananas. Johanna sighed.

"Whoops," our mother said. "Almost forgot." She bustled back into the kitchen.

Johanna wrinkled her nose. "She knows I *detest* brown bananas." She picked out the offensive banana slices and stacked them like poker chips beside her bowl.

Our mother hurried back out with a plate of graham crackers. She seemed wound up, chattering away about nothing while Johanna and I dutifully moved our spoons back and forth between our bowls and our mouths. Every so often she'd give the graham cracker plate a little nervous nudge closer to Johanna or me, but neither of us showed any interest. In the old days we would have had Mallomars. Finally her patience snapped and she shoved the plate in Johanna's face. "Take a cookie!" she ordered. "You, too," she said, turning to me.

Surprised into obedience, we each automatically grabbed a graham cracker and bit into it as she plunked the saucer back down on the table. Then we saw it, or rather them— the surprise—hidden under the boring graham crackers. Four tickets. Johanna's eyes widened and she seemed to stop breathing as she reached out and picked one up and read aloud what was printed on it: "The Beatles. Crosley Field. August 20, 1966." Then she screamed so loud the DiBernard girls froze in their tracks and looked over at us in alarm. I smiled and waved and shouted, "It's okay; she's just going to the Beatles concert!"

Johanna had her arms wrapped around our mother's neck, jumping up and down, half strangling her, shouting,

"You're the greatest, you're the greatest, thank you, thank you, thank you, thank you!"

"It's your birthday present," our mother laughed. "Happy Sweet Sixteen."

I picked up the rest of the tickets and stared down at them, not daring to ask. On the one hand, I wasn't as besotted with the Beatles as my sister and her friends, but, on the other hand, I didn't want to be left out of any major excursion. Crosley Field was in Cincinnati, over a hundred miles away.

"We're all going," my mother said, coming up for air and winking at me. "The three of us, plus Sharon." Sharon Dinsmore was Johanna's best friend.

"Oh, my *God!*" Johanna screamed again even louder. "Does Sharon know? I have to go call her."

My mother shook her head, pleased and gratified to have broken, for once, through Johanna's new usual air of cool disdain. "I asked Mrs. Dinsmore's permission, of course, but I told her to keep it a secret."

"Oh my God, I don't believe it! Wait till she hears! Oh my God." Johanna raced off to the telephone. The air around us seemed to quiver for a moment in her wake, and then her shrill, thrilled voice floated down to us from the open window upstairs.

Flushed from all the big excitement, my mother smiled across the table at me. "So, what do *you* think?"

"Are we going to stay in a hotel?" I asked. The one time we had driven to Cincinnati for a cousin's wedding we had stayed overnight at a fancy hotel where the maid left chocolate mints on our pillowcases.

"I made reservations at the Holiday Inn," she said. "It has a swimming pool."

"Wow, that's great." I dipped my graham cracker into my lukewarm glass of milk and nibbled on it. I was thinking that even *my* friends were going to be impressed by this and wishing that Johanna would get off the phone with Sharon so that I could call my best friend, Lisa.

As if reading my mind, my mother paused in clearing the table and said, "Suzanne, honey, I hope you don't mind that I didn't get a ticket for Lisa. It's just that the tickets were expensive and you know how crazy Johanna and Sharon are about the Beatles."

I nodded. This was an understatement. Our father couldn't afford to buy himself a new stereo yet, so every weekend Johanna spent most of her time lying in the front seat of his Camaro, punching the radio buttons to find Beatles songs. Her favorite was "Norwegian Wood." She practically fainted every time she heard it.

The screen door banged open and shut as my mother carried our dessert bowls into the kitchen. I reached over and ate Johanna's stack of mushy banana slices. Inside the house I could hear Johanna's squealing and my mother's humming as she ran water in the sink. She was humming "Can't Buy Me Love." Next door Mr. DiBernard came out and shut off the sprinkler. All he had on was some thin pale pajama bottoms that you could almost see through. The DiBernard girls started to whine in protest. He picked them up, one under each arm, and whirled them around in circles until they started to laugh and squeal. I got up and went inside.

Sitting in a booth at China Palace the following Saturday evening, Johanna smothered her egg roll in plum sauce, passed me the empty bowl, and announced to our father that we wouldn't be seeing him the weekend of the twentieth because we were going to Cincinnati to see the Beatles.

He frowned into his glass of beer, and I could see the objections ringing up in his mind, one after another, like prices in a cash register. One of our mother's big complaints against our father was that every time she got the spark of an idea, he dumped cold water all over it. "The thing you girls have to understand about your father is that he is essentially a very negative person," she told us as we were packing for the weekend. "Don't expect him to greet this plan with any enthusiasm."

"Well, I'm going," Johanna declared as she snapped the buckles on her suitcase shut. "No matter what he says."

"Me, too," I said.

"Your father's not going to like you missing your weekend with him. He's a stickler for the rules." She picked some stray clothes up off the floor and tossed them into our closet. "Just be diplomatic."

Our father set down his beer and said, "She should have discussed this with me first. That's a long drive and those front tires are practically bald. Not to mention your mother's lousy driving. And the expense. It's not as if we have money to throw away."

"Oh, Daddy," Johanna sighed. "You know you are essentially a very negative person."

I kicked her under the table, but I could tell from his expression it was already too late. He was really mad now.

"For your information, young lady, just because a person has a little common sense does not mean he's negative. Your mother has always considered common sense to be one of the seven deadly sins. If it was up to your mo—" He broke off as the cheerful waitress appeared and asked us if we wanted anything else. "We're fine," he answered brusquely, not sounding at all fine.

"We wish we were going with *you*," I said as the waitress was walking away, before he could start up again. "Don't we, Johanna?" I kicked her under the table again. "It would be so much more fun."

She nodded, catching on. "She drives so slow and you know how she always gets lost."

"No sense of direction," our father agreed.

"And you know how she is in restaurants," I said. "The waitress has to come back about a million times because she can never make up her mind."

"And then she always wants to eat off everyone else's plate anyway." Johanna reached over and swiped a fried wonton off my plate by way of illustration. "And then she drinks all that iced tea and has to go to the restroom about every five miles."

"World's smallest bladder." Our father was nodding, half smiling, starting to forget he was mad at us.

For a moment, I felt a twinge of guilt as we continued to assassinate our mother's character, but I knew she would understand and, what's more, approve. "Remember, the key to your father," she had said just as his car pulled up out in front of our house, "is that he likes to think he's smarter than me." Then she'd laughed, as if this were the funniest thing she'd heard in ages.

"So, how *is* your mother anyway?" our father asked, momentarily mollified, taking a casual sip of his beer.

Johanna and I shrugged and looked down at our plates. It seemed that our father was much more interested in our mother since "the separation," as they called it, than he ever was before. Before the separation, he never seemed to pay any attention when she talked. He never asked about her day. But now suddenly he was all ears.

"Forget I asked," he said, signaling the waitress for the check.

The night before the concert, Sharon slept over at our house so that we could get an early start in the morning. Normally the moment Sharon stepped through the front door, Johanna would whisk her upstairs to our room and lock me out. The two of them would spend hours up there whispering and giggling, ignoring my mother and me, walking by us as if we didn't exist on their way to the kitchen for Cokes

235

and Fritos. But the night before the Beatles concert, the four of us sat around the table on the back porch chatting like four best friends, our age differences magically leveled by the general spirit of anticipation. In the soft summer twilight our mother looked prettier and more girlish, like the girl in the old snapshots of herself from the time before she'd married our father. In those snapshots she was always in a crowd of girlfriends, all dressed up, smiling expectantly.

It was late, past our bedtime, and our mother was talking about how during the war she had worked as a nurse in the WAVES, and Sharon, who wanted to be a doctor, was asking a lot of questions and listening intently, as if our mother were the most fascinating woman on earth. I yawned. I was tired and ready for bed, but it was a point of honor not to go to bed until I was ordered to do so. Johanna, bored and peeved, was pelting me with Jiffy Pop kernels. No matter what you did, there were always a whole bunch of kernels left unpopped in the bottom of the flimsy tin pan.

"Come on," Johanna said pointedly, "let's go watch Johnny Carson. Coming?" she asked Sharon, who nodded vaguely and said she'd be there in a minute. My sister and I stomped off to the den and turned on the TV.

"Sharon's just grateful because Mom convinced Mrs. Dinsmore to let her go," Johanna said to me, as if feeling some necessity to account for her best friend's sudden perverse interest in our mother. "Her mother wasn't going to let her go because John Lennon said the Beatles were more popular than Jesus Christ. But Mom called her up and said John had apologized at a public press conference and all, so finally Mrs. Dinsmore said it was okay." Johanna turned up the volume on the TV. Johnny was talking with Zsa Zsa Gabor.

Our mother and Sharon appeared in the doorway. "I'm going to bed," our mother said. "And you girls should be hitting the hay, too."

"As soon as this part's over," Johanna said, not looking up.

"Well, good night. See you bright and early." Our mother turned and walked upstairs. Johanna and I shot each other surprised, suspicious looks. She *always* made us go to bed first. Sharon wriggled in between the two of us on her stomach. "Your Mom's really neat," she said.

"Shhh," Johanna glared at her. "I want to hear this." It was a commercial for Alka-Seltzer. Sharon gave her a weird look. Johanna reached up and snapped off the TV. "Let's go to bed."

"God," Johanna sighed and slapped down her discard, "I really don't believe this."

The three of us were sitting at a little round table in our hotel room at the Holiday Inn playing hearts. Outside it was pouring rain—not your gentle summer shower but a torrential downpour. When we checked into the hotel, the desk clerk had greeted us with the tragic news bulletin: The Beatles' Saturday-evening concert had been canceled due to rain and rescheduled for noon on Sunday.

"It's a stupid idea to hold a concert outside anyway," Johanna muttered. "What do they think this is—California?"

Sharon pulled back the drape and stared out into the flooded parking lot. "Maybe God's showing them who's boss. You know, after what John said about how they're more popular than Jesus Christ and all."

"That's ridiculous," Johanna snapped. "Why would He pick Cincinnati? I mean they've just been in Chicago, for chrissakes. You think God would pick a more important city if He were trying to make a point. Anyway, John apologized in front of the whole world, on TV and everything."

Our mother was lying on the bed nearest the door with a washcloth draped over her forehead. At dinner in the coffee shop, she had taken two Bufferin for her headache. Johanna

237

was mad because she'd wanted to go to a movie and our mother had refused to drive around a strange city in the pouring rain. She was acting as if somehow our mother were to blame for the concert being canceled.

"I'm bored with this game," Johanna tossed her cards onto the table and turned the TV on full blast. She flipped through all the channels twice and finally settled on a Western with a lot of loud shouting and shooting.

Our mother propped herself up on one elbow and lifted the edge of her washcloth blindfold in order to glare at Johanna, who ignored her. I could tell she was debating whether to ask Johanna to turn the volume down. After a second she just sighed and got up and slipped her dress back on over her black slip. Without even looking in the mirror, she ran a brush through her hair, slapped on some lipstick, and said she was going down to the lounge for a while. She emptied all the coins out of her wallet. "For the vending machines," she said, "in case you girls get thirsty."

As soon as our mother had shut the door behind her, Johanna leapt up and rummaged around on the dresser top.

"What are you looking for?" I asked.

"Car keys."

Sharon and I looked at each other apprehensively. Johanna had just gotten her driver's license the previous month after flunking the driving part the first time out.

"Damn." Johanna threw herself back onto the bed by the window. "They must be in her purse. Figures."

Sharon and I breathed a long sigh of relief.

"This movie is boring." Johanna snapped off the TV. She looked at her watch and sighed. "What a drag. Right now if it weren't for this crappy rain we'd be listening to 'Norwegian Wood.'" She banged her head against the pillow a few times in frustration.

"We're going to see them tomorrow," I said. "If you saw

them tonight, it would all be over with tomorrow. This way you have something to look forward to."

Johanna shot me a withering, scornful look. Sharon was busy searching her long dark hair for split ends. My mother's lipstick had rolled off the dresser onto the carpet next to my chair. I picked it up and drew a little dash on the top of my hand like I'd seen my mother do in the drugstore. Then I held my hand up to the light to see how this particular shade, Primrose, complemented my skin tone.

"Hey, I've got an idea," Johanna said. "Let's do makeovers, like in the magazines." She leapt up and dumped the contents of our mother's daisy-covered cosmetic case onto the bed. Most of the makeup looked new and shiny, purchased since the separation.

"You first," Johanna said to me.

I sat down in the swivel chair and Johanna draped a white towel around my neck. Then she yanked all my hair into a ponytail and skewered it to the back of my head with a couple of sharp bobby pins. "Ouch! Be careful," I protested.

"This is Sharon of New York City," Johanna said haughtily, ignoring my outburst. "And I am Johanna of Paris." She tilted my head this way and that, squinting at me in the bright lamp light. Finally she shook her head and sighed theatrically. "Have you ever considered plastic surgery?"

"Cut it out," Sharon said, elbowing Johanna aside and kneeling in front of me with the mascara wand. "Just close your eyes," she said soothingly, "and think of something nice." I thought of the DiBernard girls running through the sprinkler in our old pink bathing suits.

"I wonder what the Beatles are doing right now," Johanna said as she dabbed the powder puff over my face. The feathery little pats felt good. "I mean, really, what's there to do in Cincinnati, for chrissakes?" She sounded just like some jaded jet-setter, even though Cincinnati was the biggest city we'd ever been in outside of one trip to Chicago.

"I bet John and Cynthia are drinking champagne and doing It in a sunken bathtub," Sharon said.

"Doing what?" I said, opening my eyes.

Johanna and Sharon laughed.

"God, I'm making a real mess." Sharon spit on a Kleenex and rubbed underneath my eyes. "She looks like a raccoon."

"She's supposed to keep her eyes *open* when you do that." Johanna opened her eyes really wide and pantomimed applying mascara. She looked like an old silent film star pretending to be scared out of her wits.

Sharon tossed the blackened Kleenex onto the bed and took a step backward to assess the damage. "Look. She looks like your mother."

"Wow," Johanna nodded. "That's really weird."

I turned my head and stared at myself in the mirror on the wall opposite me and immediately turned my head away again. I had the sense that I was looking into the future, that some future me was staring back at me.

We were sound asleep when the key fumbled in the lock and a slice of bright light from the hallway slashed the dark room as my mother slipped inside and hurriedly rebolted the door. I was going to ask her what time it was, but before I could whisper anything, she tiptoed into the bathroom and shut the door. The water faucet blasted on and then I heard another sound that took me a minute to identify—the sound of my mother crying. I felt scared suddenly all alone in the queen-size bed and rolled over to see if Johanna or Sharon were awake. They were both breathing deeply and evenly in perfect unison. My mother's sobs were punctuated by low moans that scared me worse than the crying. Maybe she was sick. Appendicitis or something. I could hear her thrashing around in the tub. Maybe she was drowning.

"Johanna," I whispered into the dark space between the beds. "Wake up, Johanna."

Nothing. I climbed out of my bed and walked over to the other bed and shook my sister's shoulder.

"What?" she mumbled groggily. "What is it?" She opened her eyes and saw me standing over her. "What's your problem? What time is it, for chrissakes?"

"It's Mom," I said. "Listen."

Johanna heaved a sigh and sat up in bed. Silence except for the gentle splashing of water in the tub. She snapped on the light and squinted up at me, annoyed. "So?"

"What's the matter?" Sharon mumbled, flinging an arm over her eyes to block out the light.

Before I could say anything, defend myself, there was a loud knock on the door. In the bathroom, our mother had turned the water faucet on full blast again.

"See who's at the door," Johanna commanded.

I walked over to the door and said, "Who's there?" Our mother had repeatedly warned us never to open the door until we knew who it was.

"I have something you left," a deep male voice answered.

I hesitated and looked back at Johanna.

"Come on, Alice," he said. "I'm not such a bad guy. What did you expect?"

Alice was our mother's name. Johanna shrugged. I slid back the chain lock and opened the door a couple of inches. He was crouching down, setting a paper sack on the floor by the door. There was a little bald spot the size of a Necco wafer that glinted in the light. He started when he saw me.

"Oh," he said, running his hand through his hair. "I thought you were her. I didn't realize." When he stood up, he was tall and handsome like our father, but I didn't like him. "What's your name?" he said.

"Suzanne." I bent down and picked up the paper sack.

He was barefoot and his toenails were clear and smooth, unlike our father's, which were thick and yellow from some kind of fungus he'd picked up in the army.

As I was straightening up, he cupped a hand under my chin and frowned down into my face. "You look like her. Anybody ever tell you that?"

I shook my head.

He bent over and moved his face close to mine. His breath smelled of liquor. "Promise me something, Susie Q."

I hugged the paper sack tighter to my chest. I was staring down at his bare toes, but I felt him pulling my eyes up into his until I was looking right at him. I thought maybe he was going to kiss me. I thought maybe I even wanted him to. Something about his eyes. "What?" I said.

"Don't grow up to be a cockteaser like your mother." He winked at me, then let go of my chin, and sauntered unsteadily down the bright hall.

I slammed the door shut and looked at Johanna and Sharon, who were sitting bold upright in bed, staring at me as if they'd been electrocuted. No one said anything for a minute. We listened to the soft splashing in the bathroom.

"Give me the sack," Sharon said suddenly, breaking the spell.

I handed it over and she opened it.

"What is it?" Johanna said as if she didn't really want to know.

Sharon pulled out a black slip. Johanna and I looked at each other. Our mother's slip.

"Jesus," Johanna mumbled. "I don't believe it."

I was standing there trying to figure out how a strange man could have got hold of our mother's slip when something in my sister's expression told me not to think about it too hard. Then Johanna yanked the slip out of Sharon's hands and tried to rip it in half.

"Don't!" Sharon tugged the slip away from her and

shoved it back into the paper bag and slid the bag in between the mattress and the box spring, then threw herself back on top of the bed. "Now here's the deal," she said. "We never saw it. Nothing happened. We've been sound asleep the whole time." She leaned across Johanna and snapped off the lamp. "Okay?"

Johanna and I nodded silently in the sudden darkness. Then the three of us lay there wide awake, hearts pounding, pretending to sleep, until, a few moments later, we heard the bathwater draining away in loud gurgling gasps, the bathroom door stealthily opening and shutting, and my mother—smelling sweet and fresh, like soap and talcum—tiptoeing gingerly across the carpet and easing herself gently into bed, careful not to disturb us.

The next day the weather cleared up. We had breakfast in the hotel coffee shop, my sister silently glowering, my mother nursing a hangover. "What's with your sister?" my mother asked me when Johanna stalked back to our room to pack. I stared down at my waffle until Sharon kicked me under the table, and then I mumbled something about Johanna just being disappointed that the concert was postponed. My mother sighed and said something about my sister having a lot to learn about life. "There's not much in this world that doesn't disappoint you sooner or later," she said. Then she forced a little smile and said, "Listen to me. I sound like your father. Gloomy Gus. We're on vacation. Let's have fun."

Sharon swallowed a bite of French toast and said, "I'm having fun."

"Me, too," I lied.

My mother kept darting nervous glances at the doorway, as if afraid that any moment the strange man from last night would walk in. I thought about the black slip hidden underneath the mattress and wondered what the maid would think when she found it. Suddenly my mother excused herself and walked over to the cigarette machine and returned with a pack of Lucky Strikes. She had quit smoking—a major big deal—about three years earlier, but I didn't say anything. Her fingers fumbled as she unwrapped the pack, and her eyes slid away from mine, guiltily, as she lit a cigarette and exhaled. After a few minutes of desultory conversation, mostly initiated by Sharon, my mother looked at her watch and said we might as well get an early start, since there would be a lot of traffic. We nodded agreeably. She stubbed out her cigarette.

It was as if my sister never made the long trip home with us. As if that afternoon of the Beatles concert she vanished into some other dimension. Within a matter of days after our return from Cincinnati, Johanna got herself a job working afternoons and weekends at World Records, which was located in the mall within walking distance of our father's apartment complex, on the other side of town, and casually announced one night at dinner that she had decided that it would be more convenient if she lived with our father from now on. Our mother set down her glass of iced tea and said, "Over my dead body. You belong here, with your sister and me." My sister got up and left the dinner table without finishing her dinner. My mother sighed and looked across the table at me. "Don't worry," she said. "Your sister's not going anywhere."

That weekend she was gone. Moved out. My mother and I came back from the grocery store and found Johanna's side of the room stripped bare. Lying on the center of the bed, neatly made for a change, was a crumpled paper sack, which I recognized right away even though it looked pretty much like any other paper sack. I was about to snatch it up and hide it somewhere when my mother walked up behind me and said, "What's this?"

I didn't watch her face as she opened the bag. I busied myself pulling my sweater off over my head. All I heard was a quick intake of breath. My mother was sitting on the edge of the bed staring at the black slip as if it were a snake.

"What's that?" I said, heart pounding, trying to sound a little bored, impatient, innocent.

My mother gave me a long complicated look and then shrugged. "Ask your sister," she said, as if it were no concern of hers.

It was the night before school started, a couple of days after Labor Day. My mother, Sharon, and I were eating Eskimo Pies on the back porch. At dusk it was still sweltering. Vanilla ice cream streamed down my wrist and my tongue worked double time. A large pizza box gaped open on the table. My mother flicked a fly away from the one remaining slice of congealed pizza. After Johanna defected to my father's apartment, my mother had seemed to lose interest in the four basic food groups and we quickly drifted back into our old diet.

After I'd polished off my Eskimo Pie, I picked up the lukewarm slice of pizza and nibbled at the stringy cheese. Sharon and my mother were looking at college catalogs that Sharon had brought over. My sister and Sharon would both be going away to college the following year.

"I want to go to Berkeley," Sharon sighed, "but you know my mother. Not to mention my father."

My mother nodded and blew out a smoke ring. Ever since Cincinnati my mother had been smoking like a house afire. "Maybe you could get a scholarship. Or loans."

I had told Sharon all about how Johanna had left the slip on the bed and how my mother had found it. Sharon had called Johanna and they'd had a big fight. Since the blowup, Sharon had started spending less and less time with Johanna and more and more time at our house, just hanging out with my mother and me. It was as if Johanna had left this vacancy and Sharon had decided to fill it.

It was Saturday night and I was sitting in front of the TV alone at my father's apartment. After dinner, Johanna had taken off to the record store, which stayed open until 10 P.M. even on Saturdays, and my father had gone off to some party at his new girlfriend's place. She was a widow with a three-year-old son named Stowe, which my mother, Sharon, and I all agreed was a stupid-sounding name. He said he wouldn't stay long and asked me if I minded being left alone for a couple of hours. I said no. He rumpled my hair and promised to buy me the new sneakers I'd mentioned I wanted. I really didn't mind his going. It all felt weird now anyway, ever since Johanna had permanently installed herself at my father's. It wasn't at all the way it used to be when the two of us visited him. My sister treated me like a not-so-welcome guest. She acted like my mother— or not *my* mother but *a* mother. She had taken to doing the grocery shopping and cooking for my father. Instead of going to China Palace, we had to eat what she cooked. Revolting recipes she got out of vegetarian health-food cookbooks. Things with brown rice and tofu. She was dating some guy named Josh from the record store who played folk guitar, and now suddenly the Beatles were history. Instead she listened to Bob Dylan, Joan Baez, Judy Collins. My father had finally bought himself a new stereo, and when she wasn't working, my sister sat cross-legged on the living-room floor next to the stereo, strumming the fancy new guitar that my father had bought for her, trying to pick out the chords to "Subterranean Homesick Blues."

The following Friday I called my father and gave him some excuse about why I couldn't come stay at his place that weekend. I had a big report due in social studies, I said, and I needed to use the *Encyclopedia Britannica,* which was at our house. I expected him to argue, but he didn't. He just said, "Okay. See you next weekend," and that was that. The next night my mother, Sharon, and I went to Mona Lisa's for dinner to celebrate my mother's new job as a receptionist at an OB-GYN clinic. We ate spaghetti with clam sauce and my mother poured red wine in Sharon's and my empty water glasses. After dinner, we drove over to the mall to see a movie. In the dark my mother unwrapped a giant-size Nestlé Crunch bar and passed big squares to Sharon and me. I broke off little pieces and held each one in my mouth until all the chocolate melted and then I ate the Rice Krispies part. When the movie was over, we walked out of the dark theater, blinking in the bright lights of the lobby, and practically bumped right into my father and Johanna waiting in line for the nine-o'clock show. We all paused for an awkward moment in which nobody seemed to be able to think of anything to say. I felt a silly smile fade from my face. The look on my sister's face was hard to read. I wanted to say something. We were standing on either side of a thick blue velvet rope. My father was holding a large tub of popcorn in one hand and a Coke in the other, and I had the feeling that maybe if his hands had been free he would have done something, but as it was, all he could do was stand there. Then the lines started to move, rumbling and impatient, like two trains headed in opposite directions, passing in the night. My mother stood there for a moment, looking back at them, then she said, "The thing you have to remember about your sister is that essentially she's a lot like your father."

"She likes to think she's smarter than I am," I said, "but she's not."

"Are you sure?" My mother stopped and cupped my chin in her fingers and looked right at me.

"Positive," I lied.

When we pulled into the driveway, the DiBernard girls

were chasing each other on their front lawn in some baby-doll pajamas printed with butterflies that I recognized as having belonged to my sister and me. I walked over to them and said, "Those pajamas used to be my sister's and mine."

The little girls stopped running around and flopped down on the grass, looking up at me expectantly, as if they were waiting for me to tell them something really important. But I couldn't think of anything else to say to them—they looked so young and trusting—so I just cut across the lawn in a big hurry, as if I had suddenly heard the phone ringing or my mother calling my name.

Marly Swick

MARLY SWICK "grew up all over," she says, naming Massachusetts, Delaware, and California as former homes. Her degrees, three of them, are from Stanford (B.A.), the University of Iowa (M.F.A.), and the American University (Ph.D.). Since 1989, she has taught fiction writing at the University of Nebraska, known for having one of the top-rated creative-writing programs in the United States. An author of a collection by the same title as "The Summer Before the Summer of Love," she has the novel Paper Wings plus one other collection, A Hole in the Language, to her name.

I inquired after her views on the siblings of divorce, asking in particular if she believed that divorce must always change the relationship between sisters, or how they identify themselves as siblings.

"I do have a sister," she says, "six years younger than I, who is my only sibling, but my parents never divorced, so the effects of the divorce in my story are really just what I imagine would happen in that particular family."

Swick does add, however, "I don't think there is any one pattern [for relationships]. It depends on the dynamics of the individual family and the circumstances surrounding the divorce. In Suzanne's case, she and her mother are the ones left behind."

Swick's admirers can look forward to a new novel from her in 1999.

—C. O.

Playback

Ann Beattie

One of the most romantic evenings I ever spent was last week, with Holly curled in my lap, her knees to the side, resting against the sloping arm of the wicker rocking chair. It would have cut into her skin if I hadn't tucked my hand under her bony knees. Her satin nightgown came to midcalf when she stood but didn't cover her knees when she curled into my lap. In the breeze, tiny curls blew against my cheek, where it rested on top of her head. Ash used to say that her fine, long hair reminded him of the way ribbon curled when you held it stretched lightly across your thumb and ran a pair of scissors along the top. The nightgown had been a present from Ash: tiny pink flowers scattered here and there among the narrow pleats, a nightgown from the 1930s. He had bought it at her favorite store, Red Dog, where he had bought her the mysterious homemade rug with a chorus line of squirrels, eating what looked like shrimp. He had also gotten her a satin jacket with *Angelo* written across the back. He cut off the *o* and had a friend add embroidered wings. On cool nights, she'd wear it over the old-fashioned nightgown.

The night I held her on my lap, Ash had called from a pay phone in a bar in Tennessee to say that the rattlesnake killed in his friend Michael's garden was so big that the skin had stretched to cover Michael's fiddle case. Those were the kind of stories she wanted to hear: stories that justified her not going to Tennessee. She had a baby, Peter, who lived with her ex-husband in Boston, and a psychiatrist in Vermont: she did not want to interrupt her therapy. She had a pottery business, with her friends Andrea and Percy Green and Roger Billington, that was just starting to make a little money, and summer was the best time for selling it in the shop they had set up in Percy Green's big garage. I was visiting her for a month and a half. She knew I loved Vermont and thought I wouldn't go as far as Tennessee to visit. I think I would have. I think I would have done almost anything for her. I offered her my savings to fight her fat, villainous lawyer husband for Peter; in the winter, I drove to Vermont four weeks running to sit through group-therapy sessions, because everyone was supposed to bring someone from the family, and she had no family but her brother, in Nebraska, and an aunt in an old-age home.

I'm not the kind of woman who greets other women with little bird pecks on the cheek, and unlike Holly, I'm not used to embracing people; but when she came out to the porch, so sad from hearing Ash's voice, and shook her head and kissed me good night on the forehead, I put out my arms and she climbed into my lap. "He didn't talk long," she said. "He said he wrote me a letter that I haven't gotten yet." We must have rocked for hours, before the static on the kitchen radio got too much to put up with. Then some sort of embarrassment caught up with her: when she came back to the porch she was smiling an embarrassed smile. The angel jacket was zipped over her nightgown, and she said quietly: "Thanks, Jane. Now I can go to sleep." The lacy angel wings disappeared into the kitchen. I heard her turn on the water and knew she was doing what I'd hoped my rocking would soothe her out of, taking the nightly combination that I was convinced was deadly: two vitamin B$_6$ pills, and half a pill each of Dalmane and Valium, taken one at a time, because in spite of all the medicine she had taken in her life, she still believed that she would choke to death when swallowing a pill. One thing we all liked about Ash was that he tried to talk her out of them. He tried to get her to take a long, tiring walk with him, or to smoke a joint. He'd pull her to the old carrousel mirror in the kitchen and make her look at her guilty expression as she swallowed the pills. Lamely, she told him that two vitamin B$_6$'s couldn't hurt. Some nights he'd reason with her so that she only took half a Valium. If he ever rocked her on his lap, I don't know about it.

People often mistake us for sisters. It didn't happen at Smith, where people had watched us make friends, but later, when we went into New York to shop or to take dance classes. We were both lonely and self-sufficient—I was an only child, and her parents died when she was ten—and once we got over our jealousy because people were always comparing our looks, we realized that we were soul mates. I curled my hair to look like hers; she began to wear long, floating skirts like mine. When she got married I made the bouquet, and she threw it to me. The morning of the wedding I had wrapped thick satin ribbon around the layers of foil that held the stems together, knowing that she was marrying the wrong person, but for once too reticent to say what I thought. Fixing the flowers, I thought of the custom of binding women's feet in China: having any part of this was wrong.

She stayed married for nine years, all through her husband's time in the army and in law school, years of living in a fourth-floor walk-up in New Haven, above a restaurant. They had a big, rusty car that she was always sanding and painting. She said nothing about the dreary apartment but that the fan of stained glass above the front door was beautiful. When he became a lawyer, the house in the suburbs they moved to wasn't her taste, either, but she planted nicotiana plants that bloom at night—the most wonderful-smelling flowers I have ever known.

Peter was a breech birth, delivered, finally, by Cesarean. I sat in the waiting room with her husband, thinking: things aren't working out, and they won't even let us hear her crying. I had been spending a weekend in the country with my lover when Holly called to say she was going to the hospital. It was almost a month early—they were visiting friends in New York. I remember sitting in the waiting room, smelling of turpentine. Jason, the man I was in love with, had taken me to his house in East Hampton. A few hours before Holly called, I had been asleep in the sun, at the end of his dock, and because he thought it would be funny, because he couldn't resist, he had dipped into the bucket of gray paint—he was painting the dock—and stroked the wide brush full of cold, smooth paint over both knees as I slept. It didn't wash off in the water, and I had to use turpentine, wiping it again and again across my knees with his wife's torn blouse, more amused than I let on that he had done it, wondering how I could love a man who had a wife whose discarded blouses were from Saks. When the phone rang, a few hours before we were going to drive back to the city, Holly said: "I'm going to Lenox Hill. I'm saving myself some time." Then all at once Jason was dabbing at my knees with turpentine, telling me that I did too have time to dive off the dock, that it didn't matter if my hair was wet, that if I swam, I wouldn't have to shower. "Take it easy," he said. "You're not having the baby." No—time would pass, and then I wouldn't even have Jason. He'd reconcile with his wife, and her mysterious arthritis would disappear, and she'd be back playing the violin. But that day it seemed impossible. It was easy enough to sleep in the sun when back in the city I didn't even sleep late at night, in my dark apartment. Jason had been enough in love to pull pranks. In his house, I pulled on my jeans, no underwear underneath, borrowed a T-shirt from him, and rushed out of the house, never suspecting that it was one of the last times I'd ever see it. The very last time would be in winter, when I sat in the car and he went in to see that a pipe that had frozen had been repaired correctly. He was going back to his wife. I didn't want to see the presents I'd given him that were still inside: the moose cookie jar, the poster of a brigade of roaches: "*Con más poder de atrapar para matar bien muertas las cucarachas fuertes.*" Percy Green's drawing of a foot with a hugely elongated big toe, captioned "Stretching the Mind."

The day Holly went into labor, we had taken a fast ride back to the city, the top down on his big, white Ford, wet hair flapping against my head like dog's ears. No: I wasn't having this baby. The next spring, I would have an abortion. I would go to a restaurant with a surreally beautiful garden, and Jason would sit next to me, under the umbrella, before I went to the hospital. Pink flowers would fall into our hair, our laps, our food. I couldn't eat anything. I couldn't even tell him why. I dropped raw shrimp under the table, praying for the cat that didn't exist. Sipped a mimosa and spit the liquor back into the glass. My hand on top of his, his other hand sliding up my leg, under the big napkin—a ghastly foreshadowing of the white sheet they'd spread across me an hour later. "Eat," Jason said. "You have to eat something." Smiling. Touching. Hiding my food like a child, letting the pink flowers cover what they could.

Later that year, when Holly left her husband and moved to Vermont, she said to me: "Men are never going to be our salvation." We both believed it, enough to prick fingers and touch blood bubble to blood bubble, but of course children did that, not adults, and it was something men did, anyway. Then Holly met Ash, and for a while she was happy. It didn't last, though. I knew that there was trouble the day I went with Ash to pick berries from the scraggly blackberry bushes that grew around the crumbling foundation of what was once an old mansion. He was dropping them in his khaki cap, not caring that it would be stained forever.

"Why is Holly pulling away from me?" he said.

"Because of Peter," I told him. "Because her husband's going to win, and she knows she's losing Peter."

"Holly and I could have a baby. She sees him. Her ex-husband isn't trying to turn Peter against her, is he? I never noticed that."

"Ash," I said. "She doesn't have Peter."

He stopped picking berries. "You know what the two of you do? You condescend to me when you talk. I understand facts. Did it ever occur to either of you that there are other facts besides your facts?"

The sun was beating down on the berries, on his sad face, the stained fingers—it looked as though he had been involved in something violent, when all he had been doing was carefully picking berries. The violence was all inside his head. He was going to Tennessee, to give her time to think. Time to think about whether she could concentrate on him again, spend less time brooding about Peter, have another baby—the baby he wanted. He was staring down, dejected. A black ant ran through the berries. Many ants. He tried to flick them out, but they were quick and went to the bottom. "It's so beautiful here in the summer, and she sits in the house—"

"Ash," I said to him. "What really matters to her is having Peter."

I always wondered if what I said made him decide for sure to go to Tennessee.

Her brother, Todd, came for the last two weeks in August. He had always been suspicious of the men his sister loved, and he was suspicious of Ash. "He's one of those smiling Southern boys you outgrow. They wear the same belts all their lives," he said. But he loved Holly, and he tried to give impartial advice.

"I know it's sick," Holly said to Todd, rocking with him on the back porch, "but our father's dead and I've made you into the permission giver, and I guess what I'm hoping is that you'll tell me to go to Tennessee."

"You wouldn't leave Peter if I told you to."

"What if I made a success of myself, and I could fly back to Boston all the time?"

"It's not what you want to hear," he said, "but I remember when he was just learning to walk, and somebody took a picture of him with a flash, and he turned to you and he was blind. He was blind the way people get snowblind. I remember how the two of you felt your way toward each other—how you were both just arms and legs. You're his mother."

"And I go to a shrink in Montpelier and everybody thinks I'm very fragile, don't they?"

"Ash sat with me on this porch and told me he wanted at least three children. Kids aren't going to distract you from Peter. They're just going to remind you of him. Don't you remember when Georgia exploded that flashcube in his face and he turned around from the birthday cake like it had been a land mine? Vietnam. Fucking Vietnam."

He went into the house for iced tea, which he brought back to us on a heavy silver tray, one of those family heirlooms you can't imagine owning but can't imagine getting rid of. While he was gone, I said to Holly: "It's twelve years later, and almost every day, he gets the war into the conversation. He went to Nebraska to keep punishing himself."

When we finished drinking our tea, Todd and I decided to go swimming. Holly was a little angry at Todd, and she stayed behind to throw pots with Percy Green. Percy Green was stoned, so he didn't realize what he'd walked in on. "I pick up on something," he said. "That marvelous creative energy." He was wearing a Hawaiian shirt with men in gondolas rowing across his chest. His chest was large and well developed from lifting weights. His legs—and he was all leg, under the white shorts—were solid as trees. The only loose-ness in him anywhere was in his speech—a slight slur from being stoned. The necklace of tiny shells he had gotten in the Philippines, back in the days when he was a black belt in karate who repaired cameras for a living, dangled like a noose under one of the gondoliers' heads. He and Holly had been lovers once for a couple of weeks.

That afternoon Todd and I floated far from shore in the state park, in a rented rowboat. "She had a breech birth and a Cesarean and she's seeing a shrink twice a week and she still has a problem with drugs," he said. "Permission. Is she kidding? What could I stop her from doing, anyway?" The boat bobbled over a ripple of water. "Permission," he said. "Has she ever heard of the women's movement?"

When our boat drifted near the shoreline, I saw a tree branch curving into the lake—the split branch of a dogwood among pointed firs. Looking down into the water, I was sure that I could follow the slant of the shadow to the bottom, but I had dived into this water—I had mistaken eighteen or twenty feet for only six. The breeze was blowing, making the surface of the water ripple like patterns of lace.

"If she really needs my help," Todd said, "I could give her some advice on marketing pottery. When our aunt dies, she'll come into some inheritance money. I've been looking into debentures," he said.

Before I left for Vermont, I bought an answering machine. My friend Linda goes over to the apartment every four or five days to water the plants and listen to the tape, to see if there are any important messages. Last week she called and said that there was one she ought to play for me. She put the machine on playback and held the telephone to the microphone. It was Jason, the first message in so many months that I'd lost count: "Hello, machine. This is the voice you wanted to hear. It's calling to ask if you want to meet me for dinner. Or lunch. Or breakfast. I'm backing up, as you can tell. Doesn't this thing ever run out of tape? It's eleven o'clock Sunday morning, and I'm at the Empire Diner." A pause. Quietly: "I miss you."

"The aloe has white flies," Linda said. "I've never known an aloe to get white flies. I sprayed it with the thing from the kitchen sink, and when I go back next week, I'll zap it with bug spray."

On Monday, after Linda called, I walked down the driveway to shovel some of the gravel that had been delivered into the potholes that had deepened over the winter. I got the shovel from where it leaned against the tree, flicked caterpillars off the handle, and started digging into the pile of gravel, thinking that I shouldn't call Jason back. He didn't say he was leaving her. If I did something physical, I might not think about it. The mailman came, and I took the pile of letters. And there it was, on top: the letter from Ash, the one we all knew he'd write. Ash, with no phone, in Tennessee. Ash without Holly.

I walked to the high hedge of purple lantana—as impossible that lantana would thrive in Vermont as that an aloe would get white flies—and did one of the most awful things I've ever done. I read the letter. I slit the envelope carefully, with the long nail of my index finger, so I could patch it together and feign ignorance when Holly saw that the envelope was ripped. I was thinking of a lie before I even read it. I'd say that there might have been money in it (why would Ash send money?) and someone at the post office held it to the light and . . . No: I'd just put all the mail in the mailbox and let her get it, and look blank. The same expression I got on my face when Jason talked about himself and his wife doing the things of ordinary life. Jason had gone to get the Sunday paper. Hundreds of miles away, he had eaten French toast—that was what he always ordered at the Empire. I could hear the piano playing, see our reflections in the shiny black tabletops that gave us fun-house-mirror faces. A chic, funny place, no place Holly would ever sit with Ash. What he was asking her to do, in the letter, was to be with him. "They're probably poisoning you against me," he wrote, "but they don't know everything. They're in the country with you, but they're city people. They're the kind who cut before they're even sure the bite was from a snake. They'll try to soothe your wounds, but in the end they'll get you. I know that there isn't much for you here, but if you could come down for just a little while, the distance from that incestuous world might do you good. I don't think children are interchangeable, but there's time in life for more than one thing. I've just read a book—here's something your sophisticated friends would like—I was reading a book and I found out that because of the way space curves, there are stars that everybody thinks of as twin stars, but they're really the same one. Are you sure that I'm the naïve country boy Jane and your brother want you to think I am? Come down here, just for a week, and stand at the back door with me when the breeze is blowing and my arm is around you and look up at the sky. Then say yes or no."

A cardinal was in the road. A brightly colored, male cardinal. It stood there like a vulture—a vulture ready to feed on an animal that had been killed. But nothing was dead. The bird was small for a cardinal. No more a real omen than the little piece of paper you pull out of your fortune cookie that misspells something you should believe.

"Ash," I whispered. "How could you?"

I put all the mail in the mailbox but his letter. I ripped that to pieces as I crossed the road. The cardinal flew away. The bee that had been buzzing around me disappeared. The letter was ripped into pieces as tiny as confetti by the time I dropped them in the mud, by the stream, looking behind me for tiny white pieces I might have dropped, as guilty as a murderer whose knife drips blood. He didn't deserve her. He really didn't. That was no illusion; it was a dirty trick that if space curved, you thought that one star was two.

Todd's MG bumped slowly into the driveway. He held up something round and shiny. "Got this at a lawn sale," he said. "Can you believe it? Paella for a hundred, or we could take a bath in it. You know that Degas painting? The woman in the tub?"

I went in and poured some vodka over ice. I sat on the porch, shaking the glass. On the lawn, Todd was cleaning the gigantic pan with steel wool, washing away the dirt with a strong spray from the hose. I remembered making love to Jason at the end of the dock. Diving into the water. The long white hose that stretched from the back of the house to where the boat bobbed in the water—the East Hampton equivalent of the snake in the garden.

Simple, fortune-cookie fact: someone loved Holly more than anyone had ever loved me. Linda called again, four days later, and there was no second message from Jason. I hadn't really expected one.

Linda had sprayed the plant. The plant was sure to recover. She said she took it out of the sun for a few days, because the combination of light and chemicals might be too much.

Holly and I were mistaken for sisters, but she was more beautiful. Our long blond hair. Slender bodies. The way, in the city, people would smile at us with the same lack of embarrassment people have when they smile at twins. Oddities. Beautiful exceptions.

When I found out that I was pregnant, I had thought first about amniocentesis, because a first cousin had had a baby with a slight birth defect. My first impulse was to protect that baby in any way I could. At the end, I had just thought about what it would feel like to have my cervix

pricked, the baby sucked out. That crazy romantic lunch—
pink petals all over our laps, on the table—and I couldn't
tell him. I had on a wrap-around skirt, and he slid his chair
close to mine and was teasing, putting his hand underneath
it, and I said to him, "I *am* eating, Jason," and "I love you—I
can't eat." He wanted to go to my apartment. "I have an
appointment," I said. "Tonight," he said. "I can't tonight," I
said. "Another night. Some other night." He thought I was
kidding. When he called, hours later, expecting me to come
over, I was lying in my bed, after the abortion, Linda sitting
in a chair reading, watching, and I was trying not to sound
woozy, in spite of the fact that they'd given me so many pills
Linda almost had to carry me from the building to the cab. I
had done it because I didn't have the nerve to test him—to
find out if he loved me more than he loved his wife. Ash
loved Holly, and that went a long way toward explaining
why we looked so much alike, yet she was more beautiful.
She walked like somebody who was loved. She didn't avoid
looking into people's eyes for the same reason I did when she
walked through the city. I thought how lucky she was—even
though sometimes she could be frighteningly unhappy—the
night I held her and rocked her in my lap. I knew for sure
that I was right about her good luck a week later, when I
stood at the window, about to pull the shades in my room to
take a nap, and I looked out and saw Ash's old car, parked at
the end of the treacherous driveway, and Ash, running
toward the house, a huge torch of red gladiolas raised above
his head.

Ann Beattie

"MY CHARACTERS," Ann Beattie *wrote in an essay for the* Mississippi Review *in 1996, "who surprise and enlighten and dismay me so often, come from familiar worlds with unfamiliar subtexts. . . . Inventing characters is for me no different from inventing any day. The best days, though, are the ones that contain real inventions. The days when I write stories."*

*A native of Washington, D.C., Beattie began her writing career in 1970 at the age of twenty-two when an instructor at the University of Connecticut, where she was a graduate student, began sending off her stories to magazines. Since then, she has published a combined total of nine collections and novels, includ-*ing Another You, Chilly Scenes of Winter, Distortions, Secrets and Surprises, Love Always, *and* The Burning House, *in which "Playback" first appeared.*

Beattie loves collecting old cookbooks, postcards, and photos because they often lead to story ideas. She is married to artist Lincoln Perry. The couple divide their time between houses in Maine and Florida.

—C. O.

Sister Rue

A Personal Essay

Carol Edgarian

Not long ago, my sister came to visit. We are separated by threes—she is three years older, three inches shorter and we live nearly three hours apart. She lives in the country, I live in the city; she works in the apparel industry, I write. When my sister walked into my house, we hugged, and then, pulling away, she said, "My God, your hair."

The day before, I had called her and confessed to a spontaneous trip to the hairdresser for a semipermanent rinse. I was newly pregnant and in the throes of morning sickness, feeling awful, needing a lift. Our family had always been able to count on good hair—thick and wavy. I wore mine long and layered or boyish and short. But then I became pregnant and the bounce on top of my head turned flat and mousy. My hairdresser assured me that what I needed was an auburn rinse to jazz things up. "Anyway," he quickly added, "if you hate the color, in six weeks it will wash out." Famous words. Panicked, I returned home to my husband. "You look great," he said. "Brighter." Unconvinced, I called my sister and begged that whatever she thought when she saw me she would try to be supportive.

"Carol," she said, standing in my doorway, her critical gaze fixed on my head. "It looks orange."

She was right, of course. Now that we are older, the gift my sister and I give each other is the truth we most fear, put precisely, softened by brown eyes. We are like old crones who have had enough with niceties. We haven't time.

Sisters. The closer I get to defining what this means, the more I conclude what it is not. My sister is not my friend—she is too close, knows too much—things I would never want a friend to know. My sister knows things about me from before I was aware anyone was looking, when I was two days old and put asleep in her room, taking over the play area for her dolls. She peered at me through the bars of the crib, wondering if I would ever be of any use to her, any fun.

No, my sister is not my friend because for one thing, a friend would never deliberately make me cry by telling me my breath smells like bananas (a fruit she loathes).

Nor is she a lover, though we have certainly fought like lovers, slamming doors, spitting ugly words, carrying our grudges and jealousies into the night. No, she is not like a lover, though, come to think of it, except for my husband, I have been naked with my sister more often than with anyone else. But although lovers base a relationship on mutual attraction, choice, differing parts, ours is rooted in sameness—our bodies, our points of reference, our blood.

When I was born, or so family myth goes, my mother held me in her arms and said, "Carol, my only hope is that you won't grow up in the shadow of your sister." At the time, my mother's fears were well founded. My sister was a dynamo—bossy, strong-willed, highly emotional. In those early years, Leslie cried *every single day*. She tormented our older brother, and her bouts of hysterical sobbing left more than a few adults in tatters. At dinner, she frequently had to be excused because her stomach hurt, and among family members, the line she is most remembered for is "I don't want to." Of course, when she was happy she was London on a sunny afternoon, and everyone—friends, siblings, and parents—wanted to be near her. It was therefore understandable that our mother worried about her youngest daughter, who at first seemed so quiet.

True to our mother's fears, early on I lived in my sister's shadow, but what our mother never guessed was that I loved it. Behind my sister, I could hide. I was plain and introverted; she was dark, beautiful, and loud. She set the rules and I followed: where we played, for how long, what toys I was allowed to touch. Between her and me grew a body-knowing, an understanding we hold even now, that comes from knowing each other when we were just bodies crashing through the world, unemcumbered by words. We slept together, took baths together, sat year after year squished in the backseat of the car along with our brother. Quite often we were happy, laughing over things we found amusing. I have never worshiped anyone the way I worshiped my sister, nor has anyone been able to get under my skin so completely, to make me so blood-boiling angry.

We grew up in a house of rage and passion and that is how we fought, like primates, with our teeth, our nails, our fists—slamming, biting each other's arms, pinching each other purple. Over time, our methods became more refined and we learned how to parry and thrust, to negotiate, to wheel and deal, to hurt. It was from my sister that I discovered that false words can be worse than blows, that a withering look can last a lifetime.

One afternoon when I was eight and she was eleven, she invited me to join several of her friends in the basement. The girls were huddled together, and when I came close, they smiled at me.

My sister said, "Pull up you shirt and show them your waist."

At first I refused, but the others encouraged me.

"It's all right," my sister said. So I pulled up my blouse and the girls all gasped.

"My God," they said, "she's got *hips!*"

I ran from the room, their laughter clipping my heels. It was literally years—*years*—before I could look at myself in a mirror and believe that having hips and a waist was not something to be ashamed of.

Our mother, beautiful and childlike, kept us separate. At thirty-seven, she was bored and unhappy in her marriage, and her emotions careened while she searched in vain for a place to ground her energy—digging up the front lawn one day, redecorating our rooms the next. Our mother saw the world in extremes and her daughters were no exception. She took to saying, "Leslie is the personality; Carol is the brains." "Leslie has gorgeous legs; Carol has nice feet." "Leslie is the life of the party; Carol is the one with class." And so on. These words of our mother's stung our hearts, yet we heard them so often we began to believe them and resented each other for having those qualities that each of us lacked. To be told at a young age what you *are* before you know yourself to be anything is at best thwarting, at worse devastating. Why couldn't I be hip? Why couldn't she have class?

When I was ten and Leslie was thirteen, our parents divorced. Our brother was sent to prep school and Leslie and I took up residence in separate rooms of our mother's new house. Leslie locked her door and played the stereo, sitting Indian style on the bed, rocking back and forth with her eyes closed for hours and hours. I read. We rarely saw each other; she was always downtown with her friends, and when we were together we fought. But there were other times: when she taught me to French inhale on the roof of the garage; when she gave me her favorite purple smock blouse, which I wore until its seams fell apart in my hands; and all those hours in her room—Leslie rocking on the bed, me on the floor—listening to Joni Mitchell, Bonnie Raitt, Jackson Browne—music we loved. We did not speak much

to each other; after the divorce, even words became dangerous. That first year, I grew four inches while Leslie began to
put on weight that would take her ten years to lose. At
Christmas, our mother offered us each seventy-five dollars
to spend any way we liked. Leslie went to the thrift store
and came home with seventy-five pieces of clothing—men's
vests, flannel shirts, worn jeans—each bought for a buck. I
went to Lord & Taylor and picked out a pair of gray wool
slacks and a white angora sweater. Under the tree, Leslie
had a huge box and I had two slim ones. Our mother smiled
brightly and then, pursing her lips, she said, "How could
you girls be so different?"

There were years when we barely spoke, when we only
saw each other around the holiday table. Our mother,
unable to handle more than one daughter at a time, deepened the schism by keeping us apart; when one sister came
home for the weekend, the other was told to stay away. But
then one Christmas when Leslie was in college and I was in
boarding school, we spent a week together in the house. At
dinner that first night, our stepfather looked across the table
and said, "Carol, you've really come into your own."
Without fully knowing what he had done, our stepfather,
faced with his wife's two daughters, seemed to have chosen
one. On Christmas Eve, Leslie asked me what I was planning to wear the next day to see our father and the other relatives. I told her I didn't know but that I'd probably wear
pants. The next morning, while getting dressed, I decided at
the last minute to put on a skirt. I came upstairs and there
she was in pants. She was furious. "I hate you," she cried
and, slamming the door of her room, refused to come out for
the remainder of the morning.

When I graduated from college, Leslie decided not to
attend the ceremony, though she lived in the same town.
She disappeared for the weekend with friends. There is a
photo of us from that time taken by our brother. Leslie and I

are sitting on a park bench with our backs to each other. Now, we laugh at that picture, calling it "The War."

In our late twenties, our lives beginning to settle, we declared a truce. Our friends, who had witnessed years of ongoing drama, could not believe the sudden rash of phone calls, the weekends spent together. But we were not surprised. It was as if we had been waiting all those years for the noise of our family to die down so we could continue being sisters.

"After a certain age," Proust wrote, "the more one becomes oneself, the more obvious one's family traits become." For me, my sister is, first and last, a mirror. Within her face, her walk, the timbre of her voice, I find myself. Not that we look alike, for we don't really, but it is in her that I rediscover myself, then and now.

When we are together, we show each other our battle scars, the marks life has left on us. We talk of work, love, our houses, the way we look. All of it matters.

Once when I was on a tight deadline and had turned off the phone, Leslie left several frantic phone messages on the machine: "Carol, call me the minute you get this."

Her voice sounded dire and of course I presumed the worst. But when I called back she said, "Care, what was the name of that lipstick you loved?"

"This," I bellowed, "is why you called? *This* was what was so important?"

"*Yes,*" she shouted back, "and don't tell me it isn't!"

Last year, Leslie had a miscarriage. It was not something that happened in a day but over two long weeks she suffered with wrenching cramps. The doctor said there was nothing he could do: it would end when it ended and perhaps, just perhaps, it was not a miscarriage at all. Each day, we agonized on the phone. When at last it was over and Leslie lost the fetus, we both grieved. Having a baby was something each of us counted on, the step that for so long we had put in the future, focusing first on our careers. Now, well into our thirties, we were finally ready to have children, but what if we couldn't? What if our bodies turned against us? What if we had waited too long?

When I saw her soon afterward, we held each other for a long time, then she said to me, "You'll never guess, Care."

"What?"

"On top of everything, now I've got b.o." And she lifted up her arm for me to smell.

We have a younger sister, Jennifer, born when I was seventeen and Leslie was twenty. Jennifer grew up apart from us, practically an only child, but when we three are together, along with our brother, there is no mistaking the ties of blood. The dichotomies of our mother's personality have affected each of us differently, but at root there is much the same. There is the voice and the quickness, the shorthand phrases that serve as a bridge, making intimacy immediate. There are the eyes that look over my clothes and hair. Do I have a pimple? How many pounds have I gained or lost? Do I look happy? And there is the sorrow we all harbor, which is our mother's, too.

A month after Leslie's miscarriage, I became pregnant with another girl. My friends and my husband gathered around me, but it was to my sister that I often turned. We had talked so long about how much we wanted to be pregnant together, how we wanted our children to be like, well, sisters. But the fates had never seen us the same, and they did not then. When I was five months' pregnant, Leslie learned she had breast cancer. She found the lump and called me immediately. Then there was the wait following the biopsy. Before we knew for certain that she had cancer, my sister and her husband and my brother and his family all came up for the weekend. After visiting for a while, Leslie and I did the only thing we knew to do. We trooped upstairs to my bathroom and, shedding our clothes, stood facing each other—me with my belly, she with her lump—and we touched the belly, we touched the lump.

"It's huge," she said, awestruck, as with cold palms she felt her niece kick inside me.

"Yours too," I said, wincing.

And then, unable to help ourselves, we cried.

We didn't have much more to say, the proximity of birth and death, the mirror image of it with us, in our bodies. We didn't speak of unfairness, luck and unluck—differences— nor of our worst fears, though they were with us, too, just as they had always been, when in those earliest years we turned out the lights in our shared room. All we needed to say we said with our hands and eyes. We gamblers, grudge keepers, lonely hearts know nothing but what passes between us in a moment, what is, finally, patient and wise. Sisters.

Carol Edgarian

CAROL EDGARIAN *wrote "Sister Rue" at a time, she says, "when real life overwhelmed and temporarily silenced my fiction. As a writer, it's my inclination to watch life for moments of surprise, fear, insight, mortification . . . but rarely have I been tempted to take literal events and put them in print. Then Leslie got cancer and I was about to give birth for the first time and these things I somehow had to get down. With the birth of my daughter, my sister and I, sadly, entered another period of isolation.*

"Two weeks ago, on the second anniversary of her surgery for cancer, Leslie called to tell me she was pregnant. The love, expectation, sober caution—everything between us—was there, zinging through the lines, but also an awareness that we had been handed yet another chance to transform the old story. The sister in me hopes while the writer watches."

The writer in Edgarian won her the ANC Freedom Award for her novel, Rise the Euphrates, *which was praised by the* Washington Post *as "a book whose generosity of spirit, intelligence, humanity and finally ambition are what literature ought to be and rarely is today." Not to be outdone, the* Chicago Tribune *named it their "best first novel of 1994," and in San Francisco, where she lives with her husband, Tom Jenks, and baby daughter, Lucy, Bay Area book reviewers nominated it for their Best Fiction Prize.*

For Edgarian, *writing and life are often intertwined, evidenced by her recent effort,* The Writer's Life: Intimate Thoughts on Work, Love, Inspiration and Fame from the Diaries of the World's Greatest Writers, *coedited with her husband. Indeed, authorship has been a longtime raison d'être for her, going back to age twelve, when she won her first award for a short story "about an outcast boy, a large dog, and a disfigured old man who eventually dies. Not a jolly story, for sure," she says, "but as a child I spent hours writing under the covers, turning over What is love? What is death? All these years later, I'm still trying to work it out."*

—C. O.

Everyday Use

FOR YOUR GRANDMAMA

Alice Walker

I will wait for her in the yard that Maggie and I made so clean and wavy yesterday afternoon. A yard like this is more comfortable than most people know. It is not just a yard. It is like an extended living room. When the hard clay is swept clean as a floor and the fine sand around the edges lined with tiny, irregular grooves, anyone can come and sit and look up into the elm tree and wait for the breezes that never come inside the house.

Maggie will be nervous until after her sister goes: she will stand hopelessly in corners, homely and ashamed of the burn scars down her arms and legs, eyeing her sister with a mixture of envy and awe. She thinks her sister has held life always in the palm of one hand, that *no* is a word the world never learned to say to her.

You've no doubt seen those TV shows where the child who has "made it" is confronted, as a surprise, by her own mother and father, tottering in weakly from backstage. (A pleasant surprise, of course: What would they do if parent and child came on the show only to curse out and insult each other?) On TV mother and child embrace and smile into each other's faces. Sometimes the mother and father weep, the child wraps them in her arms and leans across the table to tell how she would not have made it without their help. I have seen these programs.

Sometimes I dream a dream in which Dee and I are suddenly brought together on a TV program of this sort. Out of a dark and soft-seated limousine I am ushered into a bright room filled with many people. There I meet a smiling, gray, sporty man like Johnny Carson who shakes my hand and tells me what a fine girl I have. Then we are on the stage and Dee is embracing me with tears in her eyes. She pins on my dress a large orchid, even though she has told me once that she thinks orchids are tacky flowers.

In real life I am a large, big-boned woman with rough, man-working hands. In the winter I wear flannel nightgowns to bed and overalls during the day. I can kill and clean a hog as mercilessly as a man. My fat keeps me hot in zero weather. I can work outside all day, breaking ice to get water for washing; I can eat pork liver cooked over the open fire minutes after it comes steaming from the hog. One winter I knocked a bull calf straight in the brain between the eyes with a sledgehammer and had the meat hung up to chill before nightfall. But of course all this does not show on television. I am the way my daughter would want me to be: a hundred pounds lighter, my skin like an uncooked barley pancake. My hair glistens in the hot bright lights. Johnny Carson has much to do to keep up with my quick and witty tongue.

But that is a mistake. I know even before I wake up. Who ever knew a Johnson with a quick tongue? Who can even imagine me looking a strange white man in the eye? It seems to me I have talked to them always with one foot raised in flight, with my head turned in whichever way is farthest from them. Dee, though, she would always look anyone in the eye. Hesitation was no part of her nature.

* * *

"How do I look, Mama?" Maggie says, showing just enough of her thin body enveloped in pink skirt and red blouse for me to know she's there, almost hidden by the door.

"Come out into the yard," I say.

Have you ever seen a lame animal, perhaps a dog run over by some careless person rich enough to own a car, sidle up to someone who is ignorant enough to be kind to him? That is the way my Maggie walks. She has been like this, chin on chest, eyes on ground, feet in shuffle, ever since the fire that burned the other house to the ground.

Dee is lighter than Maggie, with nicer hair and a fuller figure. She's a woman now, though sometimes I forget. How long ago was it that the other house burned? Ten, twelve years? Sometimes I can still hear the flames and feel Maggie's arms sticking to me, her hair smoking and her dress falling off her in little black papery flakes. Her eyes seemed stretched open, blazed open by the flames reflected in them. And Dee. I see her standing off under the sweet gum tree she used to dig gum out of; a look of concentration on her face as she watched the last dingy gray board of the house fall in toward the red-hot brick chimney. Why don't you do a dance around the ashes? I'd wanted to ask her. She had hated the house that much.

I used to think she hated Maggie, too. But that was before we raised the money, the church and me, to send her to Augusta to school. She used to read to us without pity; forcing words, lies, other folks' habits, whole lives upon us two, sitting trapped and ignorant underneath her voice. She washed us in a river of make-believe, burned us with a lot of knowledge we didn't necessarily need to know. Pressed us to her with the serious way she read, to shove us away at just the moment, like dimwits, we seemed about to understand.

Dee wanted nice things. A yellow organdy dress to wear

to her graduation from high school; black pumps to match a green suit she'd made from an old suit somebody gave me. She was determined to stare down any disaster in her efforts. Her eyelids would not flicker for minutes at a time. Often I fought off the temptation to shake her. At sixteen she had a style of her own: and knew what style was.

I never had an education myself. After second grade the school was closed down. Don't ask me why: in 1927 colored asked fewer questions than they do now. Sometimes Maggie reads to me. She stumbles along good-naturedly but can't see well. She knows she is not bright. Like good looks and money, quickness passed her by. She will marry John Thomas (who has mossy teeth in an earnest face) and then I'll be free to sit here and I guess just sing church songs to myself. Although I never was a good singer. Never could carry a tune. I was always better at a man's job. I used to love to milk till I was hooked in the side in '49. Cows are soothing and slow and don't bother you, unless you try to milk them the wrong way.

I have deliberately turned my back on the house. It is three rooms, just like the one that burned, except the roof is tin; they don't make shingle roofs anymore. There are no real windows, just some holes cut in the sides, like the portholes in a ship, but not round and not square, with rawhide holding the shutters up on the outside. This house is in a pasture, too, like the other one. No doubt when Dee sees it she will want to tear it down. She wrote me once that no matter where we "choose" to live, she will manage to come see us. But she will never bring her friends. Maggie and I thought about this and Maggie asked me, "Mama, when did Dee ever *have* any friends?"

She had a few. Furtive boys in pink shirts hanging about on washday after school. Nervous girls who never laughed. Impressed with her, they worshiped the well-turned phrase, the cute shape, the scalding humor that erupted like bubbles in lye. She read to them.

When she was courting Jimmy T she didn't have much time to pay to us, but turned all her faultfinding power on him. He *flew* to marry a cheap city girl from a family of ignorant flashy people. She hardly had time to recompose herself.

When she comes I will meet—but there they are!

Maggie attempts to make a dash for the house, in her shuffling way, but I stay her with my hand. "Come back here," I say. And she stops and tries to dig a well in the sand with her toe.

It is hard to see them clearly through the strong sun. But even the first glimpse of leg out of the car tells me it is Dee. Her feet were always neat looking, as if God himself had shaped them with a certain style. From the other side of the car comes a short, stocky man. Hair is all over his head a foot long and hanging from his chin like a kinky mule tail. I hear Maggie suck in her breath. "Uhnnnh," is what it sounds like. Like when you see the wriggling end of a snake just in front of your foot on the road. "Uhnnnh."

Dee next. A dress down to the ground, in this hot weather. A dress so loud it hurts my eyes. There are yellows and oranges enough to throw back the light of the sun. I feel my whole face warming from the heat waves it throws out. Earrings gold, too, and hanging down to her shoulders. Bracelets dangling and making noises when she moves her arm up to shake the folds of the dress out of her armpits. The dress is loose and flows, and as she walks closer, I like it. I hear Maggie go "Uhnnnh" again. It is her sister's hair. It stands straight up like the wool on a sheep. It is black as night and around the edges are two long pigtails that rope about like small lizards disappearing behind her ears.

"*Wa-su-zo-Tean-o!*" she says, coming on in that gliding

way the dress makes her move. The short stocky fellow with the hair to his navel is all grinning and he follows up with "Asalamalakim, my mother and sister!" He moves to hug Maggie, but she falls back, right up against the back of my chair. I feel her trembling there and when I look up I see the perspiration falling off her chin.

"Don't get up," says Dee. Since I am stout, it takes something of a push. You can see me trying to move a second or two before I make it. She turns, showing white heels through her sandals, and goes back to the car. Out she peeks next with a Polaroid. She stoops down quickly and lines up picture after picture of me sitting there in front of the house with Maggie cowering behind me. She never takes a shot without making sure the house is included. When a cow comes nibbling around the edge of the yard she snaps it and me and Maggie *and* the house. Then she puts the Polaroid in the backseat of the car and comes up and kisses me on the forehead.

Meanwhile Asalamalakim is going through motions with Maggie's hand. Maggie's hand is as limp as a fish, and probably as cold, despite the sweat, and she keeps trying to pull it back. It looks like Asalamalakim wants to shake hands but wants to do it fancy. Or maybe he don't know how people shake hands. Anyhow, he soon gives up on Maggie.

"Well," I say. "Dee."

"No, Mama," she says. "Not 'Dee,' Wangero Leewanika Kemanjo!"

"What happened to 'Dee'?" I wanted to know.

"She's dead," Wangero said. "I couldn't bear it any longer, being named after the people who oppress me."

"You know as well as me you was named after your aunt Dicie," I said. Dicie is my sister. She named Dee. We called her "Big Dee" after Dee was born.

"But who was *she* named after?" asked Wangero.

"I guess after Grandma Dee," I said.

"And who was she named after?" asked Wangero.

"Her mother," I said, and saw Wangero was getting tired. "That's about as far back as I can trace it," I said. Though, in fact, I probably could have carried it back beyond the Civil War through the branches.

"Well," said Asalamalakim, "there you are."

"Uhnnnh," I heard Maggie say.

"There I was not," I said, "before 'Dicie' cropped up in our family, so why should I try to trace it that far back?"

He just stood there grinning, looking down on me like somebody inspecting a Model A car. Every once in a while he and Wangero sent eye signals over my head.

"How do you pronounce this name?" I asked.

"You don't have to call me by it if you don't want to," said Wangero.

"Why shouldn't I?" I asked. "If that's what you want us to call you, we'll call you."

"I know it might sound awkward at first," said Wangero.

"I'll get used to it," I said. "Ream it out again."

Well, soon we got the name out of the way. Asalamalakim had a name twice as long and three times as hard. After I tripped over it two or three times he told me to just call him Hakim-a-barber. I wanted to ask him was he a barber, but I didn't really think he was, so I didn't ask.

"You must belong to those beef-cattle peoples down the road," I said. They said "Asalamalakim" when they met you, too, but they didn't shake hands. Always too busy: feeding the cattle, fixing the fences, putting up salt-lick shelters, throwing down hay. When the white folks poisoned some of the herd, the men stayed up all night with rifles in their hands. I walked a mile and a half just to see the sight.

Hakim-a-barber said, "I accept some of their doctrines, but farming and raising cattle is not my style." (They didn't tell me, and I didn't ask, whether Wangero [Dee] had really gone and married him.)

We sat down to eat and right away he said he didn't eat collards and pork was unclean. Wangero, though, went on through the chitlins and corn bread, the greens and everything else. She talked a blue streak over the sweet potatoes. Everything delighted her. Even the fact that we still used the benches her daddy made for the table when we couldn't afford to buy chairs.

"Oh, Mama!" she cried. Then turned to Hakim-a-barber. "I never knew how lovely these benches are. You can feel the rump prints," she said, running her hands underneath her and along the bench. Then she gave a sigh and her hand closed over Grandma Dee's butter dish. "That's it!" she said. "I knew there was something I wanted to ask you if I could have." She jumped up from the table and went over in the corner where the churn stood, the milk in it clabber by now. She looked at the churn and looked at it.

"This churn top is what I need," she said. "Didn't Uncle Buddy whittle it out of a tree you all used to have?"

"Yes," I said.

"Uh huh," she said happily. "And I want the dasher, too."

"Uncle Buddy whittle that, too?" asked the barber.

Dee (Wangero) looked up at me.

"Aunt Dee's first husband whittled the dash," said Maggie so low you almost couldn't hear her. "His name was Henry, but they called him Stash."

"Maggie's brain is like an elephant's," Wangero said, laughing. "I can use the churn top as a centerpiece for the alcove table," she said, sliding a plate over the churn, "and I'll think of something artistic to do with the dasher."

When she finished wrapping the dasher, the handle stuck out. I took it for a moment in my hands. You didn't even have to look close to see where hands pushing the dasher up and down to make butter had left a kind of sink in the wood. In fact, there were a lot of small sinks; you could see where thumbs and fingers had sunk into the wood. It was beautiful light yellow wood, from a tree that grew in the yard where Big Dee and Stash had lived.

After dinner Dee (Wangero) went to the trunk at the foot of my bed and started rifling through it. Maggie hung back in the kitchen over the dishpan. Out came Wangero with two quilts. They had been pieced by Grandma Dee and then Big Dee and me had hung them on the quilt frames on the front porch and quilted them. One was in the Lone Star pattern. The other was Walk Around the Mountain. In both of them were scraps of dresses Grandma Dee had worn fifty and more years ago. Bits and pieces of Grandpa Jarrell's paisley shirts. And one teeny faded blue piece, about the size of a penny matchbox, that was from Great Grandpa Ezra's uniform that he wore in the Civil War.

"Mama," Wangero said sweet as a bird. "Can I have these old quilts?"

I heard something fall in the kitchen, and a minute later the kitchen door slammed.

"Why don't you take one or two of the others?" I asked. "These old things was just done by me and Big Dee from some tops your grandma pieced before she died."

"No," said Wangero. "I don't want those. They are stitched around the borders by machine."

"That'll make them last better," I said.

"That's not the point," said Wangero. "These are all pieces of dresses Grandma used to wear. She did all this stitching by hand. Imagine!" She held the quilts securely in her arms, stroking them.

"Some of the pieces, like those lavender ones, come from old clothes her mother handed down to her," I said, moving up to touch the quilts. Dee (Wangero) moved back just enough so that I couldn't reach the quilts. They already belonged to her.

"Imagine!" she breathed again, clutching them closely to her bosom.

"The truth is," I said, "I promised to give them quilts to Maggie, for when she marries John Thomas."

She gasped like a bee had stung her.

"Maggie can't appreciate these quilts!" she said. "She'd probably be backward enough to put them to everyday use."

"I reckon she would," I said. "God knows I been saving 'em for long enough with nobody using 'em. I hope she will!" I didn't want to bring up how I had offered Dee (Wangero) a quilt when she went away to college. Then she had told me they were old-fashioned, out of style.

"But they're *priceless!*" she was saying now, furiously; for she has a temper. "Maggie would put them on the bed and in five years they'd be in rags. Less than that!"

"She can always make some more," I said. "Maggie knows how to quilt."

Dee (Wangero) looked at me with hatred. "You just will not understand. The point is these quilts, *these* quilts!"

"Well," I said, stumped. "What would *you* do with them?"

"Hang them," she said. As if that was the only thing you *could* do with quilts.

Maggie by now was standing in the door. I could almost hear the sound her feet made as they scraped over each other.

"She can have them, Mama," she said, like somebody used to never winning anything, or having anything reserved for her. "I can 'member Grandma Dee without the quilts."

I looked at her hard. She had filled her bottom lip with checkerberry snuff and it gave her face a kind of dopey, hangdog look. It was Grandma Dee and Big Dee who taught her how to quilt herself. She stood there with her scarred hands hidden in the folds of her skirt. She looked at her sister with something like fear but she wasn't mad at her. This was Maggie's portion. This was the way she knew God to work.

When I looked at her like that, something hit me in the top of my head and ran down to the soles of my feet. Just like when I'm in church and the spirit of God touches me and I get happy and shout. I did something I never had done before: hugged Maggie to me, then dragged her on into the room, snatched the quilts out of Miss Wangero's hands, and dumped them into Maggie's lap. Maggie just sat there on my bed with her mouth open.

"Take one or two of the others," I said to Dee.

But she turned without a word and went out to Hakim-a-barber.

"You just don't understand," she said, as Maggie and I came out to the car.

"What don't I understand?" I wanted to know.

"Your heritage," she said. And then she turned to Maggie, kissed her, and said, "You ought to try to make something of yourself, too, Maggie. It's really a new day for us. But from the way you and Mama still live you'd never know it."

She put on some sunglasses that hid everything above the tip of her nose and her chin.

Maggie smiled, maybe at the sunglasses. But a real smile, not scared. After we watched the car dust settle I asked Maggie to bring me a dip of snuff. And then the two of us sat there just enjoying, until it was time to go in the house and go to bed.

Alice Walker

BEST KNOWN *among readers for her novel* The Color Purple, *which Steven Spielberg translated into the Academy Award–honored film, Alice Walker has authored four other novels, among them* The Temple of My Familiar, *and* Possessing the Secret of Joy, *plus collections of poetry, short stories, and essays, including* In Search of Our Mothers' Gardens.

Globally, she is known not only for her books, translated into two dozen languages, but also for her activism on behalf of several causes, including efforts to end female genital mutilation worldwide; speaking out against the thirty-seven-year-old embargo against Cuba, which she believes most harms the children of that nation through starvation; and supporting the cause to ban animal-extracted estrogen. She is an active feminist and involved herself in the civil rights movement.

In the collection Anything We Love Can Be Saved: A Writer's Activism, *she traces her roots in activism to her great-great-great-great-grandmother, May Poole, who was a slave of the American South.*

Said the Pulitzer prize–winning author in a 1997 speech, "So strong was her spirit, and so clearly did I reflect some of it, that the elderly white woman to whom she'd been given as a wedding gift over three quarters of a century before recognized me as her descendant."

Walker does not consider her activism politically based alone, but culturally and spiritually inclined as well, being "rooted in my love of nature and human beings. I do not want my fear of war or starvation or bodily mutilation to steal both my pleasure in them and their own birthright."

—C. O.

A
Matter of Gifts

Cristina García

Key Biscayne
June 1991

*R*eina unsnaps the top of her bikini and lies by the pool with her back to the morning sun. It's been over a month since she arrived in Miami, and already she's grown accustomed to the uneasy indolence of exile life. The Cuba she knows is fading in the luxury of her sister's existence. Only a suitcase stuffed with her father's mementos—taxidermic bats and birds, a few books and clothes, the framed photograph of her mother—remains of that disquieting time before her departure.

It seems to Reina that she'd been on the verge of some certainty in Havana. Now she wonders whether all certainty will be kept from her, wonders, in fact, whether certainty isn't truly disaster in disguise.

At the Miami airport, Reina was stunned to see a vision of her mother rushing toward her at the gate. Constancia looks so much like Mami now, down to the minutest details, that Reina couldn't help it—she studied her sister's face like a blind woman, tried to read with her hands the grace and terror that lay hidden there.

"What a strange way of being dead!" she finally exclaimed. It was her first direct utterance to Constancia in thirty years. Later, she stared at her sister for many more hours, considered her from every angle, until it made her frantic with grief.

Her first few nights in Miami, Reina slept in the same bed with Constancia, back to stomach, Reina on the outside protecting her slight, older sister, listening for messages from the dead. She and Constancia showered together, combed one another's hair, fed each other tidbits from their dinner plates. All the while, Reina kept watch over her sister's face as if it were a compelling tragedy.

Reina wonders whether Mami's face is only a superficial membrane, like her own patches of borrowed skin, or whether it penetrates further to the bone, to some basic molecular level. She can't help thinking how everything is fundamentally electric, how natural currents flow near the surface of the earth, telluric and magnetic, how she is pulled again and again into the charged fields of her sister's face.

If only Constancia would stop talking, stay mute sufficiently long enough for Mami to emerge. Reina finds intolerable the false expectations their mother's visage sets up. There is a part of Reina that wants to address Mami directly, to risk everything—even if it means eradicating her sister—in the hope of retrieving her past.

After their mother died, Papá sent Reina and Constancia to a boarding school in Trinidad. That first rainy winter, a forest of politeness took root between them, starching the air they shared. Each time Reina tried to talk about Mami, Constancia covered her ears and hummed the national anthem. Although they spent years together at boarding school, by habit or cowardice—Reina isn't sure which—she and Constancia never discussed their mother again.

Reina dives into the deep end of the condominium's pool with her eyes wide open. There's a dime and a gold hoop earring where the bottom slopes down. She plucks them from the concrete and leaves them on the rim of the pool. Then she swims with powerful strokes to the shallow end. One stroke, then two, and she's in the deep water. Two strokes more, and she's at the shallow end again.

This is a pool for pygmies, Reina thinks. Who else could be satisfied with these few drops of blue?

The sun is high in the sky. No interference from clouds. The ocean wrinkles with the slightest breeze. The city is in the distance, strangely flat and uninviting. Reina emerges from the water and shakes herself dry, a glorious titanic beast. Near her, sunglasses are lowered, shutters flung open. Her own pungent scent steams up from her mismatched skin.

At noon. Constancia calls down to Reina from the balcony, announcing lunch. It's delicious, as usual: *arroz con pollo*, fried plantains, a coconut flan for dessert, all served on fancy flowered plates.

"This is the century that Christianity has died out," Constancia declares, picking the petit pois out of her rice. "The metaphysical is taking over. People believe in miracles now instead of God."

Reina reaches over and mashes her sister's peas with a fork, sucks them off the tines. She looks up at the past trapped in Constancia's face and doesn't know what to say.

The phone rings incessantly during their meal. One call after another from Constancia's clients, impatient for orders of lotions and creams. Her sister is nearly finished retrofitting a bowling ball factory into Cuerpo de Cuba's new manufacturing plant to meet the clamorous demand. Reina has volunteered to help Constancia with the remaining electrical work.

There's a stack of photographs on the kitchen table, taken before Constancia's affliction. Reina thumbs through the pictures, carefully examines them one by one. Her sister looks good, well groomed, younger than her fifty-two years, her body pliant and pampered, Reina notes, but lacking the tone of true succulence.

"Do you think this will pass?" Constancia is moody, restless. "I'm not extinct yet, am I?"

Reina isn't certain she can stay with her sister if Mami's face disappears, isn't certain she can stay if it remains. She takes her sister's hand and pats it. It's a child's hand, lineless and smooth. What could there possibly be here still tempting the dead?

"I wish you'd stop that!" Constancia hisses all of a sudden. "You've been doing it for days!"

Reina realizes with a start that she's been unconsciously whistling. She recognizes the melody, a traditional *changüi* from Oriente she once heard a *negrito* sing in Céspedes Park. *He nacido para ti, Nengón. Para ti, Nengón.* His singing had made Reina cry.

"I've been ingesting small amounts of sterling silver," Constancia says, calmer now. She takes a denim pouch from her apron pocket, shows Reina the silver dust inside. "I heard on the radio that it soothes hallucinations."

Reina reaches for an apple from a bowl on the kitchen table. She doesn't want to say that the entire world should be eating silver dust, then, because everyone is hallucinating.

"Someone told me this might be an equatorial disease. I must have caught it here in Miami. There are lots of people from South America." Constancia pinches a bit of silver dust and sprinkles it on the tip of her tongue. Then she washes it down with a glass of ice water. "What I want to know is where *my* face went. Where has it disappeared to?"

Reina remembers a stray snatch of a poem, she doesn't know from where, maybe something her father read to her once. *Life is in the mirror, and you are the original death.*

Of course, she doesn't tell Constancia this.

* * *

"Ayúdame, por favor." Her sister decides to prepare a batch of Muslos de Cuba, her new thigh smoothener.

Reina isn't particularly interested—the smell and the steam give her a headache—but Constancia is so overwhelmed with work that Reina reluctantly agrees to help stir up a few gallons for a department-store demonstration the next day.

"What are these for?" Reina asks, poking through a bowl of boiled avocado pits.

Constancia cracks the pits open with the blade of a knife and scrapes out the vegetal flesh. "Softens the subcutaneous cells of the thigh. Reduces the appearance of cellulite. Peel those peaches for me, will you?"

Reina leans over the tray of rotting fruit, waves away the cloud of feasting flies. She picks up a serrated knife and begins peeling. Reina is perplexed by the obsession women in Miami have for the insignificant details of their bodies, by their self-defeating crusades. She was appalled when Constancia took her to the Dade County shopping mall last Sunday. All those hipless, breastless mannequins, up to their scrawny necks in silk.

Don't women understand that their peculiarities are what endear them to men? Rarely do the most conventionally beautiful women have the greatest hold over their mates. Pepín, who adored Reina but remained an inveterate woman watcher over the years, admitted that he favored no particular female features. *Cada mujer tiene algo,* he liked to say. Every woman has something. The best lovers, Reina knows from experience, approach women this way.

"You don't have to worry; you never had to." Constancia sniffs. She opens a king-sized tub of cherry yogurt, ladles it into the steaming cauldron.

"But why should anybody?" Reina turns around, pulls up

her terry-cloth cover-up to reveal her puckered thighs. "*Oye, chica*, since when did cellulite ever deter passion?"

Constancia grabs Reina's cutting board and scrapes the peach peels into the blender. It screeches like a malfunctioning drill. The skins turn brown and pulpy, altogether unappealing. Reina watches as her sister adds them to the bubbling emollient.

"I think every woman remains fixed at a certain age in her own mind." Constancia lowers her voice to a conspiratorial degree. "A rare time when she saw herself in the mirror or through her lover's eyes and was pleased."

Reina guesses this is her sister's best cosmetics-counter voice.

"Haven't you ever noticed how often women destroy pictures of themselves, Reina? That's because nothing conforms with our private image of ourselves. My products bring back that feeling. The beauty of scent and sensation, the mingling of memory and imagination."

"Not me, *mi amor*. I live in the here and now."

"Well, you're probably the only woman on earth who actually likes the way she looks!" Constancia snaps, stirring the thigh lotion with a steady rhythm of her wooden spoon. "Definitely bad for business!"

Reina retreats to the guest room and changes into her work jumpsuit. She's putting up shelves and plywood hutches for their father's stuffed specimens. She retrieves a hammer from her toolbox and secures another bracket against the wall. Her thumbs still feel a little sore from having been broken in the mahogany tree. Then she lines the shelves with arm lengths of aluminum foil she bought at the supermarket.

Reina is bewildered each time she goes shopping in Miami. The displays of products she'd forgotten or didn't even know existed. Red pepper spaghetti. Giant artichokes, looking vaguely medieval. Bread in countless textures and shapes. And anything, it seems, can be frozen or freeze-dried here. Instant, instant everything!

In the far corner of the room, on the topmost shelf, Reina displays the *periquito* Papi shot in a virgin forest near Guantánamo. Their father's spectacular *camao*, its mantle still an enviable blue, she places in a hutch by the window, next to an earless owl called a *sijú*. Reina fondles the elfin owl, her favorite of their father's collection, recalls the faint traces of light it left in a lace of leaves. She wonders if memory is little more than this: a series of erasures and perfected selections.

Over the dresser, where a decorative crucifix has been, Reina nails up the photograph of their mother that looks exactly like Constancia today. In fact, it's identical to the antiqued photograph her sister uses for the labels on her jars of lotions and creams. Mami is pale in the picture, so pale her complexion seems more conjecture than color. Reina remembers how the summer before she died, Mami's eyelashes whitened until her green eyes looked twice their normal size.

Reina works a neat row of nails in her mouth, then pounds them into the wall one by one. She adjusts another shelf against the wall. Working up a sweat, Reina strips down to her panties and an old-fashioned bra with conical cups. She's always wanted to work in the nude, considers clothing a nuisance at best. Nothing ever fits her quite right anyway, especially in this *nalgas*-denying country. Reina knows she looks best without a stitch, even now with her patchwork skin.

It's nearly four o'clock when Reina finishes with the guest room. She finds Constancia in the kitchen, dripping vanilla extract into the cooling thigh lotion. Reina urges her sister into taking Heberto's little motorboat out for a spin.

"How hard can it be?" Reina asks. "No disrespect to your husband, *mi amor*, but how many astrophysicists do *you* know who go fishing on the planet?"

In Cuba, no one is allowed to go boating without a special permit, so Reina rarely got the opportunity to venture out on the open seas. Constancia is nervous because Heberto has been gone since March, on a covert mission against El Comandante. Reina suppresses her laughter. Nobody can bring that old *cabrón* down, much less mild-mannered Heberto Cruz. It amuses her to think that Constancia feels her husband has a fighting chance.

At the yacht club, Reina sets to repairing the rusting outboard motor before a crowd of hooting admirers. She buries her face in the motor, sharp-nosed pliers in hand, oblivious to the encircling commotion. Nobody has started the boat since Heberto's departure. Reina asks her sister for a spool of copper wire from her massive toolbox. She is always happiest with the toolbox at her side, even when she's making love. It increases her every pleasure.

Last month, she smuggled the toolbox out of Cuba by impressing the immigration officers at the airport with the name of a famous general she'd once seduced. Reina knows she could have bought a beach house in Manzanitas by selling her tools on the black market. *Coño*, it's impossible to get even a bandage in Cuba, forget a decent wrench. No way would she have left without her precious implements.

Constancia holds a stretch of wire for Reina to cut. Reina patiently winds it through the motor, then pulls on the starter. The motor shivers and dies. She tightens two more bolts with her best adjustable wrench. Reina could be dropped anywhere with her tools, in a faraway galaxy with no water and a fraction of the earth's gravity, and somehow—she grins to think of this—she knows she would survive.

On the next try, the motor roars to life. Reina is

pleased. Nothing, absolutely nothing, neither man nor machine, is immune to the resuscitative powers of her magic hands.

Constancia slips on her life jacket, but Reina doesn't bother to put one on. Instead she settles in the rear of Heberto's boat and motions for her sister to come on board. Then Reina steers her way out of the yacht club harbor as if she were born for nothing else.

The air is much too weary for wind. It's the middle of the week, and only two other boats are on the bay, sailboats barely moving in the distance. Reina has been on a boat only twice in her life, but she likes the perspective it gives her, the ocean's open contempt for destinations. Why hadn't she ever realized before the futility of living on land?

At Constancia's insistence, Reina veers left and putters through the canals of Key Biscayne.

"What would you do with this much money?" Constancia shouts over the whining motor, as if trying to impress Reina with the possibility.

Reina shrugs. She's indifferent to the mansions and yachts crowded together on the waterways. To have money and share this swamp with mosquitoes and water rats? *Por favor.* If she wins the lottery—and she's been playing religiously since she arrived in Florida—Reina would spend the rest of her life floating around the world, ravishing her choice of men. Certainly she wouldn't choose to live like this, cheek by jowl with the pathological rich.

Of course, if she won the jackpot, she'd split the money with Dulcita, coax her away from that Spanish buzzard in Madrid. Perhaps, Reina muses hopefully, she might become a grandmother. No, Dulcita is much too sensible for that. When she was fourteen and pregnant, Dulcita never said a word about it. But Reina could tell.

Her daughter slept for hours in the afternoon, kept a box of stale crackers by her bed. Reina hoped that Dulcita, by some miracle, would decide to keep the baby. But she aborted it that autumn, like something fragile and seasonal.

"I want to be a grandmother," Reina announces as she speeds around a curve. "I want to be a grandmother and mambo all night!"

Constancia turns to look at her, bemused. Reina is disconcerted by her face, by their mother's resurrected expression.

Anchored off a stub of jetty, on the deck of a yacht, a bare-chested man in madras pants types away at a portable computer. He looks up and blows a kiss at Reina.

"You're a goddess!" he shouts in badly accented Spanish, removing his baseball cap. There's a shock of gray hair on his head.

"*Caballero*, tell me something I don't know!" Reina shouts back, laughing.

The man tosses his cap in the air.

Suddenly, Reina longs for deeper waters to explore, and so she navigates her way out of the maze of canals and around the eastern tip of the island.

"Don't go too far, Reina! It's not safe!" Constancia protests. "Heberto never took the boat out of the bay!"

But Reina merely looks past her sister to the bristling blue concourse, to the broken arch of seagulls in the sky. She's impatient with Constancia's fear of adventure. Even at boarding school, her sister always asked permission for everything—to leave the breakfast table or cross the dirt road to wander through the orange grove. Then she married that boor Gonzalo, who cured her forever of any recklessness. Reina remembers how Constancia wore the loss of him like a spectacle, a holy medallion for everyone to see. But for Reina, the loss of her first lover, José Luís Fuerte, only whetted her appetite for more passion, like the ocean before them with its hunger for vulnerable men.

A concord of clouds solemnly assembles on the horizon. The sun recedes, and an unexpected wind raises tufts of monotonous waves. The little motorboat climbs and drops as the rain begins. Then nothing is visible but this realm of blue water and light.

"Turn around, Reina. *Tengo miedo.*" Constancia is shivering on her vinyl banquette, her hands raw from gripping the side of the boat.

The boat pitches in the deepening waves, spraying them with water. Reina's blouse is saturated, her sister's hair mats to her skull. The boat dips again. Another fierce spray drenches them both.

What was it Constancia told her at the boarding school? *Mercy, Reina, is more important than knowledge.* *Coño,* who had taught her sister that? Worse still, how could she have believed it? Their teachers had told them to pray for their mother's soul, to ask God for forgiveness. But Reina couldn't understand what their mother had ever done wrong.

She wants to tell Constancia again what she saw at the funeral home. Describe the colors of Mami's devastated throat. Force her to listen. Shout it loud in her sister's face. Mami couldn't have drowned, like their father said. No, she couldn't have drowned, which means their father must have lied. And if Papá lied, what the hell was the truth?

The bow of the boat tips steeply into a wave. Ocean pours in astern, up to Reina's shins. She's surprised at its beckoning warmth. She tries to imagine her mother, breathing her last breath of swamp.

Another wave slams against the side of the little boat. The motor floods and stops. Reina throws her sister a child's plastic bucket. "Start bailing!" she shouts. Constancia moves stiffly, her shoulders tight and square.

The boat rocks hard in the waves. Reina inspects the outboard, unsnaps its casing. When there's only an inch of water left at their feet, Reina blows hard on the engine, emptying her lungs. She pulls the starter, and the motor turns over without a stutter.

Reina maneuvers the boat until they're heading southwest, toward the spangle of palms on her sister's tiny island, toward the dying twilight already fraught with stars.

Cristina García

⌒

CALLING CUBAN-AMERICAN *writer Cristina García "a wise and generous storyteller,"* Time *magazine hailed* The Agüero Sisters—*from which "A Matter of Gifts" is taken—"as a beautifully rounded work of art, as warm and wry and sensuous as the island she so clearly loves."*

García was born in Havana on the Fourth of July, 1958. Her family escaped Cuba just prior to Fidel Castro's rise to power. They settled in New York City in 1960 and that's where García grew up. A graduate of Columbia University, she was a journalist, covering stories for Time *in New York and Miami, before moving to Los Angeles in 1988 and beginning her first novel,* Dreaming in Cuban.

Dreaming was published in 1992, and like the works of other authors in this anthology, was a finalist for the National Book Award, as well as a nominee to several national publications' "best books" lists. Not just a critical success, the novel climbed to best-seller status, and together perhaps with the writing of Oscar Hijuelos, brought Cuban-American fiction to the literary forefront in this country.

García is fascinated by language, its color and forms, telling an interviewer for Newsday *that it's "what drives a narrative."*

Language so captivated her that in the years between writing

Dreaming and The Agüero Sisters, *her second novel, she studied poetry in order to immerse herself in it. In fact,* Agüero Sisters *initially started as a poem. Said García of the finished novel, "I wrote it very consciously thinking in terms of musicality and rhythm and cadence."*

Divorced, García still resides in Southern California and has one daughter, Pilar.

—C. O.